THE WORLD HAPPINESS ORGANISATION

LOU GIBBONS

CENTULLE

A CENTULLE book
First edition September 2024

Cover design by victoriaheathsilk.com

For every reader - old or young - who finds a piece of themselves within these pages

Memo to The Assignments Agency

The World Happiness Organisation (W.H.O.) was founded on the recognition of happiness as a basic human right, it being infinitely and freely available to everyone.

Life challenges access to happiness in every way it can. Our work has always been in helping people navigate those bumps in the road where events don't unravel as planned or meet expectation.

As you will be aware, however, our case load has risen of late. Never before have we seen such levels of depression and anxiety as so many are pushed into fear and insecurity. We must continue our work, and continue we will, but we are called to ask if happiness should in fact be viewed as a limited commodity, reserved for some and not others. The time has come to think differently.

It is with pleasure therefore that we open our doors to Dr Cynthia Wolf from the consultancy firm West Taylor Fisher, who will work with us to understand how our Organisation can reshape itself into a resilient structure moving forward. Please address any questions to: wtf@happinessorganisation.com

CHAPTER ONE

Jeff had a square head. People said that, didn't they? A square head, or was it a square face? Mavis glanced to the ground as a twig crunched underfoot before returning her attention to the grey hair that hovered like wisps of cloud. Maybe 'angular' would be better. No head could ever be truly square after all, and Jeff held geometry in the highest esteem.

'One metre, Mavis! Any closer and you're on my heels.' Jeff paused. 'It's safer single file.'

Always the pause, tailed by the same afterthought. His trill muffling resident birdlife. A wandering mind called to heel. Just enjoy the sun, Mavis told herself, her face rising to meet its warmth. The sun that brought you here. As they approached the village, that sun rose to the right from behind a field of towering sunflowers. Precisely aligned rows of yellow and no doubt a pleasing sight for her husband, had his mind not been elsewhere. Pleasing for Mavis, had the blooms, like Jeff, not all turned their backs.

She surveyed the road ahead.

One metre. She softened her pace.

She often forgot herself, even if Jeff's directives were far from new. What people must think as they ran or cycled past, sometimes attempting a shy 'bonjour'. 'Poor sods,' they no doubt mumbled. Another old couple that has run out of things to say. Young people have no idea what life can do, particularly when things happen. Things that push you into separate cocoons and turn a one-metre gap into a deathly quiet chasm. Silence. Endless hours of nothing, with the only thing more frightening than the weight of that silence the impulse to throttle Jeff whenever he broke it. They hadn't seen it coming. Life, that is. Not realised youthful naivety was to be cherished. Even more painful for those passers-by to think those miserable old folk had once been like them.

'One metre is about two to three strides, Mavis.' Jeff's call sliced the air once more as they entered the village, this time meeting with a white Fiat 500 performing a manoeuvre that would have been more at home in *The Bourne Identity*. He ground to an abrupt halt in front of the church. 'Jesus Christ!' he muttered into the reddish-brown cloud as Mavis trod on his heels. 'Wouldn't happen if you weren't on top of me.'

Two lines, one red and one green, traced their way from the manufacturer's mascot up the car's bonnet. Gaining in thickness as they went, the tell-tale markings confirmed, the dramatic entrance having sown the seeds of suspicion, the driver was Peg. The closest Peg came to Italian heritage was a love of tiramisu in an otherwise dairy-free diet. When Giovanni at the Toulouse Club for English Pensioners had passed away, she had acquired the 'little run around', hung a fluffy dragon from the rear-view mirror and appropriated the colours as Welsh.

Peg smiled at the clock tower as she exited the car. 'Daily constitutional?'

The slightest of breezes diffused a sweet, floral smell.

'You're out and about early?' said Mavis.

'Moon ritual tonight, Mave.'

Mavis was learning that Peg attached particular importance to lunar cycles, declaring them opportune moments to converse with the dead. Her mother, Gwen, had been known right across Wales as having 'the gift'. Something Peg had inherited by all accounts.

'Sounds important, love.'

'It's only a supermoon,' said Peg, nodding. 'Closer to the Earth, the moon has greater pull.'

A supermoon. That would explain the double dose of ylang-ylang. Mavis recognised the smell now. She'd been given one of those fancy candles as a birthday present once. Supposed to be an aphrodisiac, wasn't it? Maybe a supermoon could work all kinds of magic. She observed her husband tracing pyramids with his foot. You'd need a bloody magician when it came to Jeff. She couldn't remember the last time they'd hugged or held hands, let alone any of the other. The moon could be two to three strides from Earth and Mavis doused in all essential oils known to man and it would pass unnoticed.

'Anyway, I've got news for you,' said Peg. 'Looks like the centre *is* officially opening tomorrow and we have a meeting to find volunteers for . . .' Peg scoured the fields for a handful of words, a search she quickly abandoned. 'Some World Health Organisation thing.'

'World Health Organisation?' asked Mavis. The words made some sense but she'd never heard of such a thing. 'But to do what?'

'I'd volunteer a sixteen-hour day down the mines on my hands and knees if it meant not listening to Joan and Roy bickering over that Zoom.' Peg threw her head back in laughter, a family of surprised pigeons taking flight from the church roof.

'I suppose it does mean we can meet up again,' said Mavis, thinking on the months it had taken to renovate the community centre where they ordinarily met.

'You'll have to ask *Madame la Prrrésidente* for the details. Someone sent her an email. She's all over it like a rash.'

Mavis laughed. Joan had set up the Toulouse Club for English Pensioners and managed it ever since. Whenever using Joan's self-appointed, semi-official title, Peg rolled the 'r' as hard as she could.

'World Health Organisation?' Jeff's attention rose like Lazarus from the dusty floor.

Mavis glanced sideways. Jeff shared less and less of late but he still had an opinion on most things and voiced it when many wished to God he wouldn't.

'I've heard it all now!' Jeff laughed. 'Hardly doctors, are we?'

There it was. That guttural urge to bring her hands to Jeff's throat swilled inside her. 'Martin is . . . kind of, isn't he?'

'Hadn't thought of that!' Peg slapped Jeff on the arm, knocking him off balance. 'You don't think they want to try it out on us?'

'I'm sure Joan wouldn't agree to that,' said Mavis.

'Try what out, that's the question.' Jeff shook his head.

'Could be made from fresh air and unicorn's milk for all Joan's paid attention.' Peg engulfed Mavis with unwanted aphrodisiac as she moved closer. 'She's got other problems.'

Mavis frowned.

'They're sending some fella. Said that's all she needs. Don't know why she's surprised, in'it. Like she was gonna have the run of the show.' Peg stuck out her tongue.

Mavis smiled. Roy had always been Joan's bugbear at the club. Harmless enough, or so Mavis had thought, until he had pushed for the statutes, insisting presidency an electable office however small the association. Peg was right. A new arrival would not lighten Joan's humour. There was one head chef and the broth incapable of withstanding more.

Jeff jostled from foot to foot. A tightness gripped Mavis's throat. What was wrong with him? They'd been waiting months to get back to meeting in person. Whatever Joan had signed them up for wouldn't be cause for worry. Not Joan.

'Not quite a supermoon tonight, you know,' said Jeff.

The restriction in Mavis's throat slid to seize her shoulders. Coming back to the previous discussion would offer no light relief. One thing Jeff did like was precision.

'Sorry, Jeff?' Peg squeezed Mavis's elbow.

'Well, it's technically a supermoon when less than two hundred and twenty-four thousand miles from the Earth. But tonight's moon will be two hundred and twenty-four thousand, six hundred and sixty-two miles.'

You wouldn't catch Jeff partaking in any ritualistic praising of the moon, but he knew all there was to know about the solar system. From its beginnings in the fifties, he had never missed an episode of *The Sky at Night*, watching it religiously as a boy with his father.

'I suppose six hundred miles is nothing between friends?' suggested Peg.

A lot of strides, thought Mavis, keeping it to herself as her shoulders relaxed. She didn't want Jeff upsetting Peg. She and Peg were different but that's what Mavis liked. Having been over four continents and under three husbands — Peg's words not Mavis's — Peg had arrived in Sainte-Marie only six months ago. An eagle, free and often solitary, Peg watched over proceedings, non-judgementally taking everything in. Albeit, she did have an opinion on the 'E' in T.C.E.P. That's what they called Toulouse Club for English Pensioners for short. Quite a vocal opinion too. The T.C.E.P. was open to all nationalities but Joan had insisted on the 'E' for fear of it being confused with an antiseptic.

'Right, must dash,' said Peg. 'Should be fun tomorrow. You know this fella they're sending used to sing and dance on cruise ships.'

'I told you so!' said Jeff. 'What's a cabaret act doing testing drugs?'

Just when Mavis thought they had reached dry land, he was off again. Always grumbling, but he'd turn up. Just to grumble some more.

'Sounds a right laugh. Wonder if he's single?' Peg laughed.

'A fella singing and dancing on ships? Not sure his attention would be on you, Peggy, if you know what I mean.'

'Jeff!' Mavis prodded him in the arm.

Peg's face slumped before blossoming into a smile. 'Not gonna lie to you, Jeff. Lived off the Yugoslavian coast for a few months once.' Peg searched the air. 'Suppose it's what they call Croatia now. Anyway, let me tell you there was more than one man singing and dancing on *that* boat. And I had their full and undivided attention if *you* know what *I* mean.'

Jeff's attention flooded his sandals. Peg poked Mavis in the arm. If Peg was the eagle, Mavis was the hen. Wings clipped and forced to strut around the same confined space, not forgetting her annoying cockerel who chipped in whenever the mood took him.

'Finish the crossword?' Peg asked.

Mavis attacked it first thing in the morning, leaving any unresolved clues to simmer during the morning walk. 'Stuck on one word. It's so frustrating.'

'Hit me with it.'

'Diversion,' said Mavis. 'Third letter is a "t".'

'Interruption?' said Jeff.

'It's got thirteen letters,' Mavis exhaled more loudly than intended.

The birds returned to their morning chatter and Peg searched over the horizon.

'Entertainment,' she said, turning towards her now off-white run around. 'See you both tomorrow.'

'Nothing lends itself better to planning than a balanced diet, Mavis.'

Mavis examined Jeff later that morning from a chair on their back patio. He chuckled and tilted his head. On facial expression alone, one might have thought she'd challenged the Earth being round. Standing in front of her, he eclipsed her hitherto view of the garden.

'It takes the fun out of it.' Mavis eyed the Excel printout Jeff had placed on the garden table.

They went shopping on Fridays and Jeff prepared the list the day before. Mavis had often ventured the idea of bringing more serendipity into their eating habits.

'Don't want to spend retirement thinking about shopping lists,' said Jeff, reading her mind.

Jeff had worked tirelessly on the spreadsheet broken into sections. All they needed to do was print the same sheet each week and circle the items they needed. It demanded the same energy as writing a weekly shopping list. A detail that had eluded Jeff.

'We might as well go straight after the meeting,' said Mavis, conceding to her fate as her eye tripped, as it did once a week, on the one 'c' and two 'l's in the word 'brocolli' on the page in front of her.

Jeff wasn't a man of words in any language, least of all his own. It wasn't surprising he had never invested in learning the language of Molière. Mavis was more of a dabbler. She liked words. People and words. Speaking French killed two birds with one stone.

Her husband's leg started to bounce up and down in the seat he had taken next to her. 'Can Peggy take you?' he asked in a low voice.

'You're not coming?' Mavis pushed her prescription sunglasses up her nose. She followed Jeff's gaze to the vegetable patch at the foot of the garden. Tomato plants intertwined tall metal poles, splashes of red catching the late morning sun.

'I can't.' Jeff placed a hand on his bobbing thigh.

Mavis scrutinised him. He remained concentrated on the tomatoes. He really wasn't keen on meeting this new fella after all. Or maybe he didn't know enough about what they were supposed to be doing. It was a little vague. Their move across the Channel on Jeff retiring from the maths department made them sound impulsive but they had camped in the southwest of France for over twenty-five years before that. Same ferry, same campsite, same two weeks of the year, the regularity of Manchester University's timetable feeding Jeff's love of predictability.

'I'm sure Joan knows what she's doing. There won't be any singing and dancing,' said Mavis.

'Singing and dancing?'

'You know, the World Health fella.'

'There's a delivery.' Jeff's gaze hovered at the end at the garden.

'Tomorrow?'

'I don't make the rules, Mavis.' Jeff let out a short laugh.

'Rules?'

'When they deliver.'

'Deliver what?'

'Seeds . . . Tomato seeds.'

Mavis followed her husband's gaze back to the spiralling, metal spikes. 'But we have—'

'Right, let's do this list, shall we?' Jeff picked up the spreadsheet from the table and grabbed the pen next to Mavis's crossword book.

She studied her husband. What on earth was going on? They'd both been waiting on the first meeting back at the hall. Why cancel? And why hadn't he mentioned he wasn't coming when they had seen Peg that morning? He must have placed the order days ago.

A cough brought her attention back to the patio. 'Spaghetti or macaroni, Mavis?'

Mavis joined Jeff in a forced laugh, hers more in response to the question at hand. Jeff's other Excel innovation was their weekly meal planner. On Mondays they had pasta for tea. Tuesdays, sausages (often with ratatouille). Wednesdays, curry. Thursdays, hotpot and of course on Fridays, fish. Jeff drove to pick up pizza on Saturday from Antonio's in nearby Saint-Julien and Sunday was reserved for a roast with all the trimmings.

'Wasn't it macaroni this week? Maybe we can ring the changes next week?' said Jeff.

Mavis shrugged. Jeff had already circled spaghetti. She

lingered on the word 'maccaroni' noticing the 'c' meant for broccoli had in fact eloped. Maybe once you reached a certain age, the outer limits of excitement resembled whatever shape of pasta made its way onto your plate.

She stretched her legs and took in the view. Their farmhouse sat on a hill. Late morning, its blue shutters were pinned open, eager to invite in the light. Come early afternoon, those same shutters gathered, forming a shield against the searing heat. Village life would disappear for a few hours, plunging her and Jeff into darkened silence. Jeff didn't like novelty. He liked order, structure and pattern. The fuzzy, the ever-changing and the impulsive; that was more Mavis's bag. Jeff wouldn't admit it but mathematics offered that too. An infinite decimal, that's what Mr Braithwaite had called pi back in school. Left to its own devices, it goes on producing digits forever. Even so, Jeff was acting out of character, all keen for her to go to the meeting without him. He'd never been fond of her doing things on her own, not in fifty years together. And now he was all gung-ho for her to get in a car with Peg? Despite his theory her licence had been acquired as a favour, what with the DVLA being in Swansea?

Mavis was simply tired of trying to work him out.

Jeff or no Jeff, she would go to the meeting. She didn't want to miss out. It might do her good to try something without him. She'd lost confidence along the way. Marriage does that, leaves you unable to function separately. You fade into a bigger whole, solidifying with age like those insects you see trapped in amber. Look at Peg, she was happy and more than capable of navigating life on her own.

Mavis inhaled the heavy air, her attention drifting to another majestic army of sunflowers. Starting its burning ascent to midday prowess, the sun held court as thousands of hopeful heads looked upwards, curious to know if the coming days would be any different to those that had preceded them. Just enjoy the sun, Mavis. And double-check Peg is okay to drive. Mavis didn't drive, or at least hadn't for a long time. Not since 1983.

CHAPTER TWO

It is never polite to compare anyone to a slug. As Martin slid towards Mavis, no other word came to mind. When the chair legs scored the polished concrete floor, the building's often-cited acoustics fell flat. Silencing all conversation, a piercing screech reverberated off every single exposed iron beam before paying an unwelcome visit to the wooden stage.

'For the love of God! The chairs are laid out that way for a reason,' said Joan, throwing open her arms and fanning her batwing t-shirt. Embodying a peacock, she glared at her husband in the front row, leaving Mavis to wonder what on earth that reason might be.

Martin glanced at the stage, the remnants of what resembled a *pain au chocolat* caught in his beard. Seemingly as unsure but in no mood to challenge his wife, he reverted to mouthing at Mavis from a distance. Despite a growing certitude as to the subject of Martin's enquiry, Mavis continued to frown. As Martin's teeth hit his lower lip on the last syllable, music burst through the wall. The hip-hop dance classes had to be back on too. The centre housed many halls. Whatever it was, Mavis shoulders dropped at the welcome distraction. She didn't want to explain why Jeff wasn't here. She still didn't understand herself.

'Fire regulations.' Joan's voice echoed around the hall as she forced a smile.

Martin stared at Mavis, seeming to consider his next move. Mavis returned the stare, tilting her head towards the stage and silently urging his usual marital obedience. Some may have found his scrutiny unnerving given his forty-year career and her advancing years. Mavis had come to recognise some of Martin's mannerisms and most of his poor jokes as a by-product of a lifetime spent with the dead. On many an occasion, he'd described pathology as the only branch of medicine where a patient has a one hundred percent chance of not dying.

After another brief glimpse at his wife, the slug finally returned to his original spot in the row in front of Mavis, freeing her attention to dance around the hall and count forty or so identical new chairs in the community centre that had been the *Cadeau du ciel* fig roll factory. They must have changed them with the renovation. Gone for something more modern and easier to wipe down. Looking back at the spindly legs supporting her friend, she hoped they hadn't gone for the cheapest. A self-confessed fan of any biscuit or cake, Martin was a portly man.

Deluged by a lavender mist, Mavis turned to her left.

'Natural anti-viral,' whispered Peg, returning a spray bottle to her handbag, just as Joan opened proceedings.

'Good morning, everyone. Welcome back to the hall.'

The room replied with a collective cheer.

'Nice to be back,' shouted a voice from the rear.

Joan let a laugh escape her.

Mavis leant into her chair and inhaled the unfamiliar air. Back here. After all this time. She smiled as she ran her hands down her skirt, pleats cascading like a waterfall. As quickly, she came back to Jeff's absence. Why did she do that? Notice what wasn't there, rather than what was? Questions she couldn't answer were one thing, but it also felt strange to be without him. As Joan coughed to command full attention, Mavis looked to the stage, just as Tárrega's *Gran Vals* chose the exact same moment to announce its uninvited presence. No, not now! She scrambled inside her handbag to find the culprit. Why now? Everyone would know it was her. Their David said no one had a Nokia anymore.

'Sorry, Joan, love.' She fumbled to mute her phone.

A curious cocktail of anger and relief seemed to converge on Joan's face. She coughed and briefly consulted her notes. 'As some of you may know, we have been approached by the WHO.'

'Approached by who?' came the voice from the rear once again.

'The W.H.O.' Joan spelt out the letters as she scanned the papers before her. 'World Health Organisation. To lend a hand with SMILE.'

'Smile?' shouted the same voice.

'It's a clinical trial, Roy, called S . . . M . . . I . . . L . . . E.' In enunciating the acronym, a grimace settled on Joan's face. 'It's when you test a drug to see how well it works.'

'Is that Roy?' Peg twisted. 'Been wondering what he looks like in real life.'

'I'm neither deaf nor stupid, Joan.' Roy articulated his response in an exaggerated fashion. 'What does SMILE stand for then?'

'It doesn't stand for anything, Roy.'

'It has to stand for something, doesn't it?' whispered Mavis, leaning into Peg.

'Bet the 'E' at the end is for English,' replied her friend, as they both watched Joan's attention bounce between her watch and the hall's entrance.

'It's just the name of the trial. For a drug called *Felixir* to prevent sadness.' Joan's voice rose as the room broke into chit-chat. 'I suppose you smile when you're happy, that'll be what it stands for. Anyway, as I said, we're helping them.'

A drug to prevent sadness? Could such a thing exist? Imagine always being happy, whatever happened to you. Wouldn't that be worth a try? Mavis focused on Joan.

'Something with cannabis, Joan, love?' asked Peg. 'That's in everything now, in'it?'

'These meetings not enough to get us high?' said Roy, smiling over at Peg.

'It says here, it's injected.' Joan looked up.

'Jesus Christ, Joan! Not smack?' Roy addressed the room.

Joan wouldn't get involved in anything illegal, surely not? Mavis turned to see Peg shake in silent laughter. A more raucous response rippled around the room.

'Okay, okay. I know it sounds a bit odd.' Joan glanced at her watch. 'I'm glad it makes you all laugh, but this is a serious business. A medical drug.' She returned to reading. 'Rising levels of depression and anxiety affect the lives of millions every day. No one wants that now, do they?'

'Joan, love. We're just winding you up,' said Peg.

'Get to the point,' said Roy. 'This isn't the news at ten. What exactly do you want us to do?'

Mavis shook her head. Roy had never forgiven Joan for leaving him in the waiting room during the last online meeting. Joan swore it an oversight. Mavis had her doubts.

'I'm proud to announce, Roy, that the T.C.E.P. is going to help out at one of the many European trials right here in Toulouse,' continued Joan, bringing her attention away from the main door and back to her audience.

Clapping fluttered around the room but had no time to burst into full flight.

Roy craned his neck to address everyone. 'A drug to make you always happy? Maybe life was never meant to be one gentle flowing river.'

'He's got a point here,' said Peg.

Did he? Mavis went to ask but a banging drew her attention, along with that of Joan and everyone else, to another entrance. A forgotten one in the side wall. Someone was trying to open the door that joined two halls. The room fell into silence. Roy stood to pull away a stack of chairs, leaving the door to swing open.

Shrouded in hip-hop beats stood a man, flanked by two boys in low slung sweatpants and tight vests from the dance class next door. Tanned skin offset bristly grey hair and a broad smile. He looked familiar. Mavis frowned. The complexion and crewcut reminded her of that Action Man the boys used to play with when they were little, that was it. They would move his eyes back and forth for hours with the switch at the back of his head. Mavis repositioned her glasses. Instead of fatigues, a Hawaiian shirt hung effortlessly on this GI Joe, its royal-blue fabric scattered with bright green palm trees. With at least four of the shirt's top buttons undone, a plungingly low 'v' invited Mavis's gaze downwards. Beige shorts, a pair of bronzed legs and some well-worn Birkenstocks completed the look. The absence of socks left Mavis with the mounting suspicion the new arrival wasn't British. This had to be whoever had been sent for this project. Mavis felt her lips curl into their own smile.

'Thanks lads.' Action Man fist bumped his new companions. 'You must be Joan,' he shouted towards the stage. 'How rude of me to be late. Traffic was bad and then I happened upon the wrong hall.'

A melodic accent accompanied perfect English. If the lack of socks wasn't proof enough, him stumbling on every single aitch left no doubt: the new arrival was French. Action Man walked towards the stage. Searching the room as he went, he dropped his gaze to focus on Mavis. Turning away, she cast a furtive glance at Peg.

'Pass me the factor fifty.' Peg poked Mavis in the arm.

Laughter escaped Mavis. She returned to smoothing the pleats in her skirt, choosing to associate the fluttering in her stomach with not having arrived early enough to partake in the patisserie. The stage now housed a wall of royal blue and green, Joan and Action Man stood side by side, their backs to the audience. Chiding could be heard as clear as day.

'You were meant to be here half an hour ago.'

'Joan, isn't it?' An arm encircled *Madame la Présidente.*

'They wanted to know how—'

'A perfect time to introduce me then.' Action Man cajoled an unhappy Joan to face the audience.

Joan's face deepened in colour on being greeted by the silence she had sought at the start of the meeting. She stretched out an arm, as she released herself from Action Man's grip. 'And here is Rémy. Sent to us by . . . well, I'll let him explain.'

A Mexican wave of hellos rumbled through the flabbergasted hall.

'Firstly, let me thank you. We couldn't do this without people like you.' Rémy smiled.

A second wave passed through the crowd. Silent this time, it carried the simple desire to be of use. Neither Mexican nor British, more a growing feeling that often consumes people as age traces its path.

'Peg. Nice to meet you,' shouted Peg, lifting her hand. 'Joan says it's legal, this drug.' Roy laughed out loud from the other side of the room. 'It's some kind of anti-depressant?'

'Excellent question.' Rémy broadened his attention to the entire room. 'Anti-depressants are prescribed when there is a problem. *Felixir* is quite different. It prevents sadness and worry, stopping depression before it starts.'

Mavis looked at Peg. It sounded like a vaccine against sadness. Peg rolled her eyes.

'So, down to business,' continued Rémy. 'Who wants to volunteer to try this new drug?'

'Get injected?' Joan riffled through the papers she still clenched. 'Us?'

Mavis absorbed the hall's mounting levels of surprise, as well as their inability to disturb the one person with any medical acumen. Before her, Martin had slid into deep slumber. Joan twitched on beholding the same sight. Had Jeff been right to have doubts? No one had mentioned jabbing *them*.

'I'm happy enough, thanks. I'll give your new drug a miss.' Peg offered the hall a beaming smile.

'Ms Davies . . . Peg, has a point,' said Roy. 'If you're coming here because you think us oldies are all miserable, you're wrong.'

Mavis frowned, wondering if it was the first time she had ever seen Roy smile.

'Happy or sad, bit too late for us now anyway,' chimed a new voice from the back of the room.

'Farming us out like knackered guinea pigs. Not the actions of a President, is it Joan?'

Mavis's head bobbed in indecision.

'But it's an opportunity to—' Rémy turned to Joan.

'It's an opportunity for nothing whatsoever. None of

this was in the email.' Joan folded the paperwork in her hands and ran two fingers along the crease.

Rémy's gaze ping-ponged around the room. Lines that traced a lifetime on his forehead straightened and reformed as he rubbed them with insistence. Was sending someone as old as them a tactic to sign them up wondered Mavis. Not that he had said as much.

A clapping made her jump.

On stage, his hands glued together as if in prayer, Rémy smiled. 'I bet you're all thirsty. Let's break for coffee.'

The more agile members of the audience already halfway to the table that housed the metal urn, Joan didn't have time to counter the interval. She scuttled after Rémy, prodding Martin en route.

'I told them I couldn't do two things at once,' Rémy mumbled as he descended the stairs in front of Mavis, 'let alone keep it from Mike.'

What on earth was going on? Mavis had never seen Joan so off-guard, and what could Rémy mean? Mike must be with another trial. Their David was always saying you had to keep things quiet in their line of work. But what did Rémy mean about two things at once? He was only here for this SMILE thing, wasn't he? Finding herself staring, she caught Rémy's eye. A rather deep brown one. Two, in fact, that locked her in their gaze before coordinating themselves to wink directly at her. Heat coursed through her body. She looked away. David's Action Man never used to wink. Peg hadn't seen that, had she? Nothing much got past her. Maybe the wink hadn't been intended for Mavis at all.

Mavis turned, only to relock eyes with Rémy. A second wink.

'He can stick whatever he wants in me,' Peg whispered.

'Peg!' Peg must have seen the wink. Winks, plural. No, she can't have. 'Even this drug?' asked Mavis, searching for conversation.

'Okay, anything but that. Anyway, why would you? It makes no sense.'

Eradicate sadness? Who wouldn't want to be forever happy? Life didn't let you but what if a drug could? Or were they too old to be thinking such things? Whoever had said that had a point. Mavis thought back to the winks. They were too old to be thinking a lot of things. She picked up her crossword book and flattened her skirt with her other hand.

'You'll have no pleats left. You okay?' said Peg.

'Just a bit hot.' Mavis fanned her neck.

'Let's go and see what's happening at the coffee table?'

The last thing Mavis wanted was a third wink. 'I'll stay here, catch my breath, love.'

Peg's yoga pants breezed past, leaving in their wake some badly needed thinking time.

Goodness. What was all that about? The crossword book wafted faster. Fancy winking at her like that. Not right, was it? Mavis searched the cavernous ceiling. This was when she needed Jeff. He was right to be sceptical after all. And she wouldn't be having any bother if he were here. She closed her eyes and let the book drop onto her lap. Maybe winking was Action Man's way? He'd put his arm around Joan after all. A friendly type. Mavis fidgeted in the rigid chair. Bloody uncomfortable things. Why had they gone and changed them?

'Hankering.' The voice came from behind. Breath whispered over her neck as it stumbled on the aitch.

Mavis straightened. Her eyes sprang open. There was no way she was turning around. 'I . . . sorry?'

'Craving.'

'What . . .'

'Seven down. Craving. Nine letters.'

Craving? Sweat pooled in the small of her back. Mavis looked to her knees and the open crossword book. 'Seven down. Hankering. Right you are.'

'Delighted to meet you. We must find time to chat.'

By the time Mavis had mustered the courage to turn around, Rémy was already strutting his way back to the coffee table.

CHAPTER THREE

Gab strode into the office. 'Mike! What's up?'

Mike jumped as a file dropped into his lap. 'Just thinking.'

'About what?'

'Procrastination.'

'Well, you can push that to later. We've got stuff to be getting on with.'

Mike burst out laughing.

Gab stopped in his tracks, shaking his head. 'I really don't see what's so funny. Have you seen our workload?'

'Procrastinate. Push to later. Get it?'

And that *was* what he had been thinking about. He had stumbled upon a video on YouTube. Research of sorts. Two guys in the States explaining that procrastination was at the heart of creativity. People desperately wanted to be creative nowadays, didn't they? Innovative, they called it or, even better, disruptive. No money could be made from harmony. To be honest, the two guys in question seemed to have simply repackaged the notion of 'thinking' and attached a price tag. People had become so caught up with moving from one thing to the next.

'You sure you're okay, Gab?'

Gab slapped a hand on Mike's shoulder. He seemed to force a laugh. 'I'm sorry, Mike. All this work, it's wearing me out.'

'Don't worry, they *will* ramp up the teams.'

That was what they had always done. It wasn't the first time they had experienced a spike in cases, albeit less sustained than recently. You could only do what you could do. And that YouTube video had insisted creativity lurks in the sweet spot between tackling things immediately and getting around to them when it is too late. Everyone agreed the electric car, blockchain and the latest machine learning algorithms had not burst forth from nothing at five minutes to midnight. Their case load was higher, but individual cases were getting trickier too. They needed to keep their wits about them.

Gab shrugged.

'It must have come up at the meeting?' Mike stared at Gab. 'We've been saying for weeks we need more resource.'

'Of course it came up.' Gab snapped his answer, pausing on the way back to his desk.

Mike's attention dropped to their curly spider plant, Shirley, her green ringlets cascading over the edge of his desk. He wondered how to pursue his line of questioning. Gab seemed more agitated than usual. In any case, he was cut off at the pass.

'Ignore me. It's a bit overwhelming, that's all.'

Mike had worked with Gab long enough to see signs of fatigue encroaching on the inextinguishable positivity for which his colleague was best known. He had been out of sorts for a few weeks. Not his usual chirpy self.

'Our caseload overwhelming?' Mike ventured. 'It's the uncertainty that's making it harder for everyone, isn't it?'

Not that uncertainty was new but there has always been a tendency to dupe oneself into thinking everything in life can be controlled. A realisation to the contrary can take time and stress is a sneaky little bastard. Like rodents eating away at wiring, you don't know there's a problem until the house short-circuits.

Gab nodded. 'You're right. Just a heavy caseload. No biggie.' He turned to grace Mike with a broad smile. 'But who is at hand?'

'The WHO is at hand!'

Laughing, the colleagues raised their palms to high five. Working for the World Happiness Organisation, the old joke never wore thin. Initially bemoaning acronyms as a confusing scourge of modern administration, Mike had let himself be persuaded of their useful brevity. Gab and Mike had run the Assignments Agency for years, or 'The Agency' as it was commonly called. Gab was its official director and Mike his number two. Civil servants on one hand and recruitment professionals on the other, they placed agents wherever extra support was needed.

Remembering the dossier weighing on his thighs, Mike lifted it and read. '*Toulouse Club for English Pensioners*. Is that a thing?'

'Wey aye, man.'

It was one of Gab's favoured party tricks, British regional accents. He prided himself on anything north of Watford. Mike had a passable Brummie accent, that was about it. Gab slapped his belly and dropped himself into his orange seat. An extra few pounds, Gab insisted, were essential for a trumpeter. Mike saw no need to insist he hadn't played for years. Settling in to read, Mike's arms rubbed up against the green velvet armrests. What some would call 'Instagrammable', their office boasted mismatched chairs, Gab having fallen through his old one. The eclectic seating added an inadvertent touch of cosiness. Worthy of a Swedish hashtag, no doubt. #Hygge. No one could really say that word, could they? Maybe it was a good thing communication was being pushed online. Mike pulled several plastic subfolders out of the file, each containing reams of blue paper.

'Same old. Same old,' said Mike. Having skim read the file, he looked up to see Gab's expectant face. 'Still, this one sounds a bit tricky. Who are we sending?'

'Who hev wuh sent, yee mean?'

'Someone has already gone?'

Gab pounded his keyboard. Mike remembered regional accents were also Gab's default for distracting attention.

'Wey aye. Rémy,' mumbled Gab.

'Rémy?' Mike rearranged the subfolders in the manila file. 'You're joking, right?' He craned to see Gab's expression hidden behind the monitor.

'He's the only agent we had available.' Gab abandoned the Geordie accent.

'But we pulled him out of the field for good reason.'

'Let's say the stars and moon aligned.'

'There's something you're not telling me?'

'Whey aye neet.'

'What?'

'Of course not.'

'Rémy? Really?'

'Look, I know he's a bit of a—'

'Liability?'

'Free spirit.' A nervous laugh rose from behind Gab's screen.

'I hope you know what you're doing, Gab.'

The more Mike thought about Gab's return to the office, the odder it seemed. He and Gab were both convened to the organisation-wide management meetings. Seeing no interest in both attending, they alternated their presence. At the end of each month, the meetings covered all operational areas of the Organisation and took some time. Gab had come back to the office way earlier than normal. He had never really answered the question about when they would be getting additional resource either.

'The meeting finished earlier than usual then?' asked Mike.

'Oh, I think it might go on for a while yet.' Gab drummed his fingers on the desk, his gaze wandering around the park outside.

Mike inspected his colleague more closely. Gab's earlier burst of joviality had quickly evaporated, a dark silence subsuming him whole. 'So, they don't need you?' He was determined to come back to the meeting somehow.

'You could say that.' Gab snorted.

'Could say what?'

Gab turned to face Mike. Sitting forward in his chair, he rubbed his stubbled chin. 'I suppose we have to see it through.'

Years of sharing the same office had taught Mike to recognise Gab beating around the bush. 'What happened at this meeting?'

'Changes, they said.'

'Changes?'

Mike thought about the previous monthly meeting, only then remembering it had been Gab who had attended the last two. He couldn't recall Gab sharing anything of note. 'I haven't seen any communication about changes.

No memo or mail. Have you?' Mike started to scroll his inbox.

Gab slammed the desk. 'Bloody newbies cosying up to management!'

Curly Shirley trembled.

'There were new people—'

'Three guys in suits called John.'

'What, all of them?'

'Probably.' Gab threw his arms in the air.

Mike narrowed his eyes at Araminta III. She sat on top of the new filing cabinet where Tina and Rod had once swayed. Sadly, the two palms had been relocated four doors down to make room for extra storage. Resembling no one of note, Araminta was their third attempt at a peppermint plant. Chosen for her skills in increasing alertness and lowering frustration, Mike wondered what could calm Gab today. He paused, calculating his next move. 'Want to tell me about these changes?'

'Some corporate bullshit. You know what this means?'

'They're finding other ways to help us with our workload?'

'They think our systems don't work.'

'Our systems?' Mike gave Gab a questioning look.

Systems in the plural was a stretch. The one system they deployed decided which projects took immediate priority over others, even if they ultimately treated all cases. It had never failed them, albeit basic. To be honest, calling it a system was a stretch. Their approach, if you prefer, was based on a general feeling. It was akin to noticing cows lying in their pastures or birds flying low in the sky and predicting rain. Yes, of course, satellites could observe cloud patterns and computers use numerical forecast equations. That didn't make the cows nor the birds any less reliable.

'But what are these new systems?' asked Mike.

'Doesn't matter. I told her no.'

'Who?'

'Cynthia.'

'That's a funny name for a John.' Mike attempted a chuckle.

Gab's face was stonelike. 'If it ain't broke, don't fix it.'

Mike nodded slowly. 'You left the meeting in a huff, didn't you?'

'Maybe.' Gab's lips stretched into the beginnings of a smile. 'It's not right, coming here and telling us what we've spent years understanding and fine-tuning.'

Having succeeded in initiating the beginnings of a real conversation, Mike mused on how to keep it flowing. 'I see where you're coming from, but what's wrong with being a bit open-minded? We need the extra help, whatever form it takes. You said yourself you're tired.'

'And now you're going to give me a lecture too?' Gab's smile faded.

'Let's see what it's all about before we decide.'

'The discussion is closed.' Gab retreated behind his monitor.

Mike clenched his teeth. There was no talking to Gab when he was like this. No one understood their mission better than them, Gab certainly had a point. But Cynthia, or one of these Johns, might have other ideas. All Mike was interested in was helping everyone in need. As Gab hammered his keyboard, Mike pondered on how best to retrieve the situation. He also made a mental note to attend the next meeting. There was more to this than met the eye. Why was Gab refusing to share? Mike wasn't daft. Had things been different, he could have been on YouTube, gracing the stage in a headset. Everyone saw Gab as the brains and him the brawn. That's often how it is for veterans, he knew that. For the first time, he wondered if Gab didn't think the same.

'And you're sure this never came up before?' Mike asked. 'It's a little sudden. Surely they'd let us know beforehand these changes were coming.'

There was a pause in typing.

'I'm sorry. Everyone is more worked up than usual, including me. Bet yas reet fed up wi' wer.' Gab peeped out from the side of his monitor and winked.

Mike laughed. He was right. Gab *was* hiding something from him. He heard rustling. Pursuing its trajectory over two monitors, an Everton Mint landed with a thud on his keyboard. Gab would often joke he had more than one sweet tooth. Back in the day, he used to be out in the field a lot more. They both did, but people mostly remembered Gab for that big assignment in the Middle East. They seldom went anywhere nowadays. On the rare occasion either of them did, they came back with some form of confectionary.

'One won't hurt. Keep our strength up.' Gab returned to the filing tray on his desk. 'Right, let's see who's up next.'

Liberating the black-and-white peace offering from its cellophane constraints, Mike popped it into his mouth and returned to his own files. As sure as he was Gab was keeping something from him, he hoped he was wrong. They had worked together for so long. Why wouldn't he trust him? Let Gab be unforthcoming. Mike would wait it out. The one thing about the hidden is that it always finds its way into the light. He broke into a deflective whistle, the melody echoing back. Outside a huddle of plump chests, supported by twice as many scrawny legs, perched in a nearby cherry tree. White speckles spattered the green and purple plumage, iridescent light catching the slightest of movements.

Mike whistled once more.

Starlings can mimic anything. It really is a skill. People call them greedy and selfish. They are neither. They've just learnt to eat quickly, moving as they do in flocks. People aren't that dissimilar. They merge to follow convention, subjugate themselves to the needs and expectations of others, chase whatever everyone else is pursuing. They secure their future with a job offering a decent pension scheme, rather than chasing what they believe in. They marry whoever everyone else deems suitable and endure sex by fantasising about the one who got away. They have children because that's what you do at thirty. In an effort to ignore midlife reckoning when it knocks, carving out an acceptable future for those same children then becomes their sole focus. That's what the flocks of people do. A personal quest for happiness whilst forever trying to fade into the crowd. Nowadays, that very irony constituted the mainstay of the Agency's files, not people struggling to accept that life has its fair share of unavoidable and unfortunate events. Mike glanced at the file Gab had given him. Of course, they still had those cases too.

Minty sugariness trickled down Mike's throat as he looked back out into the park. The whisper of a spritely violin came to join the fun, another starling sat on its scroll. Few were those who knew the musician's name and so people referred to him as 'The German'. A delight to listen to, he often busked outside their office or in front of the Records Office, the building that centralised all the Organisation's information. To think he had stopped playing for many years, the attitudes of others having made him doubt his true worth, or at least not pursue that which made him the happiest.

CHAPTER FOUR

The concrete walls and corrugated metal ceiling delivered on sobriety and offered a welcome escape from the rowdy midday sun. Today was registration day, with patients invited to ensure all paperwork was in place and attend a presentation about what to expect from the clinical trial. Mavis looked at the suspended strip light overhead. It flickered as if emitting an indecipherable message. She stroked the fabric of her skirt into neat lines. Showing up today had not been without hesitation. She had considered feigning a headache but it wouldn't be right to pull out.

After what, from afar, had appeared a fractious coffee break at the community centre the previous Friday, Rémy had retaken the stage to explain a dreadful misunderstanding. Joan's virulent nodding had accompanied his sincerest of apologies. He had been misinformed. T.C.E.P. members were invited as helpers to *run* the trials, not as patients themselves. Medical staff would administer the drugs but he needed administrative support. His eyes had rested on Mavis, explaining this necessitated only a handful of people. She had locked her gaze on an upside-down daisy on her skirt, deciding she was not one of them. It was only on the drive home Peg had shared the liberty she had taken of signing up both Mavis and Jeff. They didn't want to miss out after all. An invitation had followed to today's presentation.

'Bertaud, Jean-Marc.' Rémy pulled the microphone to his mouth as he called names from the list in his hand and scanned the gymnasium that had transformed itself into a windowless clinic for the duration of the trials.

Mavis had spotted him straight away, as soon as she and Peg had entered a half-open door and taken the nearest available seats. Today's green shirt was covered in pink flamingos and at the centre of the action. Compering clinical trials must be a far cry from his usual job on the boats. Peg had chattered non-stop on the way there about how Rémy knew more Greek islands than she'd had hot dinners.

'He goes by the stage name Bob McWonder, you know,' she had said as Mavis had watched her power through a red traffic light. 'He said it covers his *eclectic* repertoire from Dylan to Stevie Wonder but more than once he's been booked as a DJ.'

Mavis laughed to herself, remembering Rémy's arrival at the community centre with the hip-hop boys from the class next door. As she watched him, his hair shone in the artificial light. She felt a tickling in her palms. Closing her eyes, she imagined her hands stroking his head. Stroking his head? Her eyes sprang open. What was she thinking! Mavis shook her own head, remembering their David creasing up with laughter the day she had discovered Action Man's surprisingly soft hair.

'There's a bit of the Tony Blackbird about him, don't you think?' Peg poked Mavis.

'Tony Blackburn? He could be on the radio, I suppose.'

A smile cracked Mavis's face as she broke what Peg must have recognised as a lingering stare. Peg had as much trouble with names as any other information she was asked to retain. Mavis rubbed her hands up and down her skirt. 'Reminds me more of Maurice.'

'You've lost me, Mave.'

'Sells shoes at the market on a Wednesday.' Mavis had already noticed the two ladies in front of them, thighs spilling over the sides of the narrow chairs like generously filled muffin cases. They twisted to look at her, resembling each other enough in looks and age to suggest they were sisters. One parted her hair on the right, the other on the left. Both offered a scowl. Worried she had caused offence by talking too loudly, Mavis leant into Peg to whisper, 'Well, Maurice calls the numbers at the village bingo, doesn't he?'

Peg shrugged.

Mavis searched the room for Joan and Martin. In their absence, her attention fell on a digital clock on legs. Maybe to reassure people they would see daylight again, the outside temperature accompanied the time. Thirty-five degrees. It was hot and nearly time. Rémy hadn't seen her for the moment. If he didn't see her, he couldn't wink. That was her plan of action anyway, if only a temporary fix. Winking followed by talk of hankering had caught her off-guard. Not that he would be interested in her, not in that way. He was probably harmless and she was worrying about nothing. Safety in numbers was never a bad thing though. Where *were* Joan and Martin? From what Joan had said, she had taken the last two places, insisting that this would be right up Martin's 'medical' alley and provoking a baffling ten-minute fit of laughter from Peg. If Mavis was a gambling woman, she'd say this was more a Joan manoeuvre to keep Roy as far away as possible.

Mavis stole another glance at Rémy. Laughing, he sat in the middle of a long line of tables. Sheets were checked and cross-checked by a chain gang of paper pushers to either side, before converging on him and his microphone. Names were called and people went to the desk to sign, before wandering to the far side of the hall.

'Disclaimers,' whispered Peg.

'You what?' Mavis turned to her friend.

'Those papers. You know, if anyone carks it.'

Mavis brought her hand to her mouth. 'You don't think . . . but how would . . . that's not—'

'Unlikely, Mave, but there's always a risk with drugs, in'it?' Peg burst into laughter.

'Not right though, is it?'

From the corner of her eye, Mavis caught sight of Joan and Martin. Approaching from behind the long line of tables, they offered a wave and the beauty of hindsight. Mavis and Peg must have circumvented the main entrance. Joan strode over to the seating area, her sandals squeaking on a wooden floor that in normal times greeted basketball talent of the younger variety. Like a plane making its descent, she traced the blue line that ran the edge of the court, losing Martin as she came in to land. A familiar smell accompanied her thudding touchdown in the chair next to Mavis.

Troubled by Peg's recent comments, Mavis searched for conversation. 'Bad chest, Joan, love?'

'Bad chest?'

'Smells like Vicks VapoRub.'

Joan's eyes widened. Mavis inhaled, her certitude now feeling precipitous.

'That's my new Jo Malone.'

Peg's laugh echoed through the hall. 'Jo with an 'e'? My sister said they had loads of that knock-off Joe Malone down the market last week. You're lucky. She smelt like a damp pair of daps for three days. Tampin' she was.'

Was it the contraband perfume or Welsh vernacular that upset Joan more? Mavis couldn't tell. Joan coming from what Mavis understood to be one of the nicer parts of London, it could have been both. Not that Mavis had many reference points, just the conviction that anything below Crewe was the South. Mavis didn't have time to segue into pastures new.

'Where did you get that perfume, Martin?' Joan shouted at her husband.

Less of a controlled landing, more a plummet from the skies, Martin swooped to stand in front of them.

'It was Roy, wasn't it?' said Joan, shaking her head.

Mavis peeked sympathetically at Martin. Roy often did trips to the UK, returning with van loads of British produce. Heinz baked beans, Ginger Nuts, Yorkshire Tea, Tunnock's Teacakes, Cadbury Dairy Milk; all those tastes of home Brits abroad miss.

'Can't smell nothing now, Joan, love. Probably just this stuffy old gym,' Peg said, breaking the silence. 'You're right though. Funny place to run clinical trials, in'it?'

'I told you, Peggy. Something not quite right about it.'

Mavis smiled. She didn't know enough about clinical trials to know where you might hold them but was relieved to see the air, albeit figuratively, had cleared. Roy hadn't been the only one winding up Joan at the community centre. Peg hadn't been right with Joan since sharing her own 'gift' for the first time recently. Afflicted by Alzheimer's, Peg's mum had given up the Tarot the day she was found outside Carmarthen Greggs telling a mocking crowd a Welshman would one day host the ten o'clock news. When Joan had asked why Peg hadn't taken over her mum's stall, she had snapped. But then

Joan's 'gift' to others was often rubbing them up the wrong way.

'*Bonjour*,' said a familiar voice, this time close enough to not need a microphone.

The hairs on Mavis's neck sprang to attention, whisking her back to the community centre. She surveyed the tanned feet peeping out of a pair of Birkenstocks, the toes blurring into one.

'Tickle me,' said Peg.

'*Pardon*?' Rémy laughed.

Mavis refocused, counted Rémy's toes one by one. What the hell was Peg up to?

'Tickle me, seventy-three. Two fat ladies, twenty-two. *Le Loto*, Rémy. Thought you would make a good bingo caller, didn't we Mave?'

Mavis raised her head. She looked for the two ladies who had been in front of them. Thank God they had left and not overheard Peg's attempts at humour. The clock shouted 12.30. Everyone else must be in the presentation room. Had Rémy come over to take them there too? He seemed in no rush whatsoever. Silence reigned. Maybe interjecting would make the conversation less embarrassing, not more.

'I suppose you're used to being on the microphone,' she said.

Rémy sniffed the air, Joan tensing. Mavis watched him. His eyes didn't move from left to right and no wink in sight. Instead, he smiled, a kindness flooding his gaze. Mavis returned the smile, her shoulders dropping just as a well-worn Saint Christopher pendant caught the halogen light. She squinted, her thoughts entangling themselves in a nest of wild chest hair. She sprang as straight as a meerkat. There was that fluttering she had felt on first meeting him. She glanced back at the clock. Well, it was lunchtime after all.

'A flamboyance of flamingos, that's what they call it.' Martin pointed at Rémy's shirt.

'Flamboyant is definitely the word,' muttered Joan.

'Alone today?' Rémy asked. She could feel him looking at her. 'There's a place for Jeff, you know.'

Mavis frowned. She nodded, studying her own feet for a change. She'd explained to Jeff that Peg had reserved him a place, that they'd be one down without him. 'Couldn't come. Delivery.'

All eyes were now on her. Safety in numbers had played against her. It was embarrassing Jeff not being there again. More talk about more parcels. He was simply disinclined to help from what she could see.

'Come on, let's get to the presentation. I'll show you around afterwards.' Rémy looked up to the flickering strip light. 'That not annoying anyone else?'

No one replied, allowing the silence to return. It was the kind of silence that had a lot to say. It said that no one else believed Jeff was waiting on a delivery either.

'For the love of—'

Mavis cut Joan off at the pass with a firm stare.

'*Pardon*?' said Rémy, stood at the front of the room.

Numerous heads turned to look at Joan, Martin, Peg and Mavis sitting in the back row. In front of them, around two hundred people had been attentively listening to how a revolutionary new 'happy drug' called *Felixir* would be injected into them every day for eight weeks and their bloods tested once a week on a Friday. Mavis had zoned out after the first part and resorted to examining the finer detail of a room that had all the windowless charm of the main hall despite having windows. Going by the tiling, it must have been a changing room in former times.

'It seems a little unfair,' said Joan. 'These good people here have come to feel happier. If you inject some of them with these placebo things, they won't, will they?'

Several heads nodded in agreement. Mavis looked to Peg.

'Placebos look like the drug they're testing, but don't contain nothing,' whispered Peg. 'You don't know if you're being given the placebo or the real thing though.'

Mavis frowned, wondering the point of testing a drug that contained no drug. She'd have to ask their David. He knew about that kind of thing. They hadn't heard from him in a while now. She hoped he was okay. Probably busy with work.

'But how else would we have a control sample, Joan? We need to have the drug and its placebo to check if the drug is really working.' Rémy smiled broadly. 'And no one signed up to be happier. They signed up to trial a drug.'

'With everything going on, we'd sure like to be happier!' shouted a voice from the front row.

'Hear, hear,' said another. 'It's all doom and gloom on the news isn't it and have you seen the price of petrol now? Who wouldn't want to worry less?'

'Exactly the spirit!' said Rémy, shuffling the papers in his hands. 'Right—'

'The spirit?' asked Joan.

'The spirit.' Rémy fixed Joan with a stare. 'And without further ado, what a great time to introduce our volunteers at the back.' Rémy stretched out an arm. 'This is one of many trials taking place across Europe so all questionnaires will be undertaken in English, allowing results to be compiled at the end. These good people are here to help you. So, what's *in* the injections shouldn't concern them. The effect they have on you is what they will focus on.'

Joan's half-raised arm sank to her lap as grateful clapping trickled through the room.

'That told her,' Peg whispered, Mavis shifting her weight sideways before Peg's finger could meet her ribs.

The last time Joan had been so deftly put back in her place was when Roy had Googled 'origins of the Women's Institute'. Reading to an expectant Zoom crowd, he had shared how the first ever meeting had been held in North Wales in 1915, Joan having spent the previous ten minutes recounting her Aunt Edna single-handedly starting the movement in Surrey.

The room started to empty, people spilling past them and Rémy bringing up the rear. To Mavis's right, Joan muttered under her breath about her husband having been retired long enough to be out of the game.

'In my limited knowledge, Martin, they don't perform clinical trials on the dead,' she whispered.

'Everything will become clearer in good time.' Rémy placed his hand on Joan's shoulder and causing her to start. 'Let's do that visit now.'

One by one, they squeaked back into the main hall, rubber soling the preference of an entire generation, not only Joan. En route, Rémy revisited the clinical trials planning, evoking the importance of injecting everyone within an hour window every morning.

'Holding trials in France makes this rather challenging. People tend to arrive as and when they feel like, but then isn't it understandable to find punctuality rather restrictive?' Rémy laughed.

Joan rolled her eyes in Mavis's direction.

'And this is where people will queue for injections,' continued Rémy, stopping to point out snaking metal barriers that led to a row of tents. 'A potential bottleneck, two of you may need to man this, and with good humour.'

'People get a bit tetchy?' asked Martin.

'*Bien sûr*. The French, like any busy people, find waiting very restrictive.'

It being the second time Rémy had used the same adjective, conspiratorial glances concluded it unnecessary to point out the French seemed to find constraint in everything and its opposite.

'And so that's where the injections happen?' asked Martin, pointing to the tents.

'Exactly,' said Rémy. 'And after the injections, it is back to the waiting room for the questionnaires. It really is the most important part of the whole trial.'

Joan approached Rémy. 'The questionnaires?'

'Looking around you won't tell you where you're heading, looking inside will.'

'Sorry?'

'Important to get that stuff out there.'

'For the drugs company?' Joan shared her frown with the rest of the group.

Rémy threw back his head in laughter. 'And, of course, you can't let everyone leave straight after the injections.'

'You can't?' asked Martin.

'*Bien sûr que non!* Do you think these people would feel reassured if we didn't ask them to wait a little?'

Mavis laughed as Martin's eyebrow danced in her direction. Her body no longer carried the tension that had accompanied her to the centre. The introduction had been fun and had passed without incident. Maybe she had misjudged Rémy. Never Joan though.

Madame la Présidente took the reins. 'Let's decide who's doing what, shall we? I have a good level of French, *n'est-ce pas?* I'm happy to manage the questionnaires.'

'I'll do that queue area,' said Peg.

'Me too,' said Martin.

'And what about you, Mavis?' asked Rémy.

'Where do you want me? With Joan?'

'Well, there is one area I haven't shown you all. Come with me.'

A lingering smell of stale sweat suggested the room into which Rémy guided them had previously stored the gymnasium's equipment. That humming odour now mingled with a gentle purring that emanated from several white appliances congregated on the back wall. Some had glass doors and others were less forthcoming with their secrets.

'Fridges?' asked Mavis.

'These injections need to be kept at low temperatures, Mavis,' explained Joan.

'As do the blood samples.' Rémy walked to one of the fridges and indicated with his hand the digital thermometer on front of one of the doors. 'Welcome to the stockroom.'

Mavis scanned the room. A red light flashed in a corner of the ceiling on what seemed to be a recently installed security camera. These injections must be worth a bob or two.

'I suppose they need to be counted?' asked Mavis.

'Counted, yes. And then transported out to the injection tents, as and when we need them.' Rémy pointed to what resembled a dessert trolley to his left. He stared expectantly at Mavis. 'And when we do the blood tests, we need them collected and stored.'

Mavis nodded. She quite liked counting, especially in French. The village bingo proved challenging once you got to the higher numbers but she doubted they would be under as intense time pressure. Some of those women worked ten cards at a time. It was no wonder she had never won the leg of ham.

'I think that's it for today.' Rémy clapped his hands, pulling Mavis's attention back to the stockroom. '*Pardon*, I get a little claustrophobic.'

One by one, they left the room. Joan led the charge, followed by an obedient Martin. Peg made a quick exit too. Like Rémy, she had never appreciated closed spaces. An understandable sentiment, Mavis assumed, for anyone with a past life as a Victorian chimney sweep. Mavis followed suit but one of her sandals stuck to the floor. Her leg jammed. Feeling her balance go, she reached for the dessert trolley. Her grip tightening, she watched it wheel away from her as if in slow motion.

A cry escaped her.

She plunged into a pair of strong arms.

The door slammed shut.

The room, once flooded by light from the gymnasium, fell into semi-obscurity. Fright paralysed her limbs. A warm body squished up against her face, her nose tickling with the smell of cologne, but something else. Wiry hair. Rugged, male chest hair. Saint Christopher glued himself to her chin. Mavis jerked her head back. Rémy didn't move. Illuminated by the glow from the glass-doored fridges, his face hovered above. Deep brown eyes locked with hers. They moved neither left nor right. They didn't even blink. They simply watched her, radiating the kindness Mavis thought she had seen earlier that day.

'I've got you.' A smile traced its way across his wrinkled face. She could feel his breath. His teeth were too straight and white. Mavis was old enough and close enough to know they weren't his own. She dropped her gaze to his shirt. A flamingo, perfectly balanced on one leg, smiled back at her.'Things happen out of the blue sometimes, don't they?'

'Just a bit of a surprise.' Mavis allowed her muscles to relax. A little. The moment in itself wasn't unpleasant. She could stay there longer.

The sound of banging became louder.

'Important to be open to unexpected turns in the road, don't you think?' he said.

As she started to nod, it happened. One of the big brown eyes fell shut, leaving the other to twinkle like the North Star. Mavis jerked. Her muscles tightened. What was she thinking? What was he thinking, more to the point? There it was. The third wink she had been avoiding, and at the exact moment her mind had wandered back to running her hands over Action Man's bristly crewcut.

'Mavis. Are you okay?' Peg's voice travelled through the door, with another slam of her fist.

Mavis straightened her back. 'I stumbled. I'm fine.'

Rémy pushed her to a standing position. 'You need the keys to get in from that side. We can use the handle from here,' he shouted.

Mavis brushed her skirt and tried to smooth her hair.

'Let's continue this chat another time,' offered Rémy.

Mavis didn't reply. They wouldn't be continuing anything, at any time. She grasped for the door handle. Air, light and salvation flooded the stockroom. She rushed into Peg's open arms. Jesus Christ! If her father could see her now.

'You poor thing, Mave. No permanent damage?' asked Peg.

'Terrible thing for a claustrophobic to be trapped in a

room. No one wants that, do they?' Joan said to Rémy. 'But *you* seem quite unruffled.'

'I've been thinking,' said Rémy. 'If Jeff can't make it, let's give his place to Roy. His French is also excellent, *n'est-ce pas*? He can help you with the questionnaires.'

CHAPTER FIVE

The visor did little to block out the sunlight flooding the Peugeot 208 as Jeff slid his hands back down the steering wheel. They had inched up the plastic. Hands in a quarter to three position, that's what they advised now. Jeff glanced at the empty seat next to him, remembering that game show he and Mavis had watched together. The one that also had a wheel.

'There's nowt better than hands at ten to two!' he had shouted at the television.

That was before Mavis had Googled it. She spent more and more time on the computer lately. Jeff admired her curious mind. Airbags changed everything according to the BBC website and Jeff had been forced to concede. Old enough to remember the broadcaster as Auntie, he believed her to know best, or at least be more reliable than an exuberant TV presenter. Jeff had since resolutely focused on his hand position whenever driving. Safety first. The problem lay in old habits dying hard.

Ringing burst out of the speakers. Jeff gripped the wheel, his knuckles bulged. Bloody Bluetooth. What a mither. David had set it up and Jeff had no idea how to disconnect it. Should he answer? His phone rarely rang, in or out of the car. In fact, he had noticed a significant reduction in all forms of communication since retiring. Apart from adverts for health insurance and funeral plans, and more recent emails for Viagra. Two of those things were unavoidable realities. Did anyone still have sex at his age? Jeff's eyes darted between the road and the screen on the dashboard. He couldn't answer, not whilst driving. Too dangerous. He stretched his neck, seeking liberation from the grip of his shirt collar.

The traffic lights ahead turned to red. Jeff slowed to a stop. Ringing still echoed around the car. His eyes returned to the screen. Forty-four. An English dialling code. What if it was important? Maybe he *should* answer it. He would have a few minutes at the lights. He pressed the green button, turned towards the dashboard and raised his voice. 'Jeffery Eckersley speaking.'

Laughter trickled out of the speakers.

'David Eckersley speaking.'

'David?'

'Expecting an important call?'

'Not expecting any calls. What do you want, Son?'

'Why are you shouting?'

He wasn't shouting. Or was he? Bloody Bluetooth. You could never tell if people could hear you properly or not.

'Hurry up. The lights will change in a minute.'

The same laughter.

'Mum with you?'

Jeff hesitated. He'd told Mavis he was waiting in on another parcel. If David knew he was on his way back from Toulouse, he might tell his mum next time they spoke. Damn it. He never should have answered. Where could he say he was going? 'I'm doing the shopping.'

'So, Mum *is* with you?'

'No.'

Jeff immediately realised his mistake. David knew they did the shopping together, even if Jeff questioned how much Mavis enjoyed their supermarket trips. His latest idea of making note of all the aisle numbers for regularly bought items had met with talk of losing all spontaneity in life.

'Everything okay?'

Was everything okay? That was the big question in Jeff's mind of late. David didn't need to know that. 'Shall we call you back later, Son?'

'Actually, it's you I want to speak to.'

Jeff stared at the screen. There was no way David could know, could he? Jeff hadn't told anyone. David couldn't have worked it out. They had spoken a little but hadn't seen their David for months.

'Still there, Dad?'

Jeff nodded at the screen and made a noise to confirm. He checked the traffic lights were still on red.

'I'm thinking of changing jobs.'

Jeff felt his shoulders drop. It was something else. Hang on a minute. Changing jobs? Why the hell would David be doing that. Had he heard right? 'You've had an offer?'

'Just had enough.'

'Enough?' Jeff shouted at the dashboard.

'You're shouting again.'

He was. It was nothing to do with the Bluetooth this time. Jeff inhaled deeply, trying to sound calm. 'But you've not long been promoted.'

VP Development, that's what they called their David now. He worked for Ganz, a fifty-billion-dollar American pharmaceutical company with what seemed more like a German name. Mavis had printed out an article from

Forbes naming him one of 'Forty European Firebrands at Forty'. The alliteration had forged it on Jeff's memory, as had Mavis framing it for display on the dining room sideboard.

'We increased our turnover by thirty percent last year and they still want more. I just don't agree with the way they work,' said David.

Jeff stared at the dashboard. From memory it wasn't that long ago that David had called to justify why he'd fired half his team despite his own hefty bonus. Jeff stretched his neck and observed the lights. Still red.

'You're there to do a job, Son. What's there to agree with?'

'It's too much.'

'What do you mean too much?'

'I can't do it anymore.'

'So, tell them you'll do what you can do.'

'Doesn't work like that, Dad.'

Seemed to Jeff it did. He'd seen a documentary about these new offices and something called 'hybrid' working. Gone was the nine to five. You could do whatever you damn well pleased nowadays. Work from a bloody beach if the fancy took you. These youngsters had no idea. Jeff and Mavis had paid for David's degree and MBA. A working-class Mancunian in the 1970s, Jeff had made his way by hook or by crook. Funded himself with grants and the job uncle Vince had got him as a relief postman during the Christmas holidays.

'Just remember you've got opportunities I never had.' Jeff's leg started to bounce up and down. 'Look, I know you think the grass is greener on the other side, Son. But the grass over there is the same as the grass you're looking at now. Green is green.'

'God, you're depressing.'

Jeff jumped on hearing a beeping from behind. The seatbelt dug into his neck. He hadn't noticed the traffic lights change. Impatience rippled through the queue like a sea serpent. Engaging first gear and releasing the hand brake, Jeff turned left, offering a timid wave.

'Got to go,' shouted Jeff. 'Think of Jess. The future. Life's not always about doing whatever you please, you know.'

'Well, this was a bloody waste of time.'

'Just promise me you won't worry your mum with this.'

David hung up.

Jeff slid his hands down to quarter to three. He tightened his grip. Not only had he upset David, this was something else he had to keep from Mavis. His shirt clung to his back. And now he would have to go and do the shopping. Just to cover his tracks.

Having unpacked the bags and put the food away, Jeff sat at the dining table with a cup of Yorkshire Tea. Her seat vacant, Jeff imagined Mavis and her naturally wild hair sat opposite him. Wild hair. You didn't really say things like that, did you? Not without it appearing unflattering and it wasn't meant to be. It was exactly what had caught Jeff's eye when he had first noticed her at the pictures. Sitting two rows in front, her gravity-defying locks had quivered with every laugh. A small bird, she had chattered back and forth with her friend, her bright eyes catching the light of the projector. Happiness and adventure had radiated out of every feather. They had laughed together once.

Mavis had been thinking. He could tell. That face he had been able to read had become an illegible tome. He had leafed those pages with ease at one time. Strange to think you can forget verses learnt by heart. Or maybe over time you find yourself in front of an entirely new book, the pages having been replaced one by one. It was good Mavis was spreading her wings with these clinical trials, writing a new chapter.

Ripples travelled through his tea, troubling its surface. Jeff looked down to see his right leg bouncing. A nervous tic of his, it had been part of him for as long as he could remember. At least since that summer on coming back from Sea Scout camp. Slurping, he focused on the mantel clock on the sideboard. The hot liquid coursed his throat as he admired the timepiece's sloping sides and ordered Roman numerals. Shaped like Napoleon's hat, the Edwardian antique irritated the Englishman in Jeff but he chose to ignore it. His dad had given it to him before he had passed. He hadn't thrown everything away belonging to Mum after all. Jeff often listened to it when he didn't know quite what else to do. Just focus on the ticking, Jeff. Bring your attention to the here and now. It was a trick he had picked up. He wasn't too sure how. Focus on something in the immediate and the past and future fall away.

He heard the ticks, the tocks. His gaze dropped to his watch. 13.32. The seconds to the right on his Casio watch rolled over before his eyes. New numbers superseded old ones. Adding up. Or more counting down? The afternoon was disappearing. What was it with time? His leg twitched. The ticking wasn't working at all today. It didn't always. Jeff headed towards the patio doors, reaching for his sunhat as he went.

'Get out of it!' he shouted, cutting through the garden and the vegetable patch never leaving his sight. When he arrived at its border, the bird continued to peck away at the tomato on the ground. 'Bloody magpies.'

The bird paused. It tilted its head and stared at Jeff.

'Something to say, do you?' The coal-black eyes inspected him. 'No, I didn't think so. Easier to get on with it when no one is looking.' Jeff checked he was alone. What was he doing conversing with a magpie? You couldn't be showing any signs of the doolally. Not at his age. 'Hop it.' He clapped his hands. 'Don't let me see you here again.'

Unfazed, the bird tilted its head the other way. It turned on itself and bounced in a perfectly straight line between two rows of courgette plants and took flight.

'Where would we be if we all did as we pleased?' mumbled Jeff, thinking back to his earlier conversation.

He had been a bit short with their David. *When in doubt do nowt* was a maxim Jeff lived by. He wanted his son to slow down a bit, consider all the ramifications. He'd apologise when they spoke again. Depressing? That's what David had called him. Jeff considered himself more of a realist if anything but had that realism made life any easier? For him or for Mavis.

Jeff reached into the vegetable patch with his right foot. He coaxed the skin-pocked tomato onto the lawn to roll through the grass. He stretched out his other foot to intercept it. A smile traced his face. He knew Mavis was upset about him not participating in the clinical trials. He wasn't entirely sure she had bought his story about a second delivery either. He didn't like to lie, but he had to get his ducks in a row. He kicked again. The fruit passed awkwardly from one foot to the other as Jeff dribbled it towards the house.

'They think it's all over,' he shouted, kicking the tomato at the space between the two garden loungers. The fruit sailed cleanly through. 'It is now!'

Jeff stopped dead in his tracks, raising his arms in victory. The crowd roared. England would meet Germany in the Euros soon. Could this be it? Would England hold up a cup once more in his lifetime? When there was football, Jeff didn't need ticking. He was elsewhere. On the pitch. In the game. Studs wedged in the soil. Feeling a presence behind him, Jeff held his breath. Was the magpie back? He turned. There was no bird. No Mavis. Nothing. Just fields and hills, endless space, limited time. Jeff looked at his watch and the mounting seconds. Time to get on.

Those seconds merged into minutes and, much to Jeff's surprise, soon transformed into an hour and a half before he next checked the time. It was three o'clock when a voice called his name. From his crouched position at the edge of the vegetable patch, he saw Mavis. She squinted, her blue eyes ill-equipped for the afternoon luminescence.

'Where are your sunglasses? And your hat?'

She peered at him, her expression as fathomless as her lack of protection. She'd get burnt if she wasn't careful.

'Worst time to be outdoors between midday and four,' Jeff added. They had to be careful at their age. He had made an exception today. The vegetable patch needed work. He had all the winter plants to do. 'How was it?' he asked, berating himself for the harsh welcome. 'Bet Joan was on form?' He ventured a short laugh.

Jeff hadn't seen Joan or Martin for a while, not with the meetings at the hall having been cancelled during the renovation. With Joan's natural inclination to officiate, she probably felt threatened by the new arrival. She already had her hands full with that Roy. Funny bloke. Always looking past you. North-West Regional Manager in the early 2000s, Jeff wondered if it came with his Kwik Save training. On permanent high alert for empty boxes, spillages or shoplifters, even in retirement.

'Oh, nothing special,' said Mavis.

'What about cabaret man?' Jeff considered attempting a brief dance.

'What about him?' shouted Mavis.

Jeff stayed crouched and watched his wife shuffle from foot to foot. She was still annoyed about his absence. He hadn't wanted to change the time. They were very busy. He decided not to push it. It would only engender more questions.

'What are you planting anyway?' Mavis's voice had calmed.

'Everything for a ratatouille.'

'You and your ratatouille.'

'But you like ratatouille. We eat it every Tuesday.'

'You like to eat it, you mean. How about your delivery?'

Jeff made an 'uh-huh' noise that would pass as a white lie.

'Anyway, why did you do the shopping without me? We always do it together.' Mavis turned on her heels and walked back to the house.

Jeff pushed himself to a standing position, his fingers sinking into the lawn. Heat rushed to his head. She really hadn't bought his story. He offered his eyes the unadulterated pleasure of retracing the parallel lines of young plants. His usual aches came to join him. He tried to ignore them. They didn't understand this need to garden.

'And why is there a bloody tomato on the patio?' Mavis disappeared into the house, its blue shutters resolutely closed.

Jeff pulled out two crumpled pieces of paper from his breast pocket. In the other, he found a yellow pencil and ticked off several items on the first page. Today, he had planted fennel, courgettes and aubergines, all successfully grown from seed in the greenhouse. From the Gantt chart on the second page cascaded a multitude of colours, tracing the next three months. The fruits of today's labours would arrive in a few weeks to accompany the tomatoes and bell peppers already bursting forth. Mavis made ratatouille every year. She spent hours sterilising jars at the end of summer to squirrel away for winter. He had always thought she loved it. There was little he understood about her anymore.

A familiar sense of overwhelm started to trace a steady path from his feet to his throat. Jeff became acutely aware gardens offer many delights, but little in the way of ticking. His mind bullied him back to that morning's appointment. The room had been decorated with posters of destinations near and far. Mountains and seas, fields and open skies, and what Jeff recognised as feats of Roman engineering. All those places he had stopped himself from visiting once the fear had kicked in. The fear of what might happen. Terror-filled images of planes dropping out of the sky. To him the sea offered no such menace. The deep, dark unfathomable sea was where he rediscovered the happier times. Mavis had resented taking the ferry every summer. Those long journeys over land and sea. But some things are difficult to put into words. Just like the news he would have to announce to his wife at some point.

CHAPTER SIX

Mike watched Gab pace back and forth. A Rubik's cube rattled in his colleague's hands as squares replaced others, swathes of solid colour taking shape. Gab's dextrous fingers moved fast. He had solved it numerous times in the last ten minutes, only to immediately rejumble. The parquet groaned.

'Ridiculous, isn't it?' said Gab.

Was he talking about the slide they were currently installing to connect the four floors of their building? Or could it be the announced closure of the self-service canteen to make way for *Pulse!*, a Vegan burger bar, *Oodles*, an all-you-can-eat noodle restaurant and *Björn and Bread*, a Swedish open-sandwich bar in the park outside? The changes Gab had reported as announced only three days ago at the meeting were already well underway. All the food was free but Mike wasn't sure how gliding between floors and endless snacking would alleviate their workload. That said, there was a definite buzz about the place. A buzz Gab didn't seem to hear.

'Sorry?'

'Ridiculous that people enter competitions to solve this thing in the shortest time.' Gab waved the Rubik's cube in Mike's direction.

Mike nodded. Never playing against any clock, Gab used the toy to reflect. His thinking was however frenetic today.

'The beauty is in the impermanence, its ever-changing colour combinations.'

Mike nodded again. This was not the first time Gab had voiced that same theory. But Gab hadn't paid attention to those colour combinations for the past fifteen minutes. If Mike wasn't mistaken, Gab was agitated. A ball of energy for sure, it never ordinarily manifested itself in such frustration. He hadn't been the same since that monthly meeting.

'Why can't people see that?' insisted Gab.

'Dunno,' offered Mike hesitantly.

Gab's pace quickened. The groaning wood started to wail, emitting a smell of almond oil. Mike checked for other signs of the cleaner's visit. On running his finger over the top of his terminal, it accumulated a smudge of dust. All these changes and they couldn't find time to clean their offices? A manila file on his desk caught his eye. T.C.E.P.: Toulouse Club for English Pensioners had been crossed out to make way for a new title.

'Project Toulouse?' asked Mike.

'T.C.E.P. sounds a bit like an antiseptic, doesn't it?' said Gab, maintaining his heavy pace. 'We only have Rémy in Toulouse at the moment. Let's avoid fancy names. No need to reinvent the wheel. Sometimes the easiest solution is the best.'

Gab's rambling persistence left Mike wondering if another future directive wouldn't relate to file naming but he decided to let the subject slide. He opened the folder. A new yellow printout from the Records Office sat on the reams of otherwise blue paper. There were two types of printout: blue and yellow. The former came from the Archive Section, but the yellow ones from the other side of the building where the Forecast Analysts worked.

Mike rubbed the back of his neck and looked back at Gab. 'You seen this? A bit tight, isn't it? Can't we keep him there longer?'

Gab wafted a hand in the air, batting away the swarm of questions. 'You know what they're like once a date is set.'

'Blimey, do you think we can make this work?'

Gab stopped to stare out into the park. Mike followed his gaze to the large tree. 'I'd say Rémy is our only opportunity to make it work.' Gab returned to his pacing. 'He's as unpredictable as a handful of errors in a computer code, but he's all we've got.'

'No one has quite forgotten that incident a few years back, have they?' Mike laughed.

'What happens in Shrewsbury stays in Shrewsbury.'

Mike shook his head. Rémy had been returned to a desk job after his mission in Shrewsbury. Hadn't followed protocol and left more than one woman in tears. At least that was what Mike had heard. And now Gab had decided it wise to bring him back into the field and drop him into a group of pensioners. Well, he was there to help Jeff and Mavis, but invariably there were positive knock-on effects to all their cases. Once people start opening themselves up to happiness, their immediate entourage notice and wonder about their own.

'He's a star in his own right, that one,' said Mike, his concern now divided between Gab and their resident plants. Watering the greenery was also the cleaner's job. Shirley was dehydrated. Her locks had less bounce than usual, despite Gab's thundering tread. Mike waited for a laugh that never came. 'Are you sure you're okay?'

'They've only gone and done it,' said Gab.

'England in the last sixteen against Germany?' Mike tried to cajole volume back into Shirley's tendrils. It would be another tense penalty shootout for sure. Was that reason enough for Gab to be so upset?

'They've taken away my travel allowance,' said Gab.

'What?'

'Some SWOT thing. What the heck?'

'Swatting what?'

'They just need to give us more staff and we'll be fine.'

Mike's reply took some time to take shape, hindered not by diplomatic hesitation but pure confusion. He needed to get to the nub of the discussion one step at a time. He used the pause in Gab's pacing to cut across the office and pick up the pink watering can that sat next to Araminta III on top of the filing cabinet. She was holding up a little better than Shirley, only just. They might have to start considering a descendant. 'What is this SWAT?' he finally asked.

'S-W-O-T.' Gab spelt out the letters.

'But *what* is it? One of these new changes mentioned at the meeting?' Mike could hear his tone rise.

'Used to be at Harvard . . . or Stanford. Coming here with her big ideas.' Gab emitted a noise somewhere between a growl and a laugh.

Startled, Mike jerked and watched water spill off the parched peppermint plant. He attempted to mop up the puddle on the filing cabinet with his sleeve. 'Just answer the question, Gab. What is it?'

Mike heard the footsteps slow down behind him.

'Reporting about our current caseload I think,' said Gab. 'Not that she explained in any detail. KISS, she said.'

'You talking about Cynthia?' Mike's head swung a good ninety degrees. 'She didn't try to kiss you?'

Mike was yet to meet the famous Cynthia. They were invited to an organisation-wide meeting in the hemicycle in a few days' time. Mike had assumed it was to consult with staff about the incoming changes. Changes with which they were already steaming ahead.

Gab laughed. 'No! K-I-S-S she calls it. Keep it Sweet and Simple. Deliver information in a way people can understand.'

Noticing Gab resume walking, Mike seized the opportunity to return to his desk before the pace picked up. Wondering how to curtail Gab's dismay, he settled back into his chair. New arrivals to the Organisation often lacked humility. Not much respect for experience and an overriding certitude that everything can be brought back to an intellectual exercise.

Mike tried a different tack. 'So, *when* is this new SWOT thing coming then?'

Gab's pace slowed once more, this time to a halt. 'Wye—'

'None of that Geordie. It's already started, hasn't it?'

Gab nodded.

'When?'

'We were supposed to deliver our bit yesterday.'

'Gab!'

'I'm sorry. I never thought they'd go this far.'

'And they've taken away your travel allowance because you refused?'

'Yours too.'

'You didn't think to mention any of this before now?'

Gab walked over to Mike's desk and perched on the edge of it. 'They just don't get it, do they? What we do. I thought—'

'It did *not* help us one bit you storming out of that meeting.'

Gab's head dropped.

'Hang on a minute, why are you so bothered about the travel allowance? We never go anywhere anymore,' asked Mike.

'It's Rémy.'

'He's not done a Shrewsbury?'

'I don't know. I've not had a lot of news.'

'Not a lot?'

'None.'

Mike studied Gab. 'You seem worried?'

'I've tried everything. Even the old-fashioned methods.' Gab fiddled with the desk lamp, switching it on and off. 'I think he's ignoring me.'

Rémy was a bit of a loose cannon. Nothing new there. Mike's mind came back to the yellow printout and the questions Gab hadn't yet answered. 'Rémy hasn't seen that printout, has he? And now he doesn't know he's short on time because you can't get hold of him.'

Gab reached for the Rubik's cube, Mike picking it up before he had chance.

'Come on, Gab. We need to sort this out. Get our travel allowance back so we can tell Rémy. Let's just do their reporting thing. What's the point of digging in our heels?'

Gab growled.

'You won't get anywhere sulking.'

Gab growled again.

A silence descended on the office. Gab conceded with a reluctant nod.

'Let's do it together,' offered Mike. Something else niggled him. For the moment he couldn't quite put his finger on what. 'How hard can it be, this SWOT? What do we need to report exactly?'

Gab shrugged. 'Haven't got a clue.'

Mike shook his head and powered up his computer. They had gone from the surreal to the absurd, Gab refusing what he hadn't even seen.

'SWOT?' Mike ran a quick search. 'Right, get a pen. We need a grid of four squares. In the squares, you write the words: strengths, weaknesses, opportunities and threats.' Mike edged closer to the terminal as Gab followed his instructions.

'That's it? That's what SWOT stands for?' asked Gab.

'That's an odd way to report on our caseload.'

'You see, you find it daft too.'

'"Why do a SWOT analysis?"' Mike read out loud from the screen.

'Bloody good question.' Gab threw the pen on the desk.

'"Maybe you think you are already running a tight ship and doing everything you need to succeed", blah blah. "A SWOT forces you to look at your business in new ways and move into new directions".' Mike stopped reading and turned to a taciturn Gab. 'It's not a reporting system, Gab. This is the start of an audit.'

'I knew it when I read that memo.'

Mike's full attention turned to Gab. 'What memo?'

He'd known all along there was more to this story.

Gab's gaze dropped to his feet. 'Some ridiculous thing. I chucked it away.'

A silence descended on the office.

'But what did it say, *this memo*?' Mike stared at Gab.

'Something about happiness now being a limited commodity and how we had to rethink our whole purpose.'

'Limited commodity, those exact words?'

'I told you it was ridiculous.'

'Who *is* this Cynthia, Gab?'

'Lead consultant.'

'An external consultancy firm! You didn't mention that. And we need to rethink our purpose? Are you sure that's what that memo said?'

'You just said yourself this looks like an audit.'

It did. And why else would they have brought in other people? Never in the history of the Organisation had they opened their doors to external consultants. How could an outsider understand the intricacies of what they did? This was worse than Mike had thought. And there was Gab keeping it all from him. What seemed rushed changes, Gab had known about in advance, from the last meeting and maybe the one before. Not to mention this mysterious memo. In fact, not just keeping things from him, had he actively lied by saying it was a new form of reporting?

The many questions in Mike's head came to a motionless halt. One rose out of the dust and shouted the others into silence. That undefinable niggle he had been harbouring took on recognisable traits. 'Hang on a minute. Why are we rushing around trying to tell Rémy this now? There's no reason this yellow printout wouldn't have been in the original file.'

Gab motioned to stand.

Mike held him in place. 'Gab?'

'Well, I might need to talk to you about that too.'

'Might you now?'

'I knew they would be monitoring us more closely, so I got Rémy out quickly. Slipped Project Toulouse under the net as it were.'

The full and intricate reality of the situation now

dawned on Mike, as did the reason behind the name change. 'They don't know about this project?'

'Well, I didn't put it in the system, but they might know.' Gab rolled his eyes towards the floors above.

'But why is this case so urgent?' Mike's shoulders tensed. And why had he been kept out of the loop? Again.

Gab dropped his voice to a whisper. 'You know William, who cleans the offices?'

'Our cleaner's called Dorothy.'

'Must be a new cleaner then.' Gab glanced away for a moment. 'He said they call him Billy Whizz because of how he whips through the place.'

'So quick, he's not done half of it?'

Gab offered a hesitant laugh. 'Look, I know it's gone to pot, but we got talking. Lovely bloke, he came to me with this as a favour and . . .'

Mike laughed. It was the only recourse left to him. How much more was there to this whole story? 'You're such a soft touch. You barely know this Billy. Then you send Rémy of all people. Please tell me you aren't doing this to wind this Cynthia up?'

'Not entirely.'

'You do believe in this project though? It's not just a favour?'

'Do my instincts ever fail me?' Gab threw a friendly punch at Mike's arm. 'I'm just not sure on paper it would have made the cut. Not Cynthia paper. You know how these youngsters write off anyone over forty, let alone sixty.'

Mike gave an understanding nod. The one thing they never disagreed on was the importance of what they did, never discriminating between one person and the next. Mike was beginning to share Gab's dislike of Cynthia for softening what, to all intents and purposes, was an audit by turning the grounds of the World Happiness Organisation into a food court. Their toes were, however, up against the wall.

'Let's do this SWOT together. Keep her quiet.' Mike smiled and gave the pen back to Gab.

Gab stood, sweeping the Rubik's cube off the table. 'Out of the question,' he bellowed.

Several leaves dropped from Araminta III.

'Come on, Gab. We have to get out to see Rémy.'

Gab's pacing regained momentum as the Rubik's cube twisted faster. Mike's brow furrowed as he examined the paper containing four empty squares. Gab's tolerance levels had hit maximum and they were probably on borrowed time when it came to Cynthia. He knew how sensitive Gab could be on certain topics. If only Mike had seen that memo, he could have come to his own conclusions. Of course, he understood Gab's motivations but had Mike been right all along? Had Gab not included him because he didn't think he had the brains to navigate it. Why else would he have left him in the cold?

More to the point, what else wasn't Gab telling him? The thought pinched at Mike's insides? He reminded himself it wasn't the time to be oversensitive. Gab had overreacted enough for them both. Mike had to keep a cool head. If they were being audited, this mission needed to go well. Better than well. To achieve that, Rémy needed to know the new deadlines and quickly. Project Toulouse was under the radar but Mike had a feeling it wouldn't stay that way for long. He rubbed his chin. What exactly Cynthia was up to was still unclear but he recognised the onset of war when he saw it. He had led troops into battle when needed. Fighters may look all brawn and no brain. One thing a veteran never forgets is that to defend against whatever is attacking you, you must first understand how it works.

CHAPTER SEVEN

Scouring the somewhat quiet gymnasium for her friends and having decided to keep a low profile since her slip in the stockroom the previous day, Mavis heard him before she saw him.

'Mavis!'

Rémy had this way of putting the emphasis on the last, rather than the first, syllable of her name. All French people did that, stretched out the 'i'. The difference with Rémy was that the 's' lingered a little longer than necessary on his tongue.

'You won't be seeing your friends,' he said.

It was a statement that would have been very much at home in a Hollywood thriller, had it not been delivered by a diminutive Frenchman in yet another Hawaiian shirt. This one was bright pink and covered in white conch shells. Obediently perched in straight lines, they all turned to the right. Thunder rolled overhead. One of those tropical showers that burst forth when the sky can no longer contain the heat.

'Joan and Martin?' Mavis asked.

Avoiding eye contact, she scrutinised a basketball hoop drooping with inaction on the far side of the hall. Mavis knew Peg wasn't coming. She had received a text first thing. Peg had pulled a muscle doing the downward dog with Didier, the village baker. He had been circling Peg for weeks, encouraging her out for a drink the previous evening. A second text, explaining the downward dog to be a yoga pose, had gathered Mavis's wandering thoughts. Thoughts that were wandering again. The things she was thinking lately.

'I told them to stay at home. Are you okay?'

'Okay?'

'You're shaking your head.'

'Am I?'

Mavis tried once again to collect her thoughts. They were becoming harder to herd than cats. 'But why?' she asked.

'The accident in the stockroom.'

Blood flooded her cheeks. 'It's those shoes. The soles stick to everything. I'm wearing a different pair today.'

Mavis directed Rémy's gaze to the espadrille sandals Maurice had been selling half-price on his stall a few weeks earlier. She lifted her left foot behind her to offer an inspection of the jute sole. Rémy grabbed her right elbow. Her cheeks heated once more. Rémy laughed, his coffee-laced breath tickling her nose.

'Not your accident. It's the *Felixir* injections. There was a problem with the fridges. Happened on the afternoon shift once you'd left. The batches are all compromised and the trials on hold.'

Mavis let out a sigh of relief, trying to disguise it midway as disbelief. In any case, any solace was short-lived.

'Looks like it's just me and you, Mavis.' There was that 's'. 'Coffee?'

Ten minutes later, Rémy held open the door to reveal a reassuringly well-lit room of bright yellow walls, a sweeping mahogany bar and a distinct absence of life. Mavis didn't know what PMU stood for and had certainly never set foot in one. Dotted all over France, the one-stop establishments for eating, drinking and a flutter on the horses were known to attract daytime tipplers and a predominantly male population. Odours flirted with each other as Mavis edged inside. A definite hint of *daube de boeuf* and the pervasive tang of urine half-masked by Toilet Duck. A panoramic assessment of the room confirmed her suspicions. They were caught in the crossfire of the kitchen and the toilets, the latter accessible via a steep, metal staircase that snaked down into the bowels of the bar.

'Rémy!' A skinny man wearing wiry glasses shouted from behind the bar as he flung a tea towel over his shoulder and reached for a remote control. A greyhound breed, that's how Mavis's mother would have described him. All legs but didn't miss a trick.

As rhymes and beats spewed into the bar, Rémy shouted his order of two coffees, raising the same number of fingers in confirmation. Mavis followed the music to a once unobtrusive television hanging precariously in a corner. Navigating as best she could the damp, laminate table, she took a seat in the alcove Rémy indicated. Two men, older than her, propped up the bar, feigning sobriety with small glasses of beer. Pencils hovered thoughtfully over slips of paper. Rémy slid into the opposite side of the alcove with an agility Mavis wouldn't have associated with his years, and one she hadn't demonstrated as successfully. His Action Man eyes watched her.

Mavis pulled her phone out of her bag. Tiny espresso cups rattled in their saucers as they were placed on the table without comment. She jumped. Flipping open her phone, she silently cursed Jeff for not having called back. She had left him a message, asking him to come as soon as he could to the PMU. He was at some depot. Another parcel. She played with a paper stick of sugar with her other hand.

'Clever invention,' said Rémy.

'This old thing?' Mavis kept her eyes on her trusted Nokia. 'Peg says those smartphones are better.'

Rémy laughed. 'No, the sugar stick.'

As he took the paper packaging from her hands, his skin brushed hers. Mavis noticed his hands were soft for a man's before unsuspectingly finding herself, just for a moment, back in the stockroom. She felt herself hang desperately onto the moving trolley as the door slammed shut. She fell into his strong arms, inhaling deeply as she let the warmth of his chest press against her face. Mavis pulled back, throwing the phone into the handbag next to her feet. She brought her restless hands to heel on her knees. Rémy bent the sugar stick in half over her cup, the sugar falling effortlessly into her coffee.

'Will you look at that!' A smile escaped her.

Many a time she had fiddled with the paper tip to no avail, only to open the packet with her teeth, make the sugar soggy and abandon the idea altogether. An unfortunate outcome, not least as these French coffees, if unsweetened, were like tar on a hot day.

'Brilliant idea,' said Rémy. 'But a waste. No one knows how to use them.'

Mavis felt herself relax, not entirely. 'Like bobby pins. I saw that in a magazine before I knew about the Internet.'

'Bobby pins?'

'You know, hair grips.' Releasing her thighs from their tight grip, Mavis's hands touched her hair. A bobby pin was a female accessory and an element of English vocabulary sure to have escaped Rémy. 'The wavy side should face downwards. Gives a better grip.'

A silence fell on the table. Mavis returned her attention to the television where singers jigged energetically. Maybe too long in silence with Jeff had stripped her of the ability for small talk when it came to the opposite sex. She always managed a conversation with Martin, albeit nine times out of ten it centred around cake. But then Martin had never winked at her. Joan wouldn't stand for that.

'Joan was livid about the injections, you know,' said Rémy, as if he knew Mavis was thinking about her friend. In articulating the word livid, he stretched out the second 'i', the vowel adopting a piercing quality quite in keeping with an irate Joan.

Mavis could almost hear her. She allowed herself another smile as she picked up the spoon. 'She's probably disappointed it's all been put on hold, that's all. Not for her to say though. I mean, she doesn't run the trials.'

'People like to have someone to blame though, don't they? Be it someone else or an angry God.'

Mavis glanced up from stirring her coffee. Her and an angry God were well acquainted. He had lived with her throughout her childhood, incarnated in her father, the all-knowing Reverend Boyle. According to him, life led everyone into evil and temptation and Mavis was no exception. Only Our Father could judge, but it was *her* father that had stood guard.

'Are you a religious man?' she asked.

Rémy didn't seem like a churchgoer. All those low-buttoned shirts and cheeky looks. Her eyes dropped to his Saint Christopher. People thought of Christopher as a simple wanderer, forgetting the journey he took to carry a child across the river. The child that revealed himself to be Christ.

'I don't think anyone would call me that.' Rémy's lips curled into a smile.

Heat rushed to Mavis's head, transporting her back once again to the previous day's embrace, Saint Christopher glued to her face. Picking up a beer mat to fan herself, she brushed it off as an effect of the caffeine. The caffeine in the espresso she hadn't yet tasted.

'But living in Asia taught me to think differently,' continued Rémy.

Asia. What it must be like to travel. Mavis had always had itchy feet. As a girl, she would flip through the pages of her dad's atlas, imagining faraway places. Lives perched on African mountains, days roaming Russian plains or existences hidden away in South American jungles. Drawn once again to the television screen over Rémy's shoulder, a familiar face looked back at Mavis. David used to have her posters everywhere as a teenager. A young Madonna started to dance semi-clad and barefoot in a church.

'You seem miles away,' said Rémy.

'Tell me about Asia,' said Mavis.

'Well, I spent a lot of time in India on the ashrams. I wasn't on the boats back then.'

'You liked it out there?'

'Very much. Like I said, a whole different philosophy on life. Not the same notion of blame.'

'Blessed is the one who does not walk in step with the wicked,' muttered Mavis.

'Or stand in the way that sinners take?'

Mavis peered at Rémy. Not a religious man but he could quote the Psalms? *I'm sorry, Father, for I have sinned.* How many times had she said that growing up? Trying to wash herself of all wrong whilst floating in a bath of original sin.

'Maybe the notion of original sin is a good thing,' said Rémy.

'Original sin?' There he was, reading her mind again. 'How could that ever be a good thing?' That was definitely not one of the Psalms. They had avoided any winking but a spoonful of God was not what she had expected with coffee.

'Teaches us that no one is actually perfect or better than anyone else.'

Mavis nodded. It was an original take on the Bible, she'd give him that.

'Don't always control what comes our way, do we?' Rémy stared at her. 'That makes life less about what happens and more about how you react to whatever crosses your path, don't you think?'

There it was. The Old Testament was a strange detour, but one that had ultimately taken them back to the stockroom. Please don't wink, she thought, just as the volume on the television went up a notch. She could hear a voice, Madonna said. It was like an angel sighing.

'*Ah oui!*' shouted the bartender.

Mavis shot a look at the television. Good Lord! Reclined on a pew, Madonna was now playing with herself. In a church of all places. That wasn't right, was it? Mavis reached for the espresso and drank it in one gulp. She grimaced as the coffee clung to the inside of her cheeks like treacle.

'Say I bought you a present? Some chocolates,' said Rémy, bringing her attention back to the table.

Bloody hell! Buying her presents? This was moving a bit fast. 'I'm diabetic.'

Rémy smiled as he played with her used sugar stick.

Damn it. She'd never been a good liar.

'Some bobby pins then.' Rémy laughed. 'Just as an example. Imagine.'

'Bobby pins?' Mavis reached for her hair before letting her hand fall to her lap. Why were they imagining gifts? What the hell was he talking about now?

'If you tell me you don't want them and give them back, who does that present belong to?'

Bitterness lingered at the back of Mavis's mouth. She ran her tongue around her teeth, hoping to buy some time. *Was* he flirting with her? His eyes sparkled. What a curious little man. Mavis studied her knees. Where on earth was this conversation heading? She wasn't sure she wanted to know.

'Well, the present would belong to me. But I suppose not to you either,' she finally said.

'Same goes for guilt and regret. They are only yours if you decide to accept them.'

Guilt? Regret? Jesus Christ, he *was* talking about the stockroom. Mavis braved Rémy's gaze once more, expecting to see Action Man wink. Instead, a knowing look caught her completely off-guard.

'Sometimes, shit just happens, doesn't it? Smelly, ugly, unwanted shit.'

The discussion had most definitely moved away from the Bible. That knowing in his eyes had gone nowhere. Mavis felt it leafing through another old tome, the book of her life. Pages that spoke of much guilt and regret. A weight that clung to her like wet clothes, words that had petered into silence. She broke away from Rémy's stare to return to the fallen Madonna. In a field of burning crosses, she danced on. Life announced itself as an absolute mystery, but Madonna could hear a voice. A voice that called her name.

'Mavis?'

There was that lingering 's'.

Mavis's eyes locked with Rémy's, her silently urging his to flip left or right. Where was that bloody switch in his head? His gaze stayed with her. The knot of panic squatting in her stomach since the fall unravelled into surprise. Surprise at being somehow understood, without having to explain. Jeff hadn't looked at her like that for so long. He had stopped trying to read her a long time ago.

'But when this smelly, unwanted . . . stuff happens out of the blue. How do we move on?' asked Mavis.

'The only way out of disappointment is to accept it, not blaming anyone or anything.' Rémy's mouth stretched into a broad smile. 'And what can we do about these injections anyway?'

'Injections?'

'The wasted injections. Can't do much about them now it's done, can we?'

Mavis shook her head, coming back to what she now remembered as the conversation at hand. The *Felixir* injections, that's what they had been talking about. Not that day all those years ago that was never meant to happen. 'Not much at all, I suppose,' she said, her attention drifting to the barman.

The tea towel still gracing his shoulder like a ceremonial garment, the bespectacled greyhound placed his hands on his hips and faced the television. '*Oh putain! Et dans une église*,' he shouted.

The two elderly gentlemen turned, catching sight of a writhing Madonna. Glasses of beer clinked to the sound of cheering. Mavis turned to see Rémy roll his head back in laughter. A precariously balanced saltshaker fell from the shelf behind him and clattered its way along the floor.

A rumble of something other than sadness stirred in Mavis. A titter. Rémy was curious. An unknown concept, a bit like this bar, but there was something refreshing about that too. With unbridled determination, laughter exploded out of her. Saint Christopher winked at Mavis once more, the now ingested caffeine not making her flush in the least. There was no choice, repeated Madonna. His voice would take her there.

'*Mav*is!' The familiar trill placed the emphasis on the first syllable, in that elongated way of a born and bred Mancunian.

Mavis jumped. Jeff stood at the end of the table towering over her and Rémy. Pushing herself into the bench, she straightened her unruffled skirt with painful strokes down her thighs.

'Why aren't you answering your phone? I'm badly parked. We need to go.' Jeff nodded curtly. 'You must be Rémy?'

Mavis pulled her phone out of her bag and noticed several missed calls.

'Nice to meet you, Jeff. Get your package?'

'Package?'

'At the depot.'

'Yes. I mean, no. It's not ready. Mavis, come on!'

Mavis slid herself out of the alcove, fighting with her skirt as it rode high.

'What on earth are you doing in a PMU?' asked Jeff, already a good two to three strides ahead of her.

'It's not that bad actually.'

On the television, Madonna took a final bow as the curtain went down on her and the church. It was all pretend after all. Pretend within pretend. Things aren't always as they seem. That's what people do, isn't it, pretend? Maybe Mavis had been pretending to be satisfied for too long.

'The football this evening,' she shouted to Rémy. 'Come and watch it at our house.'

CHAPTER EIGHT

Joan, Martin and Mavis were sitting around the garden table when Jeff came downstairs smelling of sea salt and samphire. That was if you believed the label. Jeff had no idea what samphire was, their paths never having crossed outside the bathroom. Met with a steely-eyed stare from his wife, he read a full prologue of disapproval at having favoured a shower over their guests on returning from the vegetable patch. Thanks to another few hours, he was making real progress. Barely seated and without any form of briefing, he was pulled into the ongoing conversation.

'I mean he's full of his opinions, but could he run the association?' Joan stared at Jeff.

Close enough to see beads of perspiration gathering on her hairline, Jeff examined the colourless locks worthy of a soap powder ad that framed Joan's inquisitive face. Mavis had chided him on calling her White Lightening and claiming Joan had to be drinking something to come up with half her ideas. As it turned out, that was what the grammar school kids had christened their headmistress on the toilet walls. Martin had confided Joan's regret at having become Mrs Bolt. It was unheard of for a woman to keep her own name back then and, tradition or not, who could have known what was to come?

'Who?' asked Jeff, his long pause an attempt at postponing an inevitable rant.

'Roy! Asking for the statutes again.'

There it was. Joan and her long-running rivalry with Roy. Jeff observed Mavis's hair nodding in perfect time. Despite annoyance at his tardy arrival, she had a certain happiness about her today. She was asking fewer questions anyway. That made things easier. For the moment at least. The conversation was bound to turn to him at some point. *But what delivery? Why can't they deliver another day? Don't you think getting involved would be good for you?*

'Roy's not even helping with the clinical trials though, is he?' offered Mavis.

Jeff combined a shake of the head in Joan's direction with a shrug at his wife. So, he wasn't the only one not getting stuck in then? Who'd have thought Roy's custard cream and Branston Pickle empire would inadvertently divert attention.

'Couldn't do the initiation because of one of his trips back to the UK, he said. As if we believe that.' Joan shook her head. 'Claiming he wants to be president but never getting his hands dirty.'

That was Roy all over. Boasting about sixteen-hour days overseeing three of the UK's best-performing stores, conveniently forgetting that Kwik Save went bust. Admittedly, that wasn't entirely Roy's fault. What supermarket could succeed if it couldn't be bothered to unpack its boxes? Discount didn't have to equate with shambles. The Germans had gone on to prove that. The Germans. From behind his sunglasses, Jeff looked at his watch. 5.40.

'And now he's only going to ask Rémy again because you aren't there, Jeff,' said Joan.

There it was.

'Well, maybe you can cosy up to Rémy too?' Jeff tried to catch Martin's eye.

'What kind of talk is that?' Mavis smacked his leg.

Jeff yelped. What was that for?

'Can't think anyone would want to cuddle up to that man. Can you, Mavis?' asked Joan.

Jeff coughed in Martin's direction.

'It wasn't right him keeping you waiting at the first meeting,' said Mavis.

'Arrives late, wanting to jab us with some drug we've never heard of—'

Joan was in full flow. Jeff coughed again.

'—Hardly any explanation, one whistle-stop tour and now everything on hold. I don't think so.'

'But it being delayed is hardly anyone's fault, is it?' Mavis fumbled in the bowl of peanuts on the table.

'You seem to know a lot about it? Those injections wasted themselves, did they?' said Joan.

Jeff looked to his watch. 5.42. He finally caught Martin's attention. 'Shall we get some of the pre-match commentary in?'

'I may have invited him this evening.' Mavis's voice was low enough to test the notoriously sharp hearing of a bat. It immediately grabbed Joan's attention.

'Who?' Joan hit a pitch capable of terrifying any bat within a five-mile radius.

Jeff pushed back his seat.

Aware of the imminent explosion, Martin was already on his feet. 'Any of that nice cake of yours, Mavis?'

Mavis's nodded.

'You invited Rémy here?' Joan's voice filled the garden.

'Shall I get your hat, Mavis? It's cracking flags out here,' said Jeff, a growling reply confirming he was less skilled at timing questions than Martin.

As Jeff and Martin made their way inside, thoughts of hats were, in any case, soon forgotten on hearing digitalised wind chimes. Jeff looked at his watch and picked up his pace. 5.43. Pointing Martin towards a pile of cake tins in the kitchen, he marched towards the front door. He would have to find the doorbell instructions. Just to lower the volume, as Mavis had vetoed the idea of changing the tune to Rule Britannia! A recent present from David, the wireless bell had a receiver you could take into the garden. Nice idea but too late to prevent Jeff missing the first delivery attempt because of an impatient driver.

Grasping at the wrought iron handle, Jeff opened the door to reveal the flowing locks and beaming smile of Mystic Peg, as he had quietly coined her. She was chaperoned by Rémy. Talk of the devil. Jeff studied the bristly crewcut he had met at the PMU in more detail, his attention dropping to the same hideous pink shirt covered in shells. Outstretched arms offered a pack of beer. Twenty-four of those stubby bottles only the French drink.

'Jeff! They're coming on the pitch.' Martin's voice carried from the living room.

'Come on.' Jeff took the box out of Rémy's hands. He wasn't one to look a gift horse in the mouth and he couldn't miss England's one chance to beat Germany. He'd have to risk Joan's histrionics. 'I hate missing the anthems.'

Jeff shut the front door with his foot. Ushering Rémy towards the living room, he noticed the Frenchman's skin as worn as old leather. Testament, no doubt, to overexposure to the sun. From his neck hung a pendant. Saint Christopher, the patron saint of travellers. No surprise there. Rémy was one of life's eternal wanderers, that much was evident. Never planning where he would be next and doing as he pleased. Life was easy for some, but then people aren't dealt the same cards, are they? Jeff worked with the hand he had been given. Doing his best not to go bust, avoiding folding and never twisting. Up until now.

———

'Two nil!' shouted Jeff, pulling the remote control from the side of his armchair to lower the jubilant victory flooding out of the television. 'Football is on its way home!'

'Looks that way, doesn't it, Jeff?' Martin smiled as he tapped Rémy's arm. 'Suppose you're more for France winning the tournament?'

'Let's see how the cookie crumbles.'

Rémy hadn't really said much since his arrival but everything he had said had been in perfectly idiomatic English. Jeff marvelled, if not a little enviously, at his fluency. But then globetrotting afforded you time for such things, even if you could cut his accent with a knife.

'But at the group stage you beat Germany and we all like doing that.' Martin laughed, licking his finger to collect any remaining cake crumbs from the visibly empty plate next to him.

Jeff wondered what Mavis, Joan and Peg were up to. On trying to see them at half-time, he had been greeted with a plate of quiche Lorraine. Pushed through a thin gap in the doorway, it had been accompanied by Mavis's curt insistence that any communal time was a very bad idea. Not with the mood Joan was in. Mavis had also evoked the sanctified first rule of Tarot Card Club. Whatever happened in those sessions, stayed there. If Jeff was honest, that suited him just fine.

'Anyway, you can't always plan these things, can you?' said Rémy.

Jeff could feel Rémy staring. He had been miles away. Why was cabaret man looking at him like that? He had that French nonchalance alright, but there was something else. 'Can't plan what things?'

'Freedom is the only worthy goal in life. It is won by disregarding things that lie beyond our control.'

'Sorry?'

'Epictetus.'

'All Greek to me.' Martin chuckled.

Rémy continued to stare at Jeff, prompting him to counter the conversational segue with some philosophising of his own. Jeff sought his inspiration closer to home in Gary Lineker's match commentary. 'Of course you can plan for a match. You think switching to that 3-4-3 formation wasn't planned by Southgate?' Martin's nod encouraged Jeff to continue. 'Or replacing Grealish in the starting ten with Trippier?'

'Trying to make up for that missed penalty,' Martin said. 'Joan and I were on holiday in Greece for that one. Hotel full of Germans. Fancy him bringing it home now. And at Wembley too.'

Jeff ignored Martin and returned Rémy's stare.

'Southgate did play well,' said Rémy with a nod.

'Southgate? He's the manager.'

'I must be confusing it with that game Martin was talking about.'

'You're confusing what we just watched with a game from 1996?' Jeff watched Rémy shift his attention to his feet. Had he followed any of the game?

'I'm thinking of the other one.'

'Sterling?' said Martin.

Jeff shot Martin a look.

'That's the one!' Rémy slapped Martin on the arm.

Who was this strange little man and why was he coming here talking Greek philosophy? Maybe because he knew absolutely bloody nothing about football.

'So, you agree you can plan for a match?' insisted Jeff.

'Lots of preparation and delightful execution, you're right. But maybe too many plans are a waste of time.'

'A waste of time? You can't go about anything without some kind of plan.'

Who had ever approached a game of football without a plan? Looking hopefully to the heavens had never won a European cup. Typical of a Frenchman to make something as simple as football so intellectual. Just so he wouldn't pass as stupid. Not quite the song-and-dance Peg had announced.

'I'm only saying you can plan for a match, but you can't know the result. Like you can detail every single stop on a journey in advance, without ever really knowing your destination. It's all about taking it one step at a time.'

What did he just say? As Rémy peered at him, Jeff found himself back at his recent appointment, staring at a panoramic view of the Himalayas and struggling to fit the pieces together. *May seem a long haul, but let's take it one step at a time*, the woman with the red-rimmed glasses had suggested. Rémy couldn't know about that, could he?

'Well, let's see how you feel later when France plays Switzerland. More at stake for you there,' said Jeff, trying to bring the conversation back to a familiar ground.

'France won't win. But Italy might take it all the way. That wouldn't surprise me.'

Jeff nodded. For someone who had no idea about football, Rémy had pulled that out of thin air. That said, Italy was one of the tipped favourites. Spending his time in PMUs, he would know that kind of thing.

'No can do. Football is definitely coming home this time,' said Martin, just as a loud thud emanated from the still-off-limits dining room.

'Not gonna lie to you. Flew headlong into the glass door, it did.' Peg took a step back from the circle that had formed on the patio, allowing Jeff a view.

'No one wants to be doing that now, do they?' said Joan.

The lines of fairy lights that Mavis had woven across the top of the pergola illuminated the bird's jet-black feathers, revealing mysterious petrol blue hues. Small, bright eyes pleaded with Jeff. Could it be the same magpie that had been pecking around in the vegetable patch? The one he had shooed away. Jeff took the place Peg had vacated and crouched to scoop up the bird before returning to a standing position. The white-feathered chest pumped hard in his hands. To think he had warned it of coming back. As the beady eyes darted back and forth and two thin legs drooped between Jeff's fingers, the bird gradually abandoned its struggle. No! Not like this. He hadn't meant this. The garden expelled the slightest of noises.

'Come on, little fella,' whispered Jeff. He looked to Mavis, wanting to reassure her. Needing to reassure himself. 'He's scared. A bit stunned. That's all.'

'Magpies are the only birds that recognise their own reflections you know,' offered Martin.

Joan's sigh was as audible as it was tangible, her hot exhale meeting Jeff's face. 'Didn't see much of his reflection when he was diving into the window, did he?'

'I'm simply saying they are very intelligent birds.'

'Intelligent?' Joan let out a laugh.

'Joan, love! That's enough.' Mavis shot a look at Joan. She never raised her voice. She really was upset. 'Sorry. It's just a bit of a shock. And happening right when it did.'

'Right when it did?' asked Jeff.

'Peg had announced big changes in the cards.'

Here we go. Mystic Peg and her cards. It had been a while since they'd heard that story about her mum suffering a persistent headache the fortnight before JFK was shot. Jeff went to speak, Mavis catching his eye and warning him otherwise. She could chastise her friends, Jeff had to be careful. Jeff's attention was, in any case, with the bird. Its movements becoming less and less, he could feel it ebbing away.

'The tower. Not gonna lie to you. Every time this card comes out the way it just did, there are huge changes afoot. Endings.' Everyone turned to Peg. Shrouded in sparkles cascading from the fairy lights, she stood in the doorway, holding a card in one hand and a smouldering bunch of leaves in the other. 'Sage, Jeff. To cleanse the energy.'

His face must have conveyed confusion. Jeff was sure he hadn't uttered any form of question. He coughed, the smoke sickening his taste buds and hindering a full view. As far as odours went, it was more than effective at keeping the living at arm's reach. He could imagine it working for the dead too. Reminiscent of the finale to a magic trick, Peg's arm traced a semi-circle, showing the card to everyone. As the smoke cleared, another burning scene revealed itself. A flaming tower and several people jumping to their death.

'Messengers from the other side, birds,' continued Peg to Martin's nodding approval.

Should it be a missive from the other side, Jeff

suspected it would be sent via a more reliable messenger than a short-sighted magpie. If indeed there was another side. But what if this *was* the same bird back a second time? Jeff shook his head, trying to dispel the illogical thoughts. There must be millions of magpies. Impossible to tell one from the other.

'And remember, with endings always comes rebirth,' concluded Peg.

The beating in Jeff's hands had slowed to almost nothing. He peeked at Mavis, contemplating how to tell her when a violent rustling forced at his palms. Letting them part, he watched the bird stand up, stretch its wings and fly overhead into a nearby cherry tree. Jeff cried out in disbelief. As he glanced at Mystic Peg, a shiver licked his forearms. Rebirth, she had said and only seconds earlier. He went to put his arm around Mavis, her eyes inviting otherwise. He knew that expression. Mavis had misinterpreted his delight for poo-pooing. He studied his hands, thinking on the empty space where the bird had been. There one minute and gone the next. That was the way of things, he supposed.

Stood back from the main stage, Rémy and his gaudy shirt had observed the unfolding drama, never uttering a word. Jeff examined him now.

'Well, who could have planned that, eh Jeff?' said Rémy returning his stare.

Jeff dropped his gaze, embarrassed. Maybe Rémy was right about not controlling outcomes, but you could still make plans. Of course you could. Encourage life in the direction you want it to go. Tonight had worked out fine in the end. A cackling from the nearby branches offered its own confirmation.

'I have to go now,' said Rémy. 'Thanks for your hospitality.'

As he dropped the aitch on his final word of the evening, curiosity pushed Jeff to lift his head once more. He was just in time to catch what he was pretty sure was a wink and right in his direction.

CHAPTER NINE

Tripadvisor had given it four out of five stars. Mavis held onto her hat as she read the restaurant's questionable name under the black awning. Cursive red lettering glowed back at her, accompanied by a bunch of luminescent chillies and what appeared to be a freehand drawing of the Taj Mahal. Why had she accepted the lunch invitation? Her hesitation had only been further fuelled by the most recent online review. *The tikka masala! The Krakatoa-like explosions! The shame!* A review entirely formulated in nouns and exclamation marks was unsettling enough. If she was honest, it was Jeff not knowing she was there that niggled more. She wasn't in the habit of dining with other men.

She hadn't lied to her husband, more omitted to mention. Peg had announced she was leaving the centre earlier than usual that morning. On Mavis asking Jeff to pick her up at lunchtime, he had replied he wasn't sure at what time he could get there and so Mavis had asked Rémy if she could stay on at the centre. In response, Rémy had invited her to dine at the *Hot and Spicy*. More preoccupied than ever, Jeff hadn't asked any further questions. In any case, the one worrying review had awarded the restaurant three stars, quoting the mango chutney as exquisite.

With the accident soon forgotten and only a week needed to deliver extra injections to Toulouse, they had undertaken their first official shift that morning. Jeff had mentioned another delivery. Home or depot, Mavis couldn't remember. To be honest, she was done with encouraging him to come. Whatever his reasons for not wanting to help, she had decided to leave them with him. She was enjoying her job and newfound independence. Familiarising herself with the stocktaking and deliveries to the injection tents, she had already met a fair few people and Rémy said she was doing a great job. Getting to know Rémy had allowed her to see a different side to him too. He'd winked at her again after the football, but she was beginning to learn it was simply his way. A friendly sort. And what was wrong in spending time with friends?

Mavis searched up and down the street. Unsure if she would feel more uncomfortable hovering outside or waiting alone inside, she noticed a waiter appear from nowhere. Placing a firm hand in the small of her back, he ushered her into the restaurant with talk of a lunch special and a higher incidence of skin cancer in those of a fair disposition.

Inside, she let herself be guided, menu in hand. Chatter and sitar plucking accompanied the low whirring of several ceiling fans. Mavis immediately wished they would whisk her straight back home. Her eyes scanned the restaurant, searching in vain for Rémy. He had left the centre slightly earlier than her, telling her he would meet her at the restaurant. Where was he? She slid into a booth, took off her sunhat and tried to tame her hair. She served herself a glass of water and pulled out her crossword book, it falling open on the puzzle she had started that morning.

Seven down. Creating a product from raw materials. Nine letters. Starting with 'f' and ending in 'e'. She lifted her head to think. Fabricate. Of course.

Mavis rifled through the swathe of used tissues and old shopping lists inhabiting her handbag in search of a pen. Her thoughts flitted back to the PMU and Rémy making her laugh with such abandon. A tingling in her torso met with the frustration of wading through the medical paraphernalia that had also taken up residence: sunscreen, a bumper packet of Rennies, panty liners and a blister pack of cod-liver oil capsules for pain-free joints. Finally, Mavis pulled out what she had been searching for, only to see 'Flex Bomb' written in curvaceous letters. She threw the pen back into her bag, trying to rid herself of visions of gyrating hips.

She closed her eyes, remembering the offending item a gift from the chemist. Three boxes of those oil capsules and you got a free pen. Her breathing slowed. Tingling consumed her once more. She couldn't remember the last time she had laughed like that. They hadn't really had the chance to talk during the football. Joan had been on the warpath, insistent Rémy was not all he seemed. And that was before Peg had upset her with what the cards insisted to be imminent. That poor bird's near-kamikaze entrance had been disturbing, but nonetheless timely.

'Mavis.'

She jumped. There it was, that long 'i' and the lazy 's'. She opened her eyes to the same deep blue shirt as earlier that morning. She had recognised Hokusai's *Great Wave* immediately from the detailed foaming. Her head now at the height of Rémy's navel, she noticed miniature surfers riding those same waves. Not a feature she remembered.

'You like the shirt?' Rémy asked.

Mavis went to straighten her skirt, belatedly remembering she was wearing cropped pants.

'Let's see that.' Rémy nodded at the book in front of her. 'I do love a good crossword.'

Before Mavis knew it, Rémy had slid in next to her on the same side of the booth.

'Would you say you are happy, Mavis?'

The question came out of nowhere, somewhere between trying to dislodge the last of a poppadom from her back teeth and the arrival of the chicken saag. 'Sounds like something you'd ask in those questionnaires you give out.'

Mavis had read the copy Joan had passed her that morning in the stockroom. All sorts of questions like, *Why was this week a good week? What three things made you feel grateful this week?* and *At what point of the week did you feel happiest and why?* There were even questions like *What made others in the group happy this week?* It seemed odd to Mavis. Nothing about worries or fears, no mention of experiencing possible side effects. From what Martin had explained, clinical trials were used to determine the efficacy and safety of a drug. Peg said it reminded her of a meditation retreat she had once attended in Phuket.

'Bit late in the day to be thinking about being happy, isn't it?' Mavis laughed as he stirred the curry, steam rising to caress her face.

She had used a toilet break to engender a less intimate seating arrangement, although it had been fun to finish the crossword with Rémy. Jeff never showed any interest in them. Now facing Rémy's intense gaze head on, she wondered if sitting side by side wouldn't have been preferable.

'Late in the day? If everyone thought like that, how would any of us be happy? Rice?' Rémy's arm brushed hers as he leant towards her with a full serving spoon.

Mavis smiled, the hairs on her arm standing to attention. Since their coffee at the PMU, Mavis had been thinking, again. Life turns on a dime, as the Americans say, and her whole life had turned upside down on the 7th of June 1983. Spun out of control. She and Jeff had soldiered on. Done their best, even though their David resented them for just that. Rémy had seemed to be able to see it all.

'When we had coffee, you talked about how we don't always control what comes our way.' Mavis's gaze locked on Rémy's shirt. Starting at his neck, she started to count the buttons still searching buttonholes. One, two, three—

'It's all about desire,' said Rémy.

'It is?' Her eyes darted around the restaurant, before dropping to her knees. The heat from the chicken saag dissipated to her limbs. Cotton clung to her legs as she edged her hands under her thighs. Maybe thoughts of the past were not all Rémy had read in her at the PMU.

'Desire for what we don't have,' continued Rémy.

Just when she thought she understood this curious man, he confused her again. Maybe she had been right all along but fancy talking about desire of an afternoon. Or any time of the day come to that.

'Hankering.' Rémy stared at her.

'Anchoring?'

'Hankering.' Rémy tried to force an aitch with little success. 'Or craving, if you prefer.'

Mavis shook her head. She wasn't sure she did prefer. Hang on a minute. Weren't they clues in the crossword the other day?

'It's all about the Four Noble Truths.'

'You call it noble, do you?' Mavis coughed into her napkin.

'Sorry?'

Mavis shook her head. She imagined his breath once more on her neck, the aitches he frequently dropped running amok on her skin. She tried to come back to her lunch by retrieving her cutlery. She couldn't feel her tongue.

'More rice?' Rémy reached for the spoon.

Mavis retreated into her seat as his arm went to lean over hers.

'Let me do that,' said an altogether different voice.

Rémy jumped. Mavis turned to see a waiter standing at the end of the table. With his glossy, black hair and eager smile, she recognised the man who had ushered her in.

'You alright?' he asked, staring at Rémy as he took the spoon out of his hands. 'Haven't seen you for a while now, have we?'

'More work on than I expected.' Rémy returned the waiter's stare.

'Always nice to have your news though.' There was a hint of a Birmingham accent about the waiter. It faded in and out like a long-wave radio.

'You two know each other?' Mavis asked, noticing a certain familiarity and wondering if Rémy was as new to Toulouse as he made out.

'If I may, Madam.' The waiter served her a spoonful of rice. 'Life isn't as difficult as we make it.'

'I'm sorry, love?' Mavis inched her glasses up her nose.

'I overheard your conversation.' The waiter glanced at Rémy. 'It's never too late to make changes.' His eyes came to rest on Mavis once more. 'Live as if you were to die tomorrow. Learn as if you were to live forever.'

'That a famous Indian saying?'

'Dunno.' The waiter's laughter resonated around the restaurant. 'It's written on the bumper pack of Pawar Poppadoms from the cash and carry. Any naan bread for you two?'

Rémy laughed, his throat catching on whatever he was eating. 'So, tell me. From Toulouse, are you?'

As Rémy and the waiter's conversation veered into a potted history of a childhood in Solihull, Mavis rubbed the skin where Rémy's arm had touched hers. He'd caught her a little off-guard at first but her instincts about him being a cad seemed to hold true. Never too late, the waiter had said. Why *had* she come to lunch? She had never been to a restaurant with another man before today. But people did nowadays, didn't they? Their David often talked about lunch with Sam from accounts. Jess didn't seem to mind. Why was Rémy forever asking these questions about her being happy if it wasn't to flirt with her?

'You work here full-time?' Mavis asked, noticing conversation had petered into silence but the waiter still standing at the end of their table.

The waiter shook his head. 'I just step in when they need me.'

'You look a bit tired, love.'

'A lot going on. Can't say I understand it all.'

Mavis noticed Rémy's attention come back to the waiter.

'Sometimes, shit just happens, doesn't it?' said the waiter, his smile returning.

'Shit just happens?' asked Mavis. Wasn't that what Rémy had said in the PMU? Smelly, unwanted shit.

'But everything in life is simply a moment. A moment in time. Life turns on a dime.'

Mavis felt her back tense. That was exactly what she

had been saying to herself at the beginning of the meal. How could he know that? It was like talking to Rémy. Mavis studied the waiter as she swam in his gentle eyes. They were of a colour she had never seen before. Of course, a dime can turn one way, like it can turn the other, if you let it. Why had she never thought of it that way? All those years ago, she had seen so much judgement in Jeff's eyes. Nobody could have made her feel more guilty than she already did. Was that what Rémy had been trying to say? You can't change what has happened, but you can choose how to move forwards. Maybe it was time to let the past go.

'Life turns on a dime,' she repeated.

'Are you okay, Madam? You seem a little pale.'

Mavis nodded.

'Nothing's that difficult when you break it down. Keep it sweet and simple. What are the simple things in life that make you happy?'

'Doesn't he sound like that questionnaire?' said Mavis.

'Questionnaire?' asked the waiter.

'We're helping out with clinical trials for a new drug that—'

Rémy's eyes widened as he shook his head.

'Maybe I'm not meant to talk about it,' said Mavis.

'Seems like you aren't.' The waiter fixed Rémy with another firm stare as he slammed a yellow piece of paper on the table.

Mavis watched the waiter stride away, noticing she and Rémy were the last diners. Whatever she should or shouldn't have said would have gone unheard. No reason for Rémy to be upset. On unfolding the yellow piece of paper left by the waiter, his face clouded further. The meal must have been more expensive than expected. Mavis reached to her handbag, wanting to pay. She remembered she couldn't. Jeff carried the money.

An unfamiliar ringtone came from under the table. Rémy pulled a phone out of his pocket and looked at the screen.

'This is all I need.' He flashed the words MADAME LA PRESIDENTE at Mavis.

Joan wasn't on speakerphone, but Mavis heard most of her opening gambit. She had to be on her car's Bluetooth. Jeff lacked the same faith in technology when it came to any wireless connection.

'I'm still having lunch, Joan. Can I call you later?' Rémy pulled the phone away from his ear.

Ignoring his request entirely, Joan explained she had spoken to Philippe. Mavis had heard of him. He was the City Council maintenance guy who had overseen the fitting of the fridges in the stockroom. Rémy seemed impatient with the conversation but smiled across the table. Maybe Mavis hadn't said too much out of turn when the waiter had been there earlier. She smiled back. Joan said something about connected objects and data monitoring. She paused before what had to be the big reveal.

'The electricity didn't fail,' Joan's voice boomed out of the iPhone, 'but there was a gradual drop in temperature over several hours. Did you know any of this?'

'*Non, non*, Joan. Of course not.'

'You see what this means, Rémy? There's human intervention at play. Someone left those fridge doors open.'

'And no one wants that,' Mavis mouthed absent-mindedly in time with Joan, just at the exact moment Nokia's take on Tárrega's *Gran Vals* burst out of her handbag.

She jumped. Rummaging frantically once more through weeks of Jeff's Excel spreadsheets, she glanced at her watch. It was already quarter to three.

'We need to find out who,' Joan concluded.

Finding her phone, Mavis read JEFF on the screen. Her suspicions were confirmed. She was late. Scrambling to pick up her hat and bag, she edged out of the booth.

'I have to go,' she whispered, still not having answered.

'Hang on a minute,' Joan's voice reverberated out of Rémy's phone. 'Is Mavis with you? I'd recognise that ring-tone anywhere.'

CHAPTER TEN

Expectation hung in the air. It was a full house at the Records Office's hemicycle. Mike looked over the curved rows of heads that descended towards the empty stage. In normal times the room was used for training purposes as it housed the projector for the archive material. Today was something quite different. Jostling distracted his attention. Striding over knees, shaking hands and emitting the occasional laugh, Gab approached. There he was.

Dropping himself into the seat next to Mike, Gab's smile disintegrated into a tableau of resignation. 'Let's do this then.'

Mike lifted a hand for their usual high five, thinking it best to maintain appearances. It went unnoticed. In any case, first things first, they had to navigate a two-hour seminar. On receiving the email invitation, Gab had point blank refused to attend. Mike venturing the idea of keeping your friends close and your enemies closer had made him concede. That, and the promise of a bag of sweets. Mike glanced at his colleague. Gab hadn't even asked about his absence from the office earlier that day.

Only a quick trip to Toulouse, but it had allowed Mike to unearth what exactly had been going on. And what he had discovered was far worse than he could ever have imagined. Clinical trials for a happiness drug! It went against everything the Organisation stood for. An individual, and an individual alone, controls their own happiness. No one and nothing else, and certainly not injections. Everyone knows happiness comes from within.

Once Mavis had dashed out of the restaurant, Mike had cornered Rémy.

'Direct orders from above,' Rémy had said, 'I don't know any more than that. It was all in the file I was given.'

'Why wasn't it the one I was given then? Does Gab know too?' Mike had asked.

'How can't he? He's the one who gave me the file.'

Mike now observed Gab as he fidgeted in his seat. Leaving Mike with more questions than answers, the visit to Toulouse had at least allowed him to meet his initial objective: deliver Rémy the new timeframe for Mavis and Jeff. He had been a little reluctant, Rémy having careered into this new case like a bull in a china shop. Only Rémy could rock up in a half-open shirt, skirt around notions of Buddhist craving and not expect any fallout. Problems of transference weren't uncommon and Mavis had obviously taken a shine to him. That much had been evident at the restaurant. They didn't want any repeats of what had happened in Shrewsbury.

Nonetheless, Mike had shared the yellow printout, suggesting Rémy lean into more accessible subject matter and tone it down going forward. It had no doubt fallen on deaf ears, Rémy unable to digest his own frustration at having to move heaven and earth to bring two missions into one. Mike hadn't been able to order him otherwise. This went way above both of them. It had to have something to do with the audit, didn't it? But could Gab really be involved? As the screen flickered into life, Mike felt Gab relax. Let him settle in. Mike could bide his time. This was the presentation they had been waiting for since the arrival of those same auditors. Let's see what they had to say for themselves. Maybe it could offer clues as to what was afoot. Mike rummaged around on the floor for the brown paper bag he had brought with him.

'What the bloody hell is this?' Gab prodded Mike in the ribs.

Mike lifted his head to see a blue screen and 'W.H.O. Workplace Wellness' written in white lettering. What the bloody hell *was* this? Mike salvaged the bag. 'Sweet?'

Gab took out a handful. 'Where's the archive footage?'

Gab was a fan of the archive approach. Walk a mile in my shoes, he would say, and then we can talk. That was how you found happiness, he insisted, by opening yourself up to all experience.

A woman in a blue trouser suit entered the stage.

Gab crunched on the purple candies. 'These taste funny.'

Mike couldn't quite place her but, by all accounts, the woman looked familiar. 'Violet,' whispered Mike, his eyes never leaving her.

'No, that's Cynthia and no mistake.' Gab sighed.

'I mean the sweets.'

Gab sucked on the remnants of whatever had survived his frenetic munching. He frowned. 'Candied violets? You've been to Toulouse, haven't you?'

'I most certainly have.' Mike smiled, watching surprise wash over Gab like a cold shower.

'Can I have your attention please?' Cynthia's resounding voice quietened the room. She had been joined by three men. Each having swapped traditional collar and tie for a white t-shirt, they wore identical blazers the same shade of blue as Cynthia.

'Bloody hell you were right,' Mike mumbled as all three men introduced themselves as John before passing back to Cynthia with a collective laugh. This was the first time Mike had seen any of them, the team having made no visits to individual offices or the park since their arrival.

Using a remote control, Cynthia started to pass through a series of slides, Mike's ears pricking when she alluded to the SWOT analysis already undertaken for the entire organisation. Without any help from Gab, Mike had got his teeth into the exercise thanks to some Internet research. Initially confused by insistence on the three Cs – customers, competitors and corporation – when any numpty could see there wasn't one C in their business, Mike had managed to figure it out. He had handed in their contribution a couple of days ago, just in time to get to Toulouse. Cynthia and her team must have moved at lightning speed to collate all inputs before today.

'More words on a screen,' said Gab on the arrival of the next slide, as he foraged in the brown paper bag.

The noise caught Cynthia's attention. She shot a warning look across the room.

'Don't make them like the English, do they?' said Gab.

'The Americans? Presentations?' whispered Mike, surveying Cynthia as he tried to place her. Where did he know her from?

'The French. Sweets. So, what happened in—'

'Do we have a question at the back?' Cynthia's voice echoed over the microphone.

'You do actually.' Mike silenced the hemicycle.

Numerous heads turned to stare at him, including Gab's. Despite mulling over how he was going to approach the subject of Toulouse with Gab, Mike had been following the latest of Cynthia's suppositions. Having moved from the SWOT analysis to recognition of their increased workload, Cynthia had introduced the notion of resilience.

'Wellness is not a passive state but an active pursuit of lifestyle choices,' she had concluded, 'the right choices allowing everyone the level of health needed to provide that resilience.'

The word RESILIENCE was capitalised and emboldened several times on the current slide.

'Maybe you'd like to introduce yourself?' she said.

A snigger rippled through the room.

'How doesn't she know who Mike is?' said a voice from the back row.

'Ah yes, Michael, isn't it?' said Cynthia.

'Isn't this treating the symptoms rather than the cause?' Mike asked.

'The cause?'

'You know like medicating.' Mike flashed a look at Gab, who frowned back at him. 'Wouldn't a better approach be to focus on a state of wellbeing rather than wellness.'

Rifling through papers on the podium in front of her, Cynthia turned to the three Johns. The presentation cycled back through the previous slides as she clenched the remote control in her hand.

'Bloody hell. Not a second time,' muttered Gab.

'That's a great question.' Cynthia scowled at one of the Johns before jumping forward once more in the presentation.

Gab poked Mike. 'Questions won't get us through this any quicker. What are you doing?'

'And here we have it,' announced Cynthia, with a broad smile, 'your values statement.'

Mike looked at the new slide. A black circle contained the letters W.H.O. Surrounding it were five red petals, each housing words of their own. Words, Mike assumed, that were to be their new values.

'Purpose, Openness, Productivity, People and Yoga,' read Cynthia, her smile fading the closer she got to the end of the list.

Mike and Gab exchanged a speechless glance. A poppy? The fog of confusion that chilled the room was decidedly more uncomfortable than the heat of expectation it had replaced.

Cynthia used the frosty silence to continue. Her remote control transforming into a pointer, a green light danced around one of the red petals on the screen. 'Purpose. Well, we all have purpose, don't we? Most definitely. Awesome.'

'I don't remember her asking us about our values?' Gab frowned.

Mike rolled his eyes.

Gab rummaged noisily once more in the bag of sweets. 'Who but the French would make sweets out of flowers?' he whispered.

'The Turkish. Shhh. I'm trying to listen.'

'Turkish?'

'Delight!'

Cynthia paused to stare once more at Mike. A fire burned in her eyes.

'A delight, Cynthia. Your presentation, it's most enjoyable,' shouted Mike, receiving another prod in the ribs from Gab.

'Friends close,' Mike whispered, not wanting to show Gab he had been caught out.

'Openness,' continued Cynthia. 'That's about us all being open to new ideas.' She flashed another piercing look in Mike's direction. 'Open to what others have to say.

In the words of the great Sir Richard Branson . . .' Cynthia shuffled through her papers.

'We have two ears and one mouth so that we can listen twice as much as we speak,' said one of the Johns.

'Thank you, John,' said Cynthia, abandoning the array of papers before her.

'I think you'll find that was Epictetus,' said a voice from one of the front rows.

'Any more questions or comments, we'll take them at the end.' Cynthia's voice rose as a hand clenched the podium in front of her.

Mike could feel Gab become ever more irritated. Cynthia highlighted the third red petal containing the word 'Productivity'. Deploying more vigorous circling, she stayed with the subject for a good ten minutes before checking her watch and mentioning, in passing, the fourth petal called 'People'. A petal for which she didn't use the pointer once.

'And that brings us to our final value, yoga. And to your question . . .' Cynthia searched the audience. 'Michael, wasn't it? What was that question again?'

'Our wellbeing,' replied Mike.

'Well, yes, there you have it. Yoga.'

'Yoga is a value?'

'Body and Mind, Michael. Yin and Yang. We've got a guy called Wayne coming twice a week.'

'And what exactly are we meant to do with this . . . flower?'

Cynthia and the three Johns burst into smiles.

'It's your Power Poppy,' said one of the Johns.

'Purpose, Openness, Productivity, People and Yoga,' said the second.

'Spells POPPY,' concluded the third.

'Cock!' Gab's voice thundered through the hemicycle.

As he stood, sugared candies rained down on the rows in front of him.

'I beg your pardon?' shouted Cynthia.

'Poppycock, that's what this is. And I won't listen to any more of it.' Gab stormed out of the hemicycle, navigating several concerned faces and twice as many knees.

Mike looked back at the screen. Poppies only had four petals. Everyone knew that.

Mike stayed to the end of the seminar, a scarlet Cynthia rushing out as people questioned whether four of the five petals were in fact values and, more importantly, why they had never been consulted. There was no way she had had time to collate all their SWOT feedback, that much was for sure, let alone ask them what values they held dear. Only two things seemed important to Cynthia: productivity and resilience.

So how did that tie in with a new happiness drug? It had to, didn't it? There was never any talk of such a thing before the auditors turned up. Were they looking for something to numb reality and thereby lower the organisation's workload? But those things were already on the market, offering short-term relief but no long-term solutions. That was the very reason their Organisation existed. It made no sense. Cynthia had left with the parting suggestions that everyone work later that evening, having taken two hours out of their day, and that her and Mike meet next week. Some time with Cynthia was exactly what he needed, but he wouldn't be working overtime to make up for a work meeting. In protest, Mike had made his way outside to find a spot to think.

Downy blades tickled his ears as he collapsed into the

grass under the large tree, its canopy dotted with figs. Mike now remembered where he had seen Cynthia. She had been delivering a TEDx Talk about her dissertation on YouTube. She had used the same pointer, but for subject matter a million miles from the crock of shit she had just pedalled. He was sure it was her. He would research it when back at his desk. Once he had spoken to Gab, of course. He still had trouble believing Gab was involved in clinically trialling a new happiness drug, but how could he not be? It was part of his own secret Project Toulouse file.

Leaves rustled overhead, inviting him to join their opulent dance. Relaxing his shoulders, Mike let his gaze dance from branch to branch. He'd been kept out of the loop this long, talking to Gab could wait a little more. Nature had helped classify a wealth of greens, hadn't it? Olive, jade, myrtle, fern, lime . . . the list went on. Pea green, that was another one. Laughable really. When had two peas ever looked the same? The French had done their bit too. Hats off or *Chapeau*, if you prefer. Celadon and chartreuse were thanks to them. Ironic really that Paris green had been named after a rat poison. A smile escaped Mike as he closed his eyes and continued to float in the leafy mist. A thousand-metre-high building was taking shape somewhere in the Middle East. He'd read about it recently. Gone were the days when kilometres only counted horizontally. Their tree stood nowhere near that tall but power had forever been as intrinsic and misunderstood as beauty itself. *Harder, better, faster, stronger*, that's what people wanted nowadays. That song was French too, wasn't it? Mike exhaled deeply. There really were some strange things afoot at the organisation.

He heard a heavy tread and someone stop beside him.

'What are you thinking about?'

Mike opened his eyes to see Gab. His shoulders tightened. Maybe the conversation wasn't going to wait after all. He needed to approach slowly. 'Daft Punk, actually.'

'Them two fellas in helmets? Split up, didn't they? They bake bread now. Or am I confusing them?'

Mike sat up in the grass, noticing the park decidedly empty for an evening despite its all-you-can-eat makeover. Other colleagues must have taken Cynthia's suggestion of overtime more seriously. 'Maybe you should try it, baking bread.'

Gab sat down in the grass. The sweet scent of figs brought a heaviness to the air, broken only by the chirruping of sparrows. Examining the canopy, Mike now noticed hundreds of the birds camouflaged by the plump fruits ready for picking. Funny what you don't see first time around.

'You did that SWOT thing then?' asked Gab.

Mike nodded. Gab didn't seem to mind him having done it all himself and sending it to Cynthia. Mind you, playing high and mighty would be out of order.

'You didn't tell the SWOT team about Rémy though?'

'Swat team? You think they'll be taking you out next?' Mike shook his head. 'Strange times call for strange measures, isn't that what they say? But I wouldn't betray you like that.'

'You what?'

'*Work it harder, make it better. Do it faster, makes us stronger.* All getting a bit too much?'

'What are you on about, Mike?' Gab slammed down his hands. 'You've been acting odd since you got back.'

'*I've* been acting odd?'

'I don't mind you going to Toulouse, you know. I know I get a bit hot-headed. It's all these—'

'I hope you don't bloody mind.' Mike eyeballed Gab.

'You've got a cheek. You're the one who forgot to mention that Rémy is trialling a happiness drug.'

'A happiness drug? There's no such thing!'

'You don't say!'

'Have you lost your mind?' Spittle formed at the corner of Gab's mouth.

'It was in that Project Toulouse file you gave him.'

'No, it bloody wasn't. You read that file like me.'

Mike examined Gab. He seemed as surprised as him. 'You had no idea, so how—'

'Bloody Cynthia, that's how.' Gab's back straightened with the revelation. 'All these new-fangled directives were one thing, but now this.'

'Cynthia?'

'Think about it. Still no extra staff and now they are talking about some rebranding exercise. They have no intention of running this ship as it has always been run. What was it you said about treating the symptoms and not the cause?'

Mike glanced over to the Treasury, a red-brick dovecote with a conical roof. In their usual spots, legs dangling from the stone wall that ran its perimeter, sat the two artists. Their exchanges in a mix of French and Spanish were accompanied by sporadic gesticulations. Mike copied them, hoisting his shoulders and stretching his arms. It was called a Gallic shrug and handy when pure incomprehension engendered a penury of words. Could Cynthia really be at the root of all this, but how? She didn't even know about Project Toulouse. 'You don't think—'

'What did Rémy have to say?'

'Just following orders, he said.'

'But whose?' Gab snorted.

Mike looked over to the artists and shrugged once more. It was all so confusing. Gab seemed to be telling the truth and Mike wanted to believe him. It didn't make sense to tell him about one part of the file and not the other after all. But if Cynthia and her team were behind these clinical trials, this audit was more far-reaching than anyone had imagined. The sooner Mike met Cynthia the better.

'Anyway, you know Rémy, always sings to his own hymn sheet,' said Mike.

'He's pushing on with the mission I gave him too?'

'Certainly is. These mysterious clinical trials were put on hold for a week when the fridges failed and the batches were compromised, allowing him to get Mavis alone.'

'You reminded him—'

'About Shrewsbury, yes.'

Gab nodded. 'So, he's integrating well, then? That's always the toughest part at the start.'

'For the moment.'

'What do you mean?'

'Well, no one knows yet it was Rémy who intentionally left the fridge doors open.'

CHAPTER ELEVEN

Jeff was early for his appointment. He dashed across the car park, a paint-chipped bench beckoning him from the shade of a mulberry tree. The heat penetrating his sandals troubled him, as did the chat earlier that week. Surely their David wasn't serious about changing jobs. Looking back, Jeff had decided he had been short. He never meant to be, but invariably was. He thought his son might have called back but hadn't. Jeff pulled his phone out of his pocket and scrolled his limited contacts. Taking a deep breath, he pressed the green button.

'Dad?'

Was he still annoyed? Jeff couldn't tell.

'David.' Jeff paused. He hadn't really considered how to come back to their previous conversation. 'You been following the football?'

'Switching to a 3-4-3 formation was a good move by Southgate, wasn't it?'

Jeff smiled. The beautiful game facilitated moments of truce in the most difficult of times. 'Sorry I couldn't talk much the other day.'

'It didn't sound like you really wanted to, Dad.'

Not an entire laying of arms after all, but David seemed calmer.

'That's not true.'

It was a little. Jeff couldn't help but wonder about this younger generation. Always complaining, mithered by everything. Why didn't they just knuckle down and get on with it? That's what he'd done.

'Anyway, I've been thinking about what you said.'

'You have?' Jeff's voice barely hid his surprise.

'The grass is the same everywhere. Green is green. You're right. It makes no sense me moving from one pharma company to another.'

'What do you mean?'

'I need to take some time out.'

This was worse than Jeff had thought. Jobs like his weren't ten a penny. Jeff turned towards a sudden burst of screaming as it carried across the car park. An angry mass of flailing limbs, a toddler threw himself onto the floor. The more his father tugged his arm, the louder the child wailed.

'Not working isn't as fun as you think, Son.'

'Not everyone gets to live in the south of France.'

'Maybe I miss the uni.'

He did, now he thought about it. Jeff had been retired for a few years and most of the time he had no idea what to do with himself. At the university, his students had needed him. He contributed. He was someone.

'But it's normal for you to miss teaching,' said David. 'That's a real vocation.'

Vocation? It was Jeff's dad that had made him study maths. Insisted he find work he was happy to get up for in the morning rather than idle his days in a factory like him. It wasn't that Jeff didn't enjoy maths. Had he his time again and the opportunity to make the money David did, he wouldn't say no either.

'Pharma companies do good, don't they?' said Jeff. 'Thought they called you a firebrand?'

'Pharma companies make money off the back of telling people they are sick. *Doing good* is corporate bullshit speak, Dad. Surely you can see that?'

Of course, Jeff knew capitalism was about money. He had also come to learn that this younger generation had got het up in thinking work had to offer meaning. Work couldn't simply be about paying the bills anymore.

'Look, Dad, I've got to go.'

Maybe it was for the best. Jeff checked his watch. As much as he wanted to help, David never really wanted to listen. On the rare occasion he did, he turned the advice to suit him. Jeff made a mental note to never refer to green grass again. But David *was* calmer. This would all blow over, wouldn't it? David would see sense. And Jeff had other things to think about today.

'Remember, it's better to keep busy,' said Jeff, just before David hung up.

'Too much time to think otherwise, eh Jeff?'

Jeff jumped and turned to see Rémy sitting next to him on the bench. When had he arrived? Rémy stretched out his leathery brown arms in a yawn. A troop of monkeys grinned at Jeff from his yellow shirt. Some covered their ears, others their eyes or mouths.

'What are you doing here?'

'Shouldn't I be asking you that?' Rémy tilted his head towards the red-brick building behind them. A young couple milled around the entrance, smoking.

'You can't tell Mavis you saw me here.'

'You'd better let me come with you then.'

Later that day, Jeff watched Mavis and Peg gain ground, feeding his fear that, gift or no gift, Peg would soon be guiding them into the *Canal du Midi.*

'Not much further. It's just down here.' Peg held her smartphone in front of her like the proud owner of a state-of-the-art detection tool rather than someone using Google Maps.

'Are you sure you don't want me to do it?'

Jeff's words met with silence. He tried to appreciate the evening's pinkish hues as the sun descended behind them, all the time readjusting the bag on his shoulder. Sweat formed in the crease of his back. The hessian itched at his forearm. Why they had to come all this way to watch the match was beyond him. There was a perfectly good television at home but he could hardly tell Mavis he didn't want to go to Rémy's house without explaining why. What were the chances of him turning up like that that morning? Rémy now knew everything but Jeff wasn't ready to tell Mavis. Not just yet. Rémy could mither Jeff as much as he wanted. Rémy wouldn't take it upon himself to tell her, would he? He had promised he wouldn't.

'And I really don't see why we need all these baguettes, Peggy,' Jeff shouted ahead of him.

'Didier gave them to me. Would go to waste otherwise. And I won't lie to you, gluten is not my best friend, if you get my drift.' Peg's voice and hair trailed in unison behind her.

Jeff's head fell into a nod. Mavis had mentioned Peg's new suitor. Jeff wished Peggy well, but this was a conversation he'd rather not take any further, be it the intricacies of her love life or digestive tract.

'Didier not want to come today, love?' asked Mavis.

The light pink sheen of Mavis's lipstick caught the sun as she turned her head to speak to Peg. It was a shade Jeff hadn't seen before. Or maybe it was more that Mavis never ordinarily wore lipstick.

'It's the croissants. They're the worst. Get you up in the middle of the night.'

Jeff examined his sandals. They *were* going to be subjected to dietary issues after all. What was it with people of their age talking about their ailments? Some things were better kept quiet.

'I can see why getting up early to make the *viennoiserie* every morning would make him too tired to come,' replied Mavis.

Jeff's teeth unclenched as Peg came to an abrupt halt at the edge of the canal.

'You ok, Jeff?' Peg offered what Jeff suspected was a knowing grin.

His attention didn't linger to find out as it was quickly distracted. The glossy hull floated effortlessly, jet-black paint contrasting with the resident greenery and stealing the last of the day's sun. She was a beauty and most definitely French. Not surprising in these parts, but the give-away was the limited curvature. Starting at the stern, Jeff's eyes danced from one low porthole to the next. Pillar-box red licked their edges before making one final, vibrant splash where two hoisted anchors reached out like crustacean claws. *Carpe Diem* was her name. Lest anyone forget, it was written twice in capital letters, once on either side of the bow.

Inhaling deeply, he could smell it. Diesel. It was August 1964, and they were leaving the Manchester Ship Canal bound for Sea Scout camp in Ireland. Twenty-eight of them, and the majority prone to sea sickness. The smell of diesel often added to people's nausea. Jeff had come to love it that summer and crave it the summers after that. Ropes stretching out to land caught Jeff's eye. Moored, the barge floated silently. No diesel fumes after all. Just memories. Convinced they were lost and about to insist on taking over navigation from Peg, Jeff noticed a tanned figure descend the walkway that bridged the vessel and dry land.

'There you are!' Rémy beckoned them.

Rémy lived on a boat? No one had mentioned that, not even Rémy. They had only been talking about Jeff's love of the sea that morning when his appointment had been delayed. Why hadn't he said anything then? He really was odd. Jeff hoped he could trust him.

Jeff turned to see Martin coming down the towpath.

'Let's show them Ukrainians, shall we?' said Martin.

'No Joan?' asked Jeff.

'Headache.' Martin slapped Jeff on the shoulder, deftly catching the baguettes he accidentally displaced. 'No fibre in that French bread, Jeff. I won't go into how irregular it's made Joan.'

Suspecting at some point Martin would do exactly that, Jeff nodded. Pathologists were only one step on from doctors, even if they had more margin for error, and Martin only critical of his wife in her absence. Jeff didn't care. His mind was elsewhere. It was bobbing along happily on the Irish Sea.

Four-nil. The quarter-finals next. Propped up against the top of the cabin up on deck, Jeff's legs stretched before him. The final was in reach. He might get to see England hold up a cup twice in his lifetime. Craving fresh air, he opened his mouth. He let his hands stroke the decking as a smile played with his lips. He had come tonight convinced it was going to be a let-down. Why did he do that, fear the worst? It had seemed a risky business to be embarking on adventure for the quarter-finals. Initial doubts had soon been alleviated by the boat's flatscreen television and expensive satellite subscription. Offering a menu that had suited Peg's many intolerances, as well as a fair share of drinks, Rémy had been the perfect host. Where was Rémy? Probably with the others down in the cabin. The perfect host but, having rambled on about Greek philosophy again that morning, he'd said hardly anything during the match. He wasn't chatting with Mavis, was he? He'd promised he wouldn't. Jeff went to move. Head spinning, he fell back onto the cabin.

The stars were brighter tonight, closer. The thunder earlier in the week had been short-lived after all. The sky used to scare him as a child. The vast nothingness, and him floating in it. A minute speck on a tiny rock in an infinite universe. He'd felt the same lurch of existential angst when he'd watched *The Sky at Night* with Dad, just the two of them. No Mum. Every week subsumed by a desperate urge to inch closer to the man he knew nothing about. Their ritual had continued after he'd left home, but he hadn't seen a single episode since his father's death. There was no point. Jeff closed his eyes. Cigarette smoke caressed his nose as someone took a seat next to him.

'*Ça v*a, Jeff?'

Jeff lifted his head and nodded. His French was limited, not non-existent. He just hated speaking it. Foreign languages demanded a precision impossible to obtain unless you had been initiated in the womb. You couldn't just *learn* a language; not like you could pick up a textbook and learn maths. You sounded like you were trying and failing.

'You haven't been talking to Mavis, have you?'

A cigarette burned brightly as Rémy inhaled. 'It's you that needs to tell her. And soon.'

'When I'm ready. I need everything in place first. You never said you lived on a boat this morning.'

Rémy shrugged. 'You smoke?' He held out a box.

'Only when I'm on fire.' Jeff broke into a giggle.

He was drunker than he had realised. In any case, attempts at humour were in vain. Rémy looked on thoughtfully, Jeff comforting himself in the knowledge that sarcasm was invariably lost on the French. As the colours on Rémy's shirt merged into one, Jeff tried to refocus on the shapes. They were planets. Lots of tiny planets. Jupiter, Saturn, the red planet. The lurching feeling returned. He shifted his gaze straight ahead. A neat row of saplings waved back.

'The mighty oak,' said Rémy, taking a deep drag on his cigarette and flicking ash into his empty beer bottle.

'Don't look too mighty.' Jeff bent his legs as they cramped up. 'Smoking will kill you, you know.'

'We're all on borrowed time anyway,' said Rémy as idiomatically as ever.

'Hence the need to plan.'

'Hence the need to do what we have to do.'

There it was. Jeff knew he would bring the subject back to Mavis.

'You really believe that Greek stuff you talk about?' asked Jeff, thinking back to the England versus Germany match.

'About freedom being gained by letting go of what is beyond our control? *Bien sûr.*' The 'r' rolled over his tongue like butter off a hot crumpet. 'You can make choices, Jeff. You can have plans. It's not a bad thing. What people forget is that you can't control outcomes. And that's where they attach expectation.'

'Expectation?'

'To the result they want, or often the one they don't. In the process of trying to control the uncontrollable, what happens?'

Jeff shook his head.

'You forget who you are.'

Jeff turned to Rémy. 'When watching football? Yes, I suppose I do.'

Rémy laughed, before a jolt straightened his back. Jeff thought he heard something about keeping things sweet and simple. He couldn't be sure.

'I meant you forget who you are in life, Jeff. But football is a metaphor for life. You're right there.' Rémy slapped him on the arm.

'I am?'

'All rules and objectives, like those society places on us. Or we place on ourselves as we move forward. We have made life into a competition, except we are all on the same team.'

Jeff could feel his head start to turn again. Life was a bit of a game. He hadn't really thought about it that way. A start and a finish and ninety minutes of being the best you can be. 'You forget who you are,' he repeated, his voice now a whisper.

Rémy nodded. He took a last drag on his cigarette, dropped the butt in the bottle and pushed himself to a standing position. 'A bad first half doesn't have to make for a crappy second one. But you know what happens while you are busy forgetting who you are?'

Jeff could feel Rémy staring down at him.

'Those around you forget who they are too. It's not fair on anyone really, is it?'

Jeff tried to focus on the spindly oak trees once more. Mavis thought he blamed her for what happened all those years ago. He knew that. He had tried to explain otherwise. She had begged him to forgive her, and he had said there was nothing to forgive. It wasn't reproach that took hold that day, but the fear of losing her. It couldn't happen again. Fathers didn't know how to bring up children. Mavis wouldn't have spoken to Rémy about all that, would she? Jeff certainly hadn't but Rémy seemed to know more than he let on. Somehow see back into those early days with Mavis, maybe further back than that. He went to speak but turned to see Rémy's tanned calves disappear into the night, his sandals tapping the decking. Jeff's head fell backwards, his eyes closed. He let the smell of diesel come to play with him once more. He'd come back from that camp keen to tell of his adventures on the high seas, only to find a darkened living room. From the obscurity had emerged a cracked voice.

'She's gone.'

They spoke no more of Mum. Jeff would go to her dressing table to play with her jewellery and smell her handkerchiefs. One day, he came home from school and all her belongings were gone too. Jeff sailed with the Sea Scouts whenever he got the chance after that. He wanted the diesel and the sea salt. He craved smells from a time when Mum was still there and had entertained the vain hope that, on returning, she would have magically reappeared too.

Jeff stood. Running his hands through his hair, he tried to disperse thoughts of the past into the hot night air. He hobbled towards the stern, walking off the pins and needles. Thin and motionless, the young oaks mourned over what Jeff now recognised as the sorry stumps of centuries-old plane trees that had once ruled the canal. Disease ridden, thousands of them had been mercilessly felled. These would-be mighty oaks must be the new trees on the block.

He looked into the cabin, a row of thin rectangular windows offering a view of the living area and a laughing Peggy. Jeff remembered Joan's absence, only now realising she was probably still feeling threatened by Rémy. The new oak on the block as it were. She hadn't really given him a chance. Change was difficult at their age. Whether you chose it or it chose you. He would invite her and Martin over for Mah-jong. They hadn't played in a while. It might calm things down, just the four of them. You could only have four players anyway and Mavis had said Peg and Joan had had another set-to. Not a bad sort, but unlike Jeff, Joan hadn't learnt to keep her thoughts on Peg's 'gift', and most other things, strictly to herself.

'It's coming home. It's coming home. It's coming. Football's coming home!' Martin's arms swayed as he made his way up on deck.

'Not gonna lie to you. I thought you'd fallen off the edge,' said Peg, bringing up the rear.

Jeff's eyes fell on the row of windows once more. The pink lipstick that had caught his eye earlier now glided around the room, colouring the most beautiful of smiles. He watched, mesmerised. He hadn't seen Mavis dance for such a long time.

'You alright, Jeff, love? I was only joking.'

Jeff could hear talking but was fixated by the windows. 'What was that, Peggy?'

'You've been out here for ages. Are you ok? Good job I'm designated driver.' She shook a set of keys at him.

Peggy driving had been his only recourse to letting his hair down tonight. And he needed it. As Rémy and Mavis now made their way up on deck, Jeff simply nodded.

'Thank you all for coming over,' said Rémy. 'Now you know where I live, don't hesitate.'

The crew returned a chorus of thank yous and made their way down the walkway to terra firma. Mosquitos hummed menacingly close, gravel crunched underfoot and Peg explained to Mavis how her smartphone doubled up as both a torch and compass should they get lost. Jeff was disinterested in chit-chat. He blatantly ignored the tiny stones infiltrating his socks and the itching he could already feel on his neck. All he could think about was how happy Mavis had looked. And how she had not been dancing alone.

Those around you forget who they are too.

But Mavis was starting to remember. And Rémy was helping her.

CHAPTER TWELVE

Sunlight cut across the blue and yellow tablecloth as Mavis sat at the dining room table counting ivory-coloured tiles and lining them face down to build a wall. Persistent ticking drew her attention to the sideboard and the mantel clock. An ugly thing Jeff's dad had left them. She had no idea why he insisted on keeping it. Tick, tick, tick. The beating grew louder with every stroke despite the violins squealing out of the radio.

'Ah, now Mozart had a starling that helped him compose, you know.' Martin lifted a finger in the air to indicate the piece of music that had just started. 'Clever things.'

'For the love of God, Martin, I hardly think a bird wrote some of the best music ever produced,' said Joan.

'Two rows of eighteen tiles in each wall.' Jeff pointed to Mavis's half-finished construction.

'I know, I know.'

Jeff and Martin had completed their walls and were waiting on her and Joan. The four walls, once built, would all meet to form a square fortress in the middle. That's how you started a game of Mah-jong. Mavis shot a surreptitious glance across the table. It went unnoticed, Joan concentrated on stacking her own tiles. She clacked them together as she went. Clickety-clack, clickety-clack. Mavis rubbed her left temple and the headache that had taunted her since waking.

The righteous hate what is false, but the wicked make themselves a stench and bring shame on themselves.

Memories of Sunday confessions crowded her mind, interspersed with Joan's voice reverberating out of Rémy's phone. Would Joan tell Jeff about Mavis's lunch with Rémy? Mavis hadn't. As time had passed, it had become more and more awkward to mention. Reluctant to answer Joan's inevitable questions, Mavis had resolved to keep a low profile whilst working out what to do. Joan's absence at the football on Saturday had offered a reprieve, but now here she was. Hiding on a small boat would have been hard enough. Sitting within three feet of the T.C.E.P.'s answer to Jessica Fletcher all afternoon was going to be excruciating. Mavis *would* tell Jeff at some point. She just needed to consider how and when. Swapping hands to massage her right temple, Mavis found herself floating around Rémy's cabin, Tom Jones asking 'What's New Pussycat?' and two strong arms guiding her. A smile broke free. Maybe she simply enjoyed spending time with Rémy. Where was the harm in that?

Give honour to marriage and remain faithful to one another in marriage.

Clickety-clack. Clickety-clack.

Jeff stretched over to finish building Mavis's wall. She bristled as his arm touched hers. Her hands retreated to her lap. That was the problem with this game. It took an eternity to build the walls before you could start playing. Expectant faces waited on the fourth and final wall. Black-rimmed glasses magnified the *Madame la Présidente*'s all-knowing stare.

'Lovely sponge, Mavis.' Martin indicated with a flick of the eyes that his side plate was home to the lightest of remaining crumbs.

Mavis nodded her thanks, remembering her own untouched slice of carrot cake. She followed Joan's stare as it passed from her to Martin. Mavis's gaze rested on Martin's ears. Never marry a man with narrow ears, her mum would say. No chit-chat in them, not until one day it all comes flooding out. Mavis glanced back at Jeff, the same elongated forms protruding from his head. Of course, Mum had noticed Jeff's ears. Once Mavis was pregnant out of wedlock, it had proved the least of her concerns.

'How's David?' asked Martin. 'Bet he's interested in our new project.'

The dance of photos surrounding the mantel clock called to Mavis. School photos, graduation photos, former times. That article from *Forbes*.

'Busy at work. He's coming over later. In Toulouse for two days on business.'

'Still working on those drugs? Clever—'

'Right, let's start,' said Jeff, interrupting Martin.

Mavis stared at her husband as he nodded at her finished wall. He sighed and pushed it to complete a perfect square in the centre. Jeff was shorter than usual. Or was it her that was on edge? Mavis smiled at Martin, indicating they would pick up the conversation later.

Jeff threw the dice, demolished the newly built fortress and distributed thirteen tiles to everyone. Mavis turned hers to face her and studied the pictures. Circles, bamboo and characters, she recalled them as the suits now. They were easy to remember as they had numbers on. It was like playing cards in some ways. Trickier were the winds and dragons. Various Chinese characters, it was difficult to tell the winds apart and the dragons resembled in no way their fire-breathing namesakes.

'Any flowers?' asked Joan.

'Or any seasons?' added Jeff, with a small cough.

The one amusing side to games of Mah-jong was the power struggle that always ensued between Jeff and Joan, each eager to play master of ceremonies. Mavis looked at a set of tiles that resembled an unfortunate collection of crooked teeth. She scanned for anything vaguely floral. From memory, flowers and seasons didn't do much apart from bring you extra points. Hong Kong John at the uni had taught Jeff. Apparently, they hold the tiles in their palms over there, click-clacking their way through games at the speed of light. John wasn't his real name. He had adopted it on moving to the UK, saying he wanted to blend in. An unfortunate choice in retrospect. On arriving in the same department as Jeff, he had soon met the Head of Maths, John from Didsbury.

'Any flowers, Mavis?' asked Jeff.

Everyone's eyes rested on her.

'Flowers or seasons,' insisted Joan.

The dental graveyard stared back. Nothing. She shook her head.

'I've got three. Seasons, not flowers,' said Jeff with a beaming smile.

'A man for all seasons. Almost.' Martin reached for his mug of tea.

'Indeed!' Joan shot a glance at Mavis. 'We could do with your help with these clinical trials, Jeff. Hardly a man for all seasons that Rémy. What a disaster. You told him didn't you, Mavis?'

'Told him?' Heat crawled up Mavis's neck.

'About the fridges. Left open they were. That's how all those injections were ruined.'

Mavis exhaled the breath she had been retaining. Returning to her tiles, she tried to bring her house in order, moving circle tiles to sit with other circles and characters to join their counterparts, just as she would gather suits in a card game. As the table started to shake, Mavis's gaze fell to Jeff's bouncing leg.

'I can see your hand, Mavis.' Jeff nodded towards the tiles in front of her.

'Don't want to be doing that, Mavis. People will know what you are up to.' Joan's voice was firm despite an attempt at a laugh.

'Well, if you're planning getting any more of that cake, I wouldn't mind,' said Martin with a wink.

'Have my slice.' Mavis pushed her plate to Martin and forced a tight smile across the table to Joan. 'I've made extra anyway with our David coming over later.'

The clock echoed in the silence between two pieces of music.

Tick, tick, tick.

Then more violins.

It was going to be a long afternoon.

Jeff lay three north wind tiles on the table.

'A pong of winds?' said Martin with a laugh. Three of a kind was what you called a pong, a four of a kind being a kong. 'It's an ill wind that blows nobody any good.' Martin attempted to cover his face with a napkin as laughter interrupted his chewing.

'You are funny,' said Mavis, pitying Martin's recycled attempts at humour.

Martin was on his fourth slice, a kong of cakes to all intents and purposes. Joan's disgruntlement swelled like a rocky sea across the table. Gathering crumbs from in between her tiles, she collected them in a pile next to her husband. They were somewhere into their fifth game and no end in sight. They had avoided further talk of Rémy, but Mavis knew Joan. She rarely took her eye off north. Mavis checked her hand. Two identical bamboo tiles showing a parrot sat on a branch and two sixes of circles. She only needed another parrot on a branch or a six of circles to make three of a kind and go out on a pong and a final pair.

Joan paused in her crumb collection to discard a tile and call it by name, as the rules invited. 'Two of circles.'

'Kong!' Martin splattered more crumbs, this time in Mavis's direction, as he retrieved Joan's discarded two of circles from the centre and lay it face up with the three other two of circles he already had concealed in his game.

'One of circles.' Joan rolled her eyes. 'These tiles aren't mixed well. Anyway, talking of ill winds, whatever wind wafted in Rémy has brought us nothing but trouble.'

There it was.

'Trouble?' said Jeff. He took a tile from the wall and discarded it in the middle. 'Six of characters.'

Mavis double-checked her hand. It was the six of circles she was waiting on, not the six of characters. Wrong suit. And why was Jeff being pulled into the discussion?

'He's all over the place, Jeff. Here one minute, gone the next. And what a ladies' man! Flirting with everyone as we hand out those questionnaires.'

Flirting with everyone? Mavis picked up a tile from the wall, all the while trying to keep up with the conversation. A friendly sort, she would have said. Or maybe he took lots of women out to lunch? Two little sticks stared back at

Mavis. Rémy did have a habit of disappearing. Two sticks of bamboo. Damn it, she wanted the one of bamboo. The one with the parrot. No, Joan was just on her usual warpath. That was it. One little parrot sat on a bloody stick of bamboo and they could call it a day.

'Two of bamboo.' Mavis placed the tile in the centre.

'Seems a nice enough bloke,' said Jeff.

'Jeff, love. It's your go.' Mavis tapped Jeff on the arm.

Mavis hadn't seen Rémy *flirting with everyone* as Joan put it. That was an exaggeration. Come on! How much longer. A six of circles or a one of bamboo. That parrot on the stick. One of those two, that's all she needed.

'Ok, love. Why the hurry?' asked Jeff.

'Well David is coming for dinner this evening, isn't he?'

Jeff's eyes flicked between Mavis and the mantel clock. 'It's two o'clock.'

Mavis checked the clock.

Tick, tick, tick.

Two o'clock. So, it was.

'West wind,' said Jeff, pulling a tile and discarding it.

'Kong!' shouted Martin, to another audible sigh from Joan.

'You think Rémy is a nice bloke?' Joan stared at Jeff.

'Four west winds, that's got to be worth some points, no?' asked Martin, smiling.

'I mean he was nice enough to invite us all over for the football, wasn't he?' said Jeff.

'You spent most of the evening up on deck, staring at the stars.' Martin laughed. 'Not four winds, but four sheets to the wind.' He lay the retrieved west wind tile next to the three others.

'That doesn't mean I wasn't following what was going on.' Jeff looked straight at Mavis.

She froze.

Blue eyes beckoned, their regard fathomless. Was Jeff smiling? She couldn't tell. Had he seen her and Rémy dancing? How could he have? He'd been outside. He must have caught a glimpse through the narrow windows up on deck. But why wouldn't he have said anything? And what had he been doing up there all that time anyway?

Tick, tick, tick.

'But what about those wasted injections, Jeff? Points to Rémy doesn't it?' Joan had the scent of blood.

Mavis regained her breath. Maybe the injection debate was a good diversion from Rémy's flirtatious ways. The ground trembled once more as Jeff's bouncing leg gained momentum under the table.

'Whose go is it?' Jeff asked.

'Mine,' said Joan, pulling and discarding a tile and peering at Jeff. 'Six of characters. I'm convinced it was him. This kind of thing wouldn't happen if you came to help us. Then I could get rid of Roy too. He's helping with the questionnaires now he's back from his trip. There's another one, flirting away. Even making those two fat sisters laugh.'

'Hang on a minute, Joan. I'm concentrating.'

'Don't think you can say fat anymore, Joan, love,' said Mavis.

'Larger ladies,' said Martin.

'Whatever they are, there's something in those injections if they're finding Roy funny. And he's only developed some happiness calendar with three of the others. Thinks they can market it. Like we're there to make each other happy! The injections are for that. So, what do you say, Jeff? Wouldn't it be better if you were there?'

Jeff's leg was doing double time.

Mavis hadn't asked him what he had been up to the other day and why he couldn't pick her up at the centre.

That was how she had ended up at the *Hot and Spicy*. Another bloody delivery? In fact, she had no idea what he had been up to when he had disappeared on Saturday morning before the football either. She had come back from Peg's to find him gone. Told her he'd been to the chemist in Saint-Julien but came back with nothing. She watched her husband. Etched by time, she knew every wrinkle on that face, each wisp of grey hair and those watery blue eyes. She had absolutely no idea what he was thinking lately.

'Green dragon.' Jeff gestured in Mavis's general direction to indicate it was her go.

Joan widened her eyes at Jeff, awaiting a response.

'Fridge doors left open you said?' said Jeff.

A grin burgeoned on Joan's face. 'So, it was either intentional or just plain incompetence. It all points to Rémy.'

Mavis grabbed a tile. 'Green dragon.'

Clickety-clack.

Martin followed suit. 'Green dragon.'

'Not well-shuffled at all, are they?' said Mavis. 'Joan, love. Your go.'

'It's important to find out, don't you think, Jeff. Maybe you can come and help suss out the situation. Make sure it doesn't happen again. All those wasted injections. It's a crying shame. Nobody wants that.'

Jeff's leg twitched violently. Tremors rippled through Mavis's tiles.

'Oh, I don't think you need me, Joan. There have to be security cameras, don't there?' Jeff studied the tiles in front of him.

'Security cameras?' Mavis lifted her head.

'Well, I don't think they'd leave expensive drugs like that without some security.'

Jeff was right. There was a security camera. Mavis remembered a flashing red light in the corner of the stock-room. She also remembered falling into Rémy's arms. Jeff stared at her as she straightened her skirt.

'Joan, love. Your go,' repeated Mavis.

'Green dragon.'

Clickety-clack.

Mavis pulled a tile from the wall, checking in with the ugly mantel clock once more. How could she reverse and fast forward time all in one foul swoop? She discarded the tile in the centre. 'One of parrots.'

Laughter fluttered around the table.

'That's the one of bamboo, love. The parrot is sat on a piece of bamboo,' said Jeff.

'Mah-jong!' shouted Joan.

Dropping her remaining tiles to show another bamboo-perched parrot, making a pair, and the four, five and six of circles, Joan gifted her broadest smile of the afternoon in Mavis's direction.

Mavis returned to her own hand. Two parrots sitting on bamboo sticks and two sixes of circles. It was the one of bamboo she had pulled. Why had she called it the one of parrots? When had there ever been a suit of bloody parrots? Mavis folded her tiles. The game had been hers. If she hadn't discarded that tile, she would have won. Victory had been in her hands. She had taken her eye off the ball. She had let Joan win.

'You're absolutely right, Jeff,' said Joan. 'I'll check out that security footage as soon as I can. Surprising no one has thought of it before. I knew you'd have the answer. One last game before we head off?'

Mavis's eyes scaled heavenwards as the tiles were turned and Jeff assumed responsibility for building her wall. Trapped in the triangular beam, an unattainable cobweb stared back at her. She rubbed both temples. She couldn't think straight anymore. Joan had outwitted her not once, but twice. Mavis hadn't seen it coming. Game, set and God knows how the match would turn out. Jeff must have seen her dancing. What if Joan now found footage of her in Rémy's arms? How would she explain that away? Let alone that she'd been secretly dining at the *Hot and Spicy*. Even a maths lecturer would see two plus two and make five.

Clickety-clack, tick, tick, tick.

CHAPTER THIRTEEN

'After a busy week, a lively social event is just what you need?' asked Mike.

'After a busy week, what I don't need is a pile of stupid questions.' Gab snorted as he threw a ball of paper across the room to land next to the bin.

'Strongly agree, agree, disagree or strongly disagree, Gab?'

Staring at his computer screen, Mike tried to ascertain how much longer the feat of endurance may last. He had to speak to Gab about something but with his reactions so unpredictable of late, this needed to be finalised first. Mike had decided that doing whatever Cynthia and the Johns asked was the best way to better understand what was afoot. If that meant personality questionnaires, so be it. Call it reconnaissance. The progress line across the top of the page delivered the bad news that they were only ten percent through. Mike thought about the possibility of refreshments, remembering the empty space he had walked past in the hallway earlier.

'By the way, what happened to the coffee machine?'

'There's a new barista on the second floor.' Gab remained focused on his target. 'Ethiopian, Colombian and Kenyan blends and a full selection of plant milks.'

'Since when?'

Gab shrugged. 'All free. Delivered to the office. You need never leave your computer again.'

Blue and yellow printouts from the Records Office and an array of sweet wrappers littered the floor around the bin. Mike ran his finger over the desk. Dust danced in the air as if privy to good news that had escaped both colleagues.

'Cut the cleaning budget to pay for the coffee?' Mike asked.

'Poof!' Gab balled his hands into fists before stretching his fingers like an exploding firework. 'Disappeared into thin air.' He reached for a pile of disorderly papers on his desk as fresh ammunition.

'Hang on. Don't those papers need to be—'

'God knows who he was.'

'Who?'

'Billy Whizz. Here one day when I turned up, then gone the next.'

Mike glanced around the dusty office, thinking on a cleaner he had never met. 'And Dorothy isn't coming back either, then? Hang on a minute. Where does that leave us with Project Toulouse?'

'Damn it!' Gab stretched out a foot to retrieve the ball of paper that had bounced off the edge of the bin and stopped half a metre short of rolling back to him.

As the sky darkens before a storm, a cold shadow took residence over Mike. Sitting forward, he banged the table to get his colleague's full attention. 'Come on, Gab. You know what I'm talking about. If it wasn't for Billy Whizz, or whatever his name is, there wouldn't be a Project Toulouse.'

'I suppose not.' Gab stared into space, nodding.

'We wouldn't have Rémy wasting thousands of doses of some bloody happiness drug we know nothing about and we wouldn't have to back pedal on SWOT reports and—'

'Maybe we wouldn't have Cynthia on our backs.'

'You've seen her?'

Gab shook his head. 'She refuses to see me.' His voice became a whisper. 'Just sent an email to say she wants me to do an assessment exam.'

Since the arrival of the three Johns and Cynthia and their presentation at the hemicycle, most communication had been undertaken over group email. Or round-robins as Cynthia called them, virulently insisting in her first email that the term had been mistranslated from the French and was in no way sizeist. Had the email about an assessment exam only been addressed to Gab? Mike hadn't seen anything. He had received another mail though, confirming his own meeting with Cynthia tomorrow. Dare he tell Gab now?

'To assess what?' Mike lowered his own voice as he studied his colleague.

Gab's eyes met his for the first time that day. 'Whether I am the right fit for my job.'

'The job you're doing?' Mike's fingers dug into his chair's velvet armrests.

'They've given it a different name now. New name, new job.'

'KISS, my arse.'

'That's exactly right.'

'No, I mean Mrs Keep it Sweet and Simple. Cynthia's

motto. Working here is becoming as complicated as finding anyone being honest about their life on social media.'

Mike sat back in his chair, his knuckles whitening as the soft fabric warmed his hands. Things were definitely ramping up. Who in their right mind would question Gab's suitability for the job? He had been erratic of late, but the job and Gab were one and the same. Mike had thought over and over about Cynthia's presentation and his subsequent chat with Gab. He wanted to believe Gab was in no way involved in the drug trialling. Pulling him in for some kind of assessment seemed to further support his colleague's innocence. But if it was all Cynthia, there was no way Project Toulouse could be the secret they thought. She had to know the other reason Rémy was in Toulouse. Could it also have been Cynthia who sent Billy Whizz to Gab? That would explain why they hadn't seen him again. But the two projects didn't sit together. One was to minimise their caseload; the other would increase it by ensuring they didn't discriminate on age. The question that troubled Mike most was what on earth was in those injections.

'Heard from Rémy since my visit?' asked Mike.

'Diddly squat. Or should I say diddly swot? Did just see a huge bill out of nowhere for houseboat rental through.' Gab let out a dry laugh.

Mike's bottom jaw dropped. 'What's wrong with you, Gab? You've been bouncing off the walls and suddenly you don't care?'

Gab's anger during the presentation had since petered into silence, Mike having not only toyed with the idea that Gab wasn't all innocent but that he might have even been trialling the drug himself. The silence Gab had sunk into was however far from happy. It was a pit of apathy.

'What do you want me to say? You know Rémy. For

someone who has never set foot on a cruise boat or an ashram, he spins a good yarn.'

Yarn wasn't high on Mike's list of priorities. They needed to skip the spinning and get straight to the knitwear, not to mention the yarn Rémy span was often colourful. At the Indian restaurant, Rémy had reassured Mike he knew the dates and what was at stake. He would get back to them to tell them more about the trialling too. If it wasn't Gab and Mike managing it, Rémy felt sure someone else would contact him soon. Here they were and still no news.

'And what is my opinion worth to Cynthia. She won't even deign to see me.' Gab looked to his feet. 'I'm being pushed out, Mike.'

Mike studied his colleague. The freshly mixed cocktail of pessimism and *laisser faire* was more disconcerting than the pacing to which Mike had become accustomed. Could Gab be right and he was being shown the door? It was best not to mention his own meeting with Cynthia tomorrow after all. Face-to-face, Mike would have the chance to work her out. He'd speak to Gab afterwards. It was a possible Cynthia would advocate a drug to reduce their caseload. Only yesterday, a good few of the Forecast Analysts and all the Archivists at the Records Office were let go, and in direct contradiction to their demands for more staff. But why wouldn't she be open about it?

'Shall we give this a go then?' Mike pointed to his monitor.

'Why are we doing these personality tests again?'

'Better understanding of staff.'

'She could just come and talk to me.'

Of course, it was a valid point. Here was Cynthia questioning Gab's suitability for the job without even talking to him. For the moment, however, reconnaissance was more important. Mike decided on a diversionary response. 'Quicker this way?'

'Another way to see if we're good enough or not.'

'It's the people petal.'

'People petal?'

'Power Poppy.'

The words fell from Mike's mouth like fruit from a shaken tree. He immediately regretted mentioning what Gab had coined 'that shitty flower'. Once fruit has fallen, it's impossible to pin it back on the branch.

Mike raised his hand as Gab went to speak. 'Please Gab. We've been at this forever and we are barely a tenth of the—'

'How many bloody questions are there?' That's the other thing with fallen fruit. Once on the ground, it rots. Gab slammed the desk causing the newly resident plant to tremble. 'And what the hell is that?'

Sat next to Curly Shirley, her thinning hair now cropped into a bob, was a small and bulbous cactus that had gone largely unnoticed. Mike regretted having classed Gab's mood as apathetic. He was as angry as ever.

'Meet Napoleon.' Mike attempted a laugh.

'Napoleon?'

'Napoleon the Cactus. Small and prickly. I thought it suited him.'

Gab tilted his head towards the filing cabinet. 'Araminta not make it?'

'Afraid not. This little fella smells of absolutely nothing at all but is appeasing to the mind in his lack of need for attention. Maybe Napoleon wasn't a great name after all.'

'Small and prickly? I could have thought of a better—'

'Agree or disagree, Gab?' Mike nodded at his monitor.

'What was the question again?'

Deciding it was easier to answer for Gab, Mike clicked

on the circle labelled 'Disagree strongly' and set about finding a simpler question.

'Look. This is a funny one. You have always been fascinated by what happens, if anything, after death?' asked Mike. 'Fancy asking us that. I wonder where she got this questionnaire from?' Mike scrolled the page as he laughed. He soon realised he was alone in his mirth.

'I'm not sure anything fascinates me anymore,' said Gab flatly.

They had slid back into apathy. Mike rescanned the questions. 'Ok, try this one. You find it easy to empathise with a person whose experiences are very different from yours?' The room went silent once more. Disturbingly so. 'Walk a mile in my shoes? The archive footage? Come on, Gab. That's completely you, no?' Mike peeked around the side of his monitor.

'I'm beginning to wonder, Mike. Maybe I'm not as good as I think.'

'The great Gab?' Mike let out an encouraging laugh.

Gab looked out of the window towards the large tree, before pushing himself out of his chair. 'Cynthia sent me another mail. Said our backlog of cases reflects the need to better prioritise my time.'

'But we have twice the cases compared to ten years ago. And it was already bad then.'

'We're doing two and a half jobs, Mike, what with no more Archivists, and the Analysts halved. And there she is saying we need to learn to say no.'

'She's suggesting we turn people away?'

'I'm not sure what she's saying. She's also pushing increased targets at me.'

Mike thought on how Gab had said the original memo had spoken of happiness being for a select few. Was Cynthia going to get there by pushing them to their limits?

How on earth would they ever decide who would benefit from their services and who wouldn't? No one really felt comfortable in that situation. That's why artificial intelligence had been invented. Be it inflated insurance premiums or drone strikes, put an algorithm in between you and a decision and any notion of moral responsibility evaporates. Mike's head bobbed. Of course! That was how Cynthia would sell them the idea of happiness injections once the cat got out of the bag. She'd play on their aversion to prioritising some people over others. Mike looked at his rather pale colleague.

'It's all leading to those injections, Mike.'

Mike realised the same conclusion was the reason behind Gab's lack of colour. But something still didn't make sense. Mike would have to watch that YouTube video again.

'I'll be off early if you don't mind? Terrible headache,' said Gab, pulling Mike from his thoughts.

'Are you sure you're feeling okay?'

'Just tired. So very tired.'

The wooden floor creaked as Gab took the few paces needed to reach the door. Alone, Mike stared at the unfinished personality quiz on his screen. In its crossfire of cheery questions, Mike sank into a velvet bunker of solitude. That solitude that comes with aligning to your true convictions. The loneliness of the battlefield. The silence that is the essence of all existence.

Long brown hair cascaded over her shoulders. She wore jeans, a loose t-shirt and white trainers. The latter Mike had gleaned, after watching many TEDx Talks, the chosen footwear of any bright young thing. Sustainably sourced, of course. No navy suit in sight. Had things turned out differently Mike would have loved to deliver talks, share his thoughts on life. Her dissertation wasn't from Stanford as he had thought, but Berkeley. She had studied for a doctorate at their Happiness Research Center. Mike had watched the video six times, like now, whenever Gab was out of the office. It was definitely Cynthia. He raised the volume to listen to the conclusion of her talk once more.

'The flow state is hard to describe. It's a feeling of being totally immersed in whatever you are doing.' She spoke into her headset as she glided across the floor, highlighting elements on the diagram behind her with her green pointer. 'It is less goal-driven and more experience-driven. Since the dawn of time, humans have been purpose-driven creatures, but internal and external gratification have been confused. True happiness comes from within. From people wanting to do something good because it's satisfying, not because there are external objectives and rewards attached to it.'

Mike paused the video. She was captivating. Enchanting in many ways. It wasn't the same woman who had presented in the hemicycle, and yet it was her, Dr Cynthia Wolf, albeit using what had to be her maiden name, Spielmann. A self-proclaimed expert in happiness who, when asked about focusing on wellbeing rather than wellness, had presented a five-petalled Power Poppy. Something didn't add up. This Cynthia talked about ideas a million miles removed from happiness drugs. Her chestnut brown eyes stared at him.

Mike clicked on the red dot in the corner of his screen to close his browser, noticing two new mails in his inbox. They had to be the personality test results. Having taken it upon himself to answer the questions as Gab would have answered them, back when he had been known for being in a perpetual flow state, Mike had then filled out his own test. Clicking on the first mail, he skimmed the results.

'INFJ,' Mike read out loud.

It was what they also called an 'advocate' and was the rarest of all personality types. Mike recognised Gab immediately in the characterisation: always striving to do right and wanting to create a world where others do right too. That was Gab, imbued with a mission. Everyone in the Organisation looked up to him. Mike knew he was respected for what they had achieved, but Gab was seen as the insight and creativity behind their partnership.

'Sensitive to criticism.' Mike laughed as he read through an advocate's weaknesses. 'Reluctant to open up,' he continued reading. That was playing out currently. It was like treading on eggshells.

Having skim-read Gab's results, Mike came out of the first mail to click on the second, curious to discover his own.

'ISFP,' he said, leaning towards the screen, 'showing introverted, observant, feeling and prospecting personality traits.' What on earth could that mean? 'Adventurer!' he shouted to an empty office, a smile consuming his face on discovering what his personality type was more commonly called. Scrolling down he searched for his strengths. 'Charming, imaginative, passionate and artistic, adventurers challenge traditional expectations with experiments in behaviour and beauty. They loathe sitting in the same four walls for too long.'

It was all so true. Mike smiled, rather pleased with an outcome he had expected to fade into insignificance next to Gab's ultra-rare profile. He glimpsed at the weaknesses. 'Easily stressed, overly competitive, fluctuating self-esteem.' Overly competitive? Hardly. He arrived at the conclusion. 'Adventurers are full of the insight and creativity to form bold ideas that speak to those around them. Whereas ideas are good, what adventurers really need is to explore and prove those ideas for themselves.'

A sense of pride filled Mike as another smile played with his lips. There you had it. This was his time to shine. Show everyone that the brains behind the Agency were not only Gab's, but his too. His real calling, this was how he could show everyone it wasn't bravery alone that led to victory.

Solitude welcomed its old friend nostalgia as Mike thought on how the workplace used to be. What Mike hadn't told Gab was that on chatting with Avi who ran *Björn and Bread*, he had learnt these personality tests were part of what they were calling a three-hundred-and-sixty-degree assessment, whereby anonymous feedback was gathered from direct reports, peers and managers about all employees. No doubt the exam Gab had been invited to sit was all part of the same process. What others thought about you would be compared with how you saw yourself. Mike couldn't help thinking the veil of anonymity would be easily lifted. Thoughts flipped back to Cynthia. Their meeting tomorrow couldn't come soon enough. He would go it alone. He was ready. A strategist always observes their opponent before going into battle, warfare a combination of a handful of enduring principals.

'So, Napoleon.' Mike looked to the cactus. 'Let's start with surprise, shall we?'

CHAPTER FOURTEEN

Jeff hovered. At least, that's what he had been informed he was doing as he paced the patio and inspected the garden. Evening light bounced off the vegetable patch. Green, red and yellow bell peppers sunned themselves, catching the last rays. It had been months since David's last visit. He would be here soon. He had told Mavis he had something to tell them both. Jeff had watched her hang up the telephone to excitedly rifle though dog-eared knitting patterns. He hadn't had the heart to suggest otherwise. Hadn't mentioned their David's talk of leaving his job. Mavis was so proud. Jeff had no idea why Mavis would think it could be a baby anyway. Their son had never spoken of wanting children. Jeff paused to examine the flowerbeds. David and Jessica had been married for at least five years, he supposed. It was in the order of things.

He peered over Mavis's shoulder as she sat at the table. The crossword book lay open and a pen hung reflectively in her hand. Jeff imagined Mavis's thoughtful frown. A sleeveless blouse exposed her wiry arms, reminding him they were both getting older. No one ever had the time they once thought they had, did they? If only it could be a baby. And sooner rather than later. Kids would take David's mind off work. A familiar smell engulfed Jeff as he inched closer. Tea and honey. Mavis always smelt of tea and honey. And maybe perspiration, but it had been a scorcher of a day. Jeff lifted his hat to cool his head, the clammy air offering little respite. He craned his neck to see past Mavis's hair.

Four across. Hide. Seven letters.

Mavis had once bought him a Sudoku book, thinking with his love of maths and what she termed 'a blatant disregard for spelling' he would favour number combinations. To be honest, words intrigued him. Maybe as they so often escaped him. Hide? What could that be? Suppress, or withhold? No, both too long. What about conceal? Seven letters. That fitted. Jeff went to speak, his wife's stiff back dissuading him. Mavis wouldn't like him butting in like that. She'd been testy since Joan and Martin's visit that afternoon. She'd been different in many ways of late.

Jeff picked up his gentle pacing of the patio, kicking an errant stone towards the flowerbeds. Mah-jong with their friends had seemed a good idea. The favourite pastime had only left Mavis displeased and Joan on a mission. She really had it in for Rémy. It must drive Martin mad, her trying to control everything all the time. He paused. The image of Mavis gliding across the impromptu dance floor the previous weekend waltzed through his mind. She had seemed so happy. They had both been like that once. So much so, they had got carried away. Reverend Boyle had looked at Jeff like dog shit walked into the vicarage on Mavis's shoe. Told them to marry before his daughter showed she was expecting. That had been the only way back then. Times had changed. They had changed. What had Rémy said? *In forgetting who you are, those around you forget who they are too*. Mavis was remembering who she was. Jeff wanted to remember who he was too.

Passing by Mavis, he rechecked the crossword to see an 'L' at the beginning of four across. The pen scratched out the final letters. Leather. Seven letters. Jeff nodded. Of course, the other kind of hide. He'd talk to Mavis soon enough, once everything was in place.

Aromatic notes of cumin and coriander tickled his nose. A hint of coconut too. He noticed the kitchen window was slightly ajar.

'Smells like a curry, love?'

'That's because it is a curry, Jeff.' Mavis's attention didn't leave the crossword.

'But it's Tuesday. We always have sausages on a Tuesday.'

'Vegan?' Jeff looked over at David.

'It means using nothing derived from an animal.' Mavis laid a dish on the table with a thud. It was a cast iron apparatus the French use to cook hearty casseroles of beef, veal or lamb. Those dishes where the meat is left to tenderise for hours until the toughest cuts fall off the bone to melt in the mouth.

'I know what it means, love. I'm wondering what prompted it.'

Jeff was quickly coming to the realisation that the only thing melting in his mouth tonight would be five of his five-a-day. Newfound veganism would indeed explain the lack of sausages. Mavis must have known already. Something to do with Jessica, no doubt. Working in food marketing, their daughter-in-law was prone to the whims of her clients.

'Eating meat increases your risk of all kinds of diseases, Dad. Why would anything need to prompt it?' asked David.

'Don't want you lacking in protein.'

'It's a balanced diet, is it? Eating the same thing Monday, the same thing Tuesday.'

Mavis sighed as she started to serve the rice. Jeff brought his attention to the mantel clock. It was already gone half past nine. David had arrived later than expected and Jeff hadn't managed to get him alone. No time to find out what the announcement might be and if it was as he feared. They usually ate earlier. Jeff found himself in no way hungry.

Just focus on the ticking.

'He's looking after himself, Jeff. Doesn't he look well?'

Jeff nodded. David was looking well, reassuringly so considering recent conversations. Dark blond hair sat over his ears and, despite his forty-five years, showed only the faintest signs of grey around the temples. He seemed to have lost a few pounds too. It was more a lightness of being Jeff noticed. Maybe that upset at work had blown over. You could only hope.

'I don't know why you can't just accept my choices.'

Damn it. They had made it this far. David was obviously coming to it. Mavis's stare bore a hole in Jeff's head as she slopped curry onto his plate, sauce splashing his shirt.

'Mavis, love. Be careful. I tell you, your mum has been a bag of nerves all day.' Jeff offered her a pardoning smile.

Mavis glared back. 'Well, maybe next time you could cook instead of leaving it all to me.'

'But I never cook, Mavis.'

'That's exactly my point, Jeff.'

A silence descended on the room. Jeff tried to focus on

the clock's steady ticking. He reached for the wine in the centre of the table. The evening had already descended into discontent before David sharing his big news. His last comment had confirmed his resignation was exactly what he had come to announce. Mavis would be beside herself once she knew. She scowled at Jeff as he offered himself a top-up. He gestured the bottle towards David, who placed his hand over his glass. Maybe he really was looking after himself. Jeff let the cool white nectar trickle down his throat. He examined the swathe of spinach, courgettes and other less recognisable vegetables drowning on his plate.

'What about you two anyway?' David broke the silence.

Jeff decided to keep a low profile.

'I've been busy helping with a clinical trials project. It's really interesting.' Mavis stroked her hair, a smile creeping over her face.

'Clinical trials?' David lifted his head. 'For what?'

'It's called SMILE. For a happiness drug.'

'They're testing it on you?' David frowned, looking between Jeff and Mavis.

'No, love. The T.C.E.P. has been called in to help run it. They needed extra manpower. Or womanpower.' Mavis let out a giggle.

Jeff pulled the wine glass to his lips. There it was. More talk about that bloody drug. The next question would be why he wasn't involved.

'You there too, Dad?'

'Your dad doesn't want to help, do you, Jeff? Would rather wait in on parcels.'

David cast him a confused look. Jeff chose not to respond. David seemed to sense it was dangerous territory. He must have also noticed the heightened levels of agitation in his mother.

'A happiness drug? I haven't heard of it,' said David. 'Who's running these trials?'

Jeff stopped chewing. Their David knew everything going on in the world of pharmaceuticals. From what Joan had said about wasted batches, whatever she had got them involved in was far from a tight-run ship. 'The WHO, your mum said.'

'The World Health Organisation? But they don't develop pharmaceuticals. What did you say it's called, Mum?' David looked intently at Mavis.

'*Felixir*, love. Something to do with happiness in Latin.'

'And what do you do there?'

Mavis placed her cutlery on her plate. Dropping her hands to her legs, she straightened her skirt. She did that when she was nervous. One hand made a short reappearance to push her glasses up her nose. Jeff noticed she had that lipstick on again. And that her sleeveless blouse was red. She never wore red. She said it drained the colour from her.

'I help out where I can. Actually, I run the stockroom.' Her cheeks flushed.

Mavis had barely spoken about the clinical trials since she had started helping. Jeff didn't know she was in the stockroom. He had assumed she was in the waiting room or manning the door. Joan had said the fridges had been left open. Were they in the stockroom?

'Tablets or inj—' started David.

'You like the curry, love?' asked Mavis.

'Err.' David looked back to his plate. 'It's lovely.'

'Thai green. Five veg.' Mavis smiled. 'Spinach, Aubergine—'

'The stockroom?' Jeff took another sip of wine.

'Careful on that wine, Jeff. Don't want to end up like the other night,' said Mavis.

'Other night?' asked David.

'As drunk as a skunk, your dad, after that match with the Russians.'

'Ukrainians,' said Jeff and David simultaneously.

'You're not drinking too much again, are you Dad?'

Jeff noticed his empty glass. He raised his head to see everyone else had noticed it too. He had dipped into drinking for a moment. After everything that had happened, it had been his way of coping. Jeff searched for the clock. Tried to count the ticks. The tocks. Why was Mavis mentioning him having one too many? She knew it would upset their David. Jeff looked at Mavis's plate. She had barely eaten.

Tick tock, tick tock.

'So, Joan and Martin are helping too?' David asked.

Mavis nodded. 'Martin was asking after you today. Ate most of my carrot cake, but I made sure I kept you some. Shall I get it?' Mavis went to stand.

David looked to his half-eaten plate. 'Might finish this curry first, Mum. You two not eating?'

Jeff noticed he had barely touched his own food either.

'Your dad wanted sausages, didn't you, Jeff?'

Jeff eyed the wine bottle. Could he attempt a refill? He had no idea what had got into Mavis again tonight. She couldn't be involved in that wasted batch, could she? That might explain her agitation. Her general mood had deteriorated since Joan had talked about it over Mah-jong. Joan could be overbearing, but harmless enough. Mavis had been provocative too, fattening Martin with cake all afternoon. That man had left half a stone heavier. Happy, but heavier. And now Mavis was turning on him. God help them when David made his announcement. Jeff stared at his wife long enough to catch her eye. They both knew the evening was going off the rails. It was forever a delicate balance with their David. He was so sensitive. Maybe it wasn't Joan, but the thought of David coming home after all this time that had got to Mavis. His reactions were hard to predict and they both misjudged him in one way or another. Mavis gave a gentle nod.

'Anyway, love. Tell us about you. How's work?' Mavis smiled, flicking a glance at the *Forbes* article on the sideboard.

Jeff's eyes followed hers, lingering on the subheading: *Saving the world by bringing his personal passion to pharma.*

David shook his head. 'Not so good.'

Jeff leant back in his chair. 'You didn't go and quit though?'

The clock ticked louder. Jeff looked to his wine glass. Why had he blurted that out?

'Why would he do that, Jeff? You wouldn't do that, would you, love?'

'They fired me.'

'What do you mean fired you?' Jeff tried to focus on the beats. Tick tock, tick tock.

'I wasn't happy with the way we were manipulating clinical data. It's all about monetising people's health.'

'Well of course it is,' Jeff shouted. 'They have to make money.'

David dropped his cutlery onto his plate, curry splattering the tablecloth. 'By making people think the only recourse is medication?'

'But *Felixir* is getting great results, love,' said Mavis. 'After just a few weeks, most people are happier. It's all being proved by the questionnaires.'

'Maybe it's because they have been *told* it will make them happier, Mum. The mind is a powerful thing.' David turned to Jeff. 'Come on, even you're not getting involved in this shitshow.'

'David! Language!' Mavis threw her napkin on the table.

'That's a different subject altogether,' said Jeff.

'Is it, Dad? Or is this you trying to dictate every single fucking part of my life again?'

Jeff shook his head at his son. What on earth was he doing, messing up a well-paid career? Getting fired was worse than leaving. How would he find another job now. As if pharma companies were in the business simply for the glory. Of course it was about money. Why had David just woken up to that now? Jeff looked over to see tears in Mavis's eyes. There would have been a million better ways to announce it.

'No, it's time it was said,' shouted David. 'It's suffocating . . . You're suffocating.'

Mavis's face froze. Jeff went to speak.

David raised his hand. 'Let me talk. That's enough now. This constant trying to control things so that you can't lose anything else.'

His son's stare pierced into him. Jeff searched across the table for help. Mavis was still on pause.

'You're always ready to comment on my life. Tell me what to do down to the last detail, but what about yours? You've wasted too much of it, Dad.' David turned to Mavis. 'And you too, Mum. Holding on to something, but to what? Matthew is never coming back. And you can't do anything about it.'

Pain and shock consumed Mavis's face.

'Son—' Jeff began.

'Carry on. Sit here living in fear if you want. Of getting on a plane or eating sausages on any other fucking day than Tuesday.'

'Let's not—' Jeff reached out to touch his son's arm.

'Not talk about it? Not the time, is it? So, when would

be a good time? Why don't you come back to me when you have a thirty-minute window? You know, somewhere between now and never, so we can talk about how I feel.'

Tears welled in his son's eyes. Jeff hadn't seen David cry since he was a boy. He opened his mouth and tried to find words. Words he knew he had somewhere. Words of love that had got buried by fear. In his peripheral vision, he saw Mavis push back her chair. He reached out his arm to David. He pulled away.

'Jesus Bloody Christ!' shouted Mavis, as a plate hurtled through the air above them.

Wilted spinach leaves and diced courgette hit the tablecloth. A moment later, the plate smashed into the wall behind the sideboard and the mantel clock fell as collateral damage to what remained of its coconut-based ammunition.

'Not the clock, Mavis.' Jeff jumped out of his seat to salvage the only memory of his mother.

'Mum!'

'I've had a guts full!'

Jeff turned to see Mavis, hands on her hips, white as a sheet. Unable to mentally connect the perpetrator with the attack, Jeff returned his attention to the clock. A drip of green coconut milk traced an almost perfect line between twelve and six. Mavis left the room in tears, mumbling about him caring more about an ugly old clock than her.

'It's always the bloody same with you two,' said David. 'Why can't we just be a normal family? Forget what I came here to tell you.'

'There was another—'

The door slammed shut, shaking the house.

Jeff picked up the clock and the framed photo sat next to it, the one of David graduating. He placed them on the table, before opening the lower drawer of the sideboard and pulling out another photo. His legs twinged as he sat back down. Opening the back of the gilt frame, he replaced one photo with another, his one son with two. From the beach in Blackpool, mismatched clothes of the eighties and two scruffy heads grinned back at him. David and Matthew. With his sleeve, Jeff wiped the curry from the clock and sat it next to his boys. He poured himself another glass of wine. The wooden chair dug into his back as he gulped. He urged the nectar to trickle into every limb. Prayed it would numb each cell. Stroking the photo, he wondered where Matthew might be, if he was happy. And then the sadness returned. A tsunami, it pushed at his insides, wanting to leak out. Needing an escape. Jeff thought of the poster on the wall, the one with the wide-open sea. He was going back in a few days to confirm things. He implored the timepiece to soothe him. Its ticking had stopped.

CHAPTER FIFTEEN

Peg's farmhouse was not dissimilar in layout to Mavis's. Where there had once been a dividing wall stood a vertical wooden pillar propping up two equally imposing beams. Three pieces of wood holding up an entire house. Mavis's eyes danced between the cobwebs lacing the multitude of purlins crossing the ceiling like train tracks. Why did rustic charm always come with additional housework?

'Now, with your palms face up, let those feet fall out to the sides,' said Peg, lying on the yoga mat next to hers.

Melodic Welsh tones floated on a balmy wind of sandalwood incense, momentarily drowning out what sounded like scratching. Mavis thought back to the previous evening and winced. It would be preferable to eke out the rest of her days in hot, uncomfortable inertia rather than having to face Jeff and David. She'd heard the shouting and before she knew it David had left.

'Close your eyes and relax those shoulders. Let your body sink into the mat.'

Music played. A sparse set of notes accompanied a meandering stream. A steady trickle of water. Her bladder pinched as Mavis tried to relax into the sticky foam. The scratching returned. Like claws on wood. Opening one eye, she stared at the low ceiling. Peg didn't have rats, did she?

'And with every inhale, feel your body expand.'

Eaten alive by rats. Maybe that was still preferable to facing Jeff. He had been on his hands and knees in the vegetable patch when Mavis had got up that morning. They'd slept in separate rooms since Dr Bourdon had confirmed Jeff's snoring equivalent in volume to a jack-hammer, so Mavis had managed to avoid him. Thankful for the invitation to pop around to Peg's house, she had left a note. What had come over her last night? No wonder David had left in a rage, and before he had time to tell them his real news. Jeff had cleaned up her mess and pulled out an old photo of Matthew. Why on earth would he do that? Like they needed a reminder. Like she didn't think about it all the time. It would only prompt questions from visitors and neither of them wanted to talk about it, with each other or anyone else.

'And on every exhale, breath out whatever is weighing you down.'

Scratch. Scratch.

'Feel yourself sink deeper into the mat.'

Mavis's calves itched.

'And let it all go.'

She squeezed what she remembered to be her pelvic floor.

Scratch, scratch.

Mavis clenched her fists. 'I can't let it go! I threw a curry at the wall. I'm trying to see life a bit differently but look what it's doing to me. Let the rats eat me!'

Scratch, scratch.

'That shit of a cat! In and out more than a fiddler's

elbow that one.' Peg pushed herself up and went to open the back door.

Mavis heard a disgruntled meow and Peg pad her way back to the yoga mats. Mavis opened her eyes, tears trickling down her face, to see a confused smile and dark locks towering over her.

'You did what, Mave?'

'Threw a Thai vegan curry at the wall.' Mavis turned her head in shame.

'Veganism is a big step. Tuesday is sausages, isn't it? Maybe not the easiest night to start?' Peg failed in her attempts to make Mavis laugh. 'Look, don't cry. I'll make us a cuppa and you can tell me all about it.' Peg scuttled off, shouting as she went. 'And let me change this music. I'm gonna piss myself otherwise.'

'Apart from penguins and maybe wolves,' concluded Peg as Mavis tuned back in.

'Wolves?'

Having shared a potted update of the last few days and regained her composure, Mavis sat at Peg's breakfast bar. Silently chewing over endless permutations of recent shame, she had let Peg return to stories of free love in mid-seventies Bangkok. She didn't have the faintest idea what she was now talking about.

'Monogamy, Mave. Humans are one of the few animals to mate for life.'

'Who's talking about not being monogamous? I only went for a curry.'

'So why are you feeling so guilty?'

Mavis stared speechlessly at Peg, feeling somewhat tricked into her response. Duped into accepting that having lunch with another man needn't come with a side helping of Catholic guilt. Peg hummed, stirring the pot of tea in front of her. Mavis wrinkled her nose. Peg's tea smelt strange and never came in bags.

'Green tea and cardamom. It's that or nothing.'

Trying to gather her thoughts, Mavis gazed past her friend to the jars of nuts and seeds lining the shelves next to the extractor fan. Crowning the array of potential protein, a piece of driftwood declared: *What we think, we become*. What had she been thinking and what had she become of late? Even if Mavis's guilt did result from needless blame, what niggled her was having kept it all from Jeff. The tormenting buzzing of a hidden mosquito, pushing you towards madness. Encouraging you to hurl curries.

'You can't spend all your time wanting things to have been different, Mave.'

Mavis cast a questioning glance at Peg. A capacity to read thoughts must come with her gift.

'The Four Noble Truths say that's what creates suffering.'

Rémy had also spoken of things noble, oddly packaged in that talk of craving, hadn't he? Mavis patted her sticky neck. Maybe Peg could shed some light. 'Wanting people to change creates suffering?'

'Wanting *things* to change, Mave. But I suppose people too.'

If Mavis could change what had happened last night, she would. They hadn't seen their David for so long. But then there were so many moments to change, not just last night. She cupped the mug Peg had placed in front of her. Taking a tentative gulp, she ran her tongue around her teeth to rinse the brew's astringent taste.

'Your Jeff's a leopard though,' said Peg.

Mavis remembered the enduringly faithful wolves and penguins. 'He's playing away?'

'Huh?'

Mavis thought on recent parcel deliveries. How many seeds did one man need? If indeed there were deliveries. She hadn't seen any packaging in the recycling, had she? Now pulling out old photos, Jeff had been odd in a few ways of late.

'Goodness. You don't think he's got a fancy woman, do you?'

'A fancy woman? Jeff?' Peg burst into laughter. 'Why would you think that? He's a leopard and leopards never change their spots. You want change, but he'll be the way he is 'til the day he dies.'

'And that's a noble truth?'

Having known Jeff before he became the spotty worrier he was today, Mavis silently questioned Peg's theory. Cubs are born with grey fur after all. It's life that causes them to develop spots. When they had met at the pictures, Jeff's bright blue eyes had twinkled out from under his floppy fringe, like the stars they watched with his father on *The Sky at Night*.

'You keep looking up there but what about down here?' Mavis had asked. 'If you could go anywhere in the world, where would it be?'

'The Himalayas. Some of the highest peaks in the world,' Jeff had answered without hesitation. 'Or the Great Pyramid of Giza. Now that's a mathematician's dream.'

But before having the chance, Jeff had developed a fear of flying, never declaring it as such but simply refusing to get on a plane. The tents at *Beausoleil* campsite every summer were the closest they had ever got to anything pyramidal.

'Life is all about letting go of the need to control,

Mave. Not counting on others. Look at me, I don't have anyone and I'm perfectly happy.' Peg's arm swung around her kitchen to illustrate her point.

Mavis followed the circular motion, appreciating in passing a rather unnecessary family collection of Denby tableware arranged in an imposing glass-doored cabinet. Mavis and Jeff had been happy together once. Something about being with Rémy had brought back those early days. They had rushed to marry because of being pregnant but Jeff had been all the fun and escape she craved. Then life had happened. Turned up with an industrial-sized tin of paint and splattered them both with ugly black spots. Maybe Peg was right, once life has daubed you, you're marked for life.

Mavis let out a shy laugh. 'Do you think letting plates fly can be noble too?'

'Definitely not one of the seven deadly sins you think it is. Better to let anger and disappointment out than leave them to fester inside. Swansea wasn't built in a day. And it was the capital long before someone decided it was Cardiff. Want to see what the cards have to say?'

Mavis wasn't sure she did but Peg had recently confided that, until her dying day, her own mother had been adamant the gift skipped a generation. Not wanting Peg to think her friends also doubted her abilities, especially after that set-to with Joan, Mavis nodded reluctantly. Having already moved the teapot, Peg took the elastic band off a deck that had lain unnoticed under a pile of magazines.

'Time to focus on the future. Only got one life. Leave the past where it belongs.' Peg offered Mavis a knowing look, as she shuffled the cards.

Peg's looks were all of the knowing variety, but this one reached a little deeper than usual. Peg knew about that day. The day Matthew had left them. She hadn't needed any photo on a mantelpiece. If Mavis was reticent about Peg pulling cards, it wasn't scepticism but fear of what they might reveal. *What we think, we become.* Mavis took another gulp of the tea, the taste growing on her.

'You feel suffocated,' said Peg.

Mavis coughed. That was what David had called Jeff. Probably what he thought about them both. The card on the breakfast bar featured a blindfolded and bound woman surrounded by a circle of swords. Suffocating. Maybe she and Jeff were as suffocating for each other as they were collectively for him.

Peg continued to deal cards. 'There's a trip for you. Over the water.'

'Overseas? I can't see that with Jeff.'

'No, more on the water,' Peg corrected, turning more cards. She winked at Mavis. 'If only we knew someone with a boat.'

Mavis held her breath as she stared at a picture of a woman huddled in a canoe.

'You're going to discover yourself on this trip. Show the real you.' The smile on Peg's face vanished with the arrival of more cards. 'But hang on, there is someone around you who is not telling the truth. I can see tears and—'

'What?'

Peg shook her head. She gathered the cards, denying Mavis the time to examine the remaining pictures. Peg closed her eyes, her face regaining its serenity. 'It's Rémy. Something has happened, hasn't it?' she whispered on opening her eyes. 'What at first seemed like an accident.'

Mavis dropped her hands to her thighs, the creases in her cropped pants catching her palms. She stared at her unmanicured feet. 'Well, maybe I didn't tell you everything.'

'Mavis Eckersley!'

'That day the stockroom door slammed shut, I sort of fell into Rémy's arms.'

'You've been having it away in the stockroom after all!'

'Peg!'

'Hot as they come, that one. I told you so. Don't worry. You didn't do anything, I know. Got you thinking though, I bet?' Peg poked Mavis in the arm, provoking a shy giggle.

'Hang on, what did you say? Seemed like an accident? Are you suggesting it wasn't?'

'I'm not suggesting anything. I'm telling you. An accident of his own doing. Maybe you did the falling, but the cards say it was all planned.'

A familiar fluttering tickled her stomach. Had she been right all along to think Rémy was flirting with her? He could do what he wanted, she supposed, but Peg's strange-smelling brew had prompted the realisation that Mavis was enjoying the attention. *What we think, we become.* The guilt she felt had roots that ran deep. Nothing to do with what people may think she had done, and everything to do with what *she* had been thinking of doing. The fluttering rose to her chest. Mavis wanted it to be hunger but knew otherwise.

'Been meaning to ask you. What's up with Joan now?' Peg slid the deck of cards back under the magazine.

Mavis shrugged.

'Accused poor Roy of smuggling the other day. Could hear her from the other side of the centre.'

Mavis must have been in the stockroom as she hadn't heard any argument. Going head-to-head with Roy would only add to Joan's tetchiness. Not a good thing. She'd be wound up like a spring when she came over to watch the football with Martin later. Mavis thought back to the previous afternoon and Jeff's leg bouncing at Joan's suggestion he take Roy's space at the clinical trials. It wasn't just Mavis's skin Joan was crawling under lately, was it?

'Poor Roy?' asked Mavis, recalling Peg's choice of adjective. 'Smuggling what?'

'Pork pies.'

Mavis laughed. 'You sure you can smuggle a pork pie?'

'It's a Brexit thing. Anyway, maybe the upside of it all is Martin will get a break. She was ripping strips of him too before the treasury meeting yesterday. Poor sod. No idea why.'

'She's not been right since finding out them fridge doors were left open.'

'That's how the injections were ruined?'

'Joan didn't tell you at the meeting?'

Peg shook her head as Mavis explained how Joan was now on the hunt for the security footage. Seeming to understand the ramifications for Mavis in terms of what other stockroom events such footage could reveal, she squeezed Mavis's arm. 'Don't worry. You know Joan. She'd love something to pin on Rémy, but she won't drop you in the shit. She just likes being top dog.'

Harbouring doubts about Joan's notion of solidarity since Mah-jong, Mavis hesitated before replying, 'I'm not sure your cards announcing she wouldn't be president much longer helped.'

'It's a gift, Mavis. I'm told what I'm told. I don't make this shit up.'

Tarot aside, Mavis wondered if you could make up half of everything that had happened lately. A thought she kept to herself as Peg's attention drifted once more.

'But why wouldn't she mention those fridges. It doesn't make any . . .' Peg's forehead crumpled.

'You'll see her later. Football at ours. Why not bring Didier?'

'I might just do that. I think we'd both love to see the Danes give the English a walloping.' Peg looked back at Mavis as she took a sharp intake of breath. 'I know what I forgot to ask you. Is your Jeff off to pastures new?'

Mavis frowned. 'Pastures new? You said Jeff was a leopard. So, you *did* see something else in the cards?'

'Not those kind of pastures. And don't need the cards. Didier was on his way back from the cash and carry and saw him. Nowhere near the hall, but on the other side of town.'

If they went to Toulouse, it was only ever to go to the T.C.E.P. meetings or for Jeff to drop off or collect Mavis at the clinical trials centre, both in proximity of each other.

'When was that then?'

'Saturday morning.'

Jeff had said he was at the chemist in Saint-Julien on Saturday morning. Mavis continued to frown at Peg. 'But why was he there?'

'You see, Mave. Your Jeff doesn't tell you absolutely everything either.'

CHAPTER SIXTEEN

Early for his appointment, Mike brought his ear to the heavy wooden door. A shrill female voice accompanied that of a radio songstress. Together, they sang of nights when the wind was so cold. He pushed the door without knocking. 'Hope I'm not late?'

'Michael!' Leaning back on her desk, one leg perched on a chair, Cynthia hurried to bring herself to a standing position.

As she tidied her hair, tendrils rebelling against the bun perched on her head, Mike's mind flipped to the TEDx video and her long locks roaming free. The radio continued to sing of things never to be repeated even though they'd always seemed right.

Mike retrieved the remote control from the floor. 'Didn't have you down as a fan?'

Cynthia snatched the remote control out of his hand. 'You're early.'

'Am I?' Mike smiled. 'Well, you know what they say about the early bird.'

Cynthia's cheeks flushed as she turned off the music.

Mike's gaze travelled the spacious office. To the right of the recently vacated desk sat a smoothie maker and an exercise bike, both flanked by shelves of books. As Mike's eyes danced over the colour-classified tomes that offered a rainbow of reading, Cynthia finished straightening her jacket. She moved to kneel on what appeared to be a cross between a stool and a church pew. One of those designs to support good posture.

She followed his gaze. 'The classics.'

'Austen, Zola, Kafka?' Mike's eyes widened.

'Leadership, management, strategy.'

A heavy pause descended on the room. They seemed worlds apart and yet, even closer now, he was sure it was her. Cynthia Wolf, with a doctorate in happiness and flow states. There was the same beauty spot above her right eyebrow. Mike took a seat opposite Cynthia in what appeared to be a run-of-the-mill chair. He tried to hide a smile. He'd been observing Cynthia since her arrival. Ordered and structured, he knew arriving early would catch her off-guard.

'Right then, Mike. Can I call you Mike?' Cynthia fumbled with a pile of folders on her desk. 'Shall we have an update?'

'Sure.' Mike's eyes lingered on the smoothie maker. Next to it, peaches, plums and pomegranates gathered in a precarious pyramid. Maybe it was a new dieting fad, combining foods beginning with the same letter.

'We'll come back to the reasons behind your declining performance. First your SWOT. Remember, strengths, weaknesses—'

'Opportunities, threats,' mumbled Mike, smiling.

It had taken him half a day to research SWOT analyses over the Internet. It was a minefield of sorts, and yet fascinating how what one person might perceive as a threat could present itself as an opportunity to someone else. Something he hadn't considered before.

'I'd like to thank you for your efforts . . .' Cynthia pulled out a file. She stared at him until his gaze met hers. 'But what is this shit?'

'Pardon?' Mike straightened in his chair.

'It's hardly enough to say one of your strengths is helping people, now is it?'

'That's a good thing, isn't it?' Mike held his breath. The strategy he hadn't expected from Cynthia was good old-fashioned frontal attack.

'Mike, you're stuck in the *what* you do, rather than *how* you do it.' A talon-like fingernail tapped the desk. 'Remember the poppy?'

'How could I forget?'

'Think P for productivity. We need more for less.'

Maybe the fruit wasn't a dieting fad and Cynthia simply liked the letter 'P'.

'I'm not sure I—'

'Do you know what the definition of stupid is, Mike?'

'Sorry?'

'Doing the same thing over and over again, thinking you'll get the same results.'

'But we *are* getting the same results.'

'Are we though?' Cynthia tilted her head, offering the question with a strained smile. 'Seems to me we have a little backlog at the Agency.'

'But we have never had this many files!' Mike clenched his fists. 'Shouldn't we be bringing in more—'

'More. Yes, Mike. Back to my point. More for less.'

Cynthia hauled herself up from her knees. She rubbed the small of her back as she made her way to the other side of the desk. Perching on its edge, she smiled. 'Gabriel seems a bit off-colour.' Her perfume ambushed him. An earthy smell. 'We're wondering if it's not time for him to hang up the saddle.'

'We?'

'Let's just say the three-hundred-and-sixty-degree assessment showed you in a much more cooperative light. People think Gabriel has become a little too . . .' Cynthia dragged a hand through the air, 'emotional.'

'Who are these people? I mean, I was never . . . I can't believe—'

Bringing a finger to her lips and leaning in closer, Cynthia locked eyes with his. Mike centred his attention on the beauty spot.

'Of course, I can't say, Mike. Anonymous, you understand. No room for emotion in the workplace, I'm sure you'll agree. We need a cool mind at the Agency. It's all about keeping your eye on true north.'

'I think he has been trying to—'

'You know what the hardest word to say is, Mike?' Cynthia's hand traced the air once more in its search for words. Words, that Mike was beginning to realise had been gathered in her head long before their meeting.

'Sorry?'

'No.'

'Pardon?'

'The hardest word to say is "no". We need someone who can see our purpose is in fact productivity.'

The Power Poppy. Damn it. Cynthia had him well and truly cornered. What to do when trapped? Throw a grenade.

'Have you spoken to Rémy?' asked Mike.

Cynthia returned to standing position. 'Rémy? Isn't he one of the agents Gabriel told me had retired?'

'But it was you that got him sent to Toulouse.'

'Toulouse?'

She'd had him on the back foot momentarily, but now he was back in control. It was time to find out the truth.

'You asked him to run clinical trials for a new drug. Is that really how you think we'll lower our caseload?'

Cynthia straightened her jacket and picked a hair from her sleeve, before pinning Mike to his seat with a firm stare. 'Isn't it time we all got real in this organisation, Michael?'

'I—'

'You've lived off fresh air for long enough. Not only is *Felixir* going to lower your caseload, it will make us some decent cash.'

'But we've always been a non-profit.'

'Not exactly working though, is it?'

'What doesn't work is your drug. Everyone knows there is no pill or injection to *make* people happy. It's all about people changing how they see life. What's in it?'

Cynthia rolled her eyes. 'Does it matter what's in it?'

'Well—'

'Everyone has been conditioned to think happiness doesn't come easily, Mike. You tell them this will make them happy, they'll buy it. Easy. But the real beauty of *Felixir* is that people are so used to being unhappy, whenever they feel the effects wearing off, they'll just ask to be prescribed more. It's the model all the tech giants use. What phone lasts a lifetime now? If batteries weren't made to die after three years, these companies would go bust. Think about it, the economy doesn't turn on giving people long-term solutions. And certainly not free ones!'

'But—'

'Jeez, not you too. Gab threw his toys out of the cot but we thought you'd understand.'

'Gab?'

'Good old Gab.' Cynthia's mouth cracked into a smile 'Didn't tell you, did he?'

Mike stared at Cynthia. So, Gab *had* known about this?

'Come on, Mike. We can count on you to go with the flow, can't we?'

'The flow? But you know all about real flow.' Mike's voice rose as he withdrew his chair.

'Sorry?'

'Your TEDx Talk.' Mike stopped talking. Like a novice corporal, he'd just let the enemy know their encryption codes had been cracked. But now Cynthia knew what he knew, wasn't it better to continue? 'How can you believe happiness comes from within but back a happiness drug? It doesn't make sense.'

Cynthia looked past Mike and smiled. 'Saw my video, did you?'

'You were inspirational!' Mike checked himself. 'I just don't know how it's possible to go from that to this.'

Cynthia stared into the distance. She crossed her arms. 'You're clever, Mike. I've read about you too. The Great Defender of Good. But you're more than a fighter. You have a sharp mind. A very sharp mind. We need that.'

'I—'

'Had things been different, you'd have given talks. I'm sure of it. Did you not think to come to me with your ideas when you saw the memo announcing our arrival? Don't tell me, knowing Gabriel it went straight in the bin, am I right?' Cynthia stared into Mike's eyes as her hand rested on his shoulder and picked at fluff. 'This was never meant to cause such a problem, you know. Such a shame he never brought you to that first meeting.'

The earthy odour of perfume played with Mike's nostrils once more as a beauty spot danced before him. Ambushed by all his senses, he searched past Cynthia. To the left of the door hung a poster advertising the film *I'm No Angel*. A rouged, bare-shouldered woman in a velvet dress winked at Mike, her hair as yellow as the capital letters that spelt out the actress's name.

'I think you and I could work well together, Mike. You're pragmatic.'

Mike's eyes traced the yellow lettering. Over and over, as he tried to think. *Mae West. Mae West. Mae West.* He glanced at the fruit bowl. Pragmatic. That also began with a 'P'.

'It's just our vision is challenged sometimes, isn't it? Things happen.'

'Sorry?'

'You asked why I am now running this audit and not giving TEDx Talks.'

Mike nodded.

Cynthia's hand cupped his upper arm. 'Men are disturbed not by things, but by the view which they take of them.'

'Epictetus.' Mike squeaked out the four syllables.

'Epictetus indeed.'

So, she *was* familiar with ancient Greek philosophy.

So, you'll help us then?' said Cynthia, exposing a set of perfectly straight, white teeth.

'Help you?'

'Get Rémy back.'

'Back? But he's not finished.'

'The trials are well underway now. We are getting the results we need.'

'And Project Toulouse?'

'That project you've been trying so hard to hide from me.' Cynthia stared down at Mike. 'What is that anyway? We send agents out to anyone and everyone now, do we? On the wish of a cleaner who was passing through. They refused to take the injections and they're too old to do anything with now. Leave those pensioners to it.'

Mike's mouth ventured a form of words only to find all vocabulary had been hijacked. Too old for happiness? Judging by the way she had spat her last comments, he had found one word beginning with 'P' that Cynthia definitely didn't care for. Pensioners. She was more than well-briefed on Project Toulouse too. Fully informed of everything, as it went.

'And make Gabriel understand he is no longer needed.' Cynthia's breath lingered over Mike's face. With no trace of plums or pomegranate, the peach smell nauseated him. 'Think of it as a favour to him. That man is in burnout.'

Not wanting to face Gab, Mike lingered in the park that was eerily quiet. He stood facing their building, his eyes tracing out the words: *World Happiness Organisation*. Cheering rumbled out of the video games room in the basement. Between the free food, amusements and sleeping pods installed on the roof, Mike had come to recognise these work 'perks' as a disguised means of making people stay longer at the office, simply by giving them no reason to go home. Was this what they had become? Filling days with distraction and monetising mental health?

Mike kicked a tuft of grass. He didn't know what to believe anymore. Gab had seemed genuinely surprised when Mike had told him about the *Felixir* trials but Cynthia maintained Gab had known all along. Why wouldn't he have shared that with Mike? It made no sense unless Cynthia was right about one thing. Could Gab be in burnout? Mike had read about it online. The depression-like symptoms brought on by stress in the workplace, the disillusionment, the evaporating self-esteem and the fatigue. It had become more common than the common cold. Once stress had been recognised as an essential ingredient of work, burnout had been accepted as the result. Maybe the trials going ahead pushed Gab over the edge. Could burnout explain Gab stepping back? Could it explain him giving up on their cause?

Across the park, a thin man in glasses gave instructions to people examining the same façade as him. Mike scratched at his nose, wondering what was going on. The smell of peach clung to him as did Cynthia's instructions. Bring back Rémy and get rid of Gab. A break would be good for Gab but she meant him never coming back, didn't she?

'That'll be Steve.'

Startled, Mike turned to see Gab standing next to him. Talk of the devil. He followed Gab's gaze back to the man in glasses 'Steve?'

'The guy brought in to develop our new slogan, not that they'll be wanting our opinion.'

'What's wrong with *Quod est superius est sicut quod inferius*?'

As above, so below. It made perfect sense and had been embedded in their crest for as long as Mike could remember.

'I've no idea, Mike.'

'Not that a new slogan will make anything better,' said Mike quietly.

'Something up?'

Gab's eyes bore into him, leaving Mike to regret his unconsidered response. But their problems had all started with them not communicating.

'I just met with Cynthia.'

'So, she'll see you, not me?'

Mike chose to ignore the bigger question and test the

water with the easier of Cynthia's two parting requests. 'She wants Rémy back. Still no news?'

Rémy really was their only other link to the clinical trials programme. As much as he had promised to keep them up to speed, Rémy had reverted to his usual modus operandi.

Gab shook his head. 'It's too soon to pull him out.'

'I know. Everyone has forgotten about those wasted injections.'

'But what's on that video will come out soon.'

They'd both been following progress, it seemed. Hands in his pockets, Gab studied the crest etched into the marble edifice.

'She knew about Billy Whizz, you know?' said Mike.

'Billy Whizz?'

'The one-time cleaner.'

'I know who he is, Mike.' Gab's voice echoed around the park causing Steve and his team to turn around.

It was now or never. 'She also said she'd spoken to you about the drug trialling down in Toulouse before it started. That you'd known all along.'

'She did no such thing!' shouted Gab. 'She wouldn't bloody dare! So, this happiness drug *is* her doing?'

Mike studied Gab jigging from foot to foot, listing all the many things he resented about Cynthia's arrival. If Gab was telling the truth, that meant Cynthia was lying about Gab knowing about *Felixir*. Cynthia wasn't all she seemed, but why lie about that? Mike didn't know what to think. He'd never doubted Gab before, but he'd also never seen him like this.

Gab grabbed Mike's arm, causing him to start. Violent sobs jerked out of his colleague, tears filling his eyes. Maybe secrecy and lying were part of burning out too? Because one thing now seemed certain to Mike, burnout was exactly what was happening to Gab. They'd never had any cases at the Organisation before. How could they? The Organisation that managed everyone else's happiness pushing its staff to burnout! The whole idea was ridiculous and yet here they were. Mike wrapped an arm around Gab. It was as clear as day now. Cynthia was right. Gab had lost his cool head. It was time for Mike to take charge.

'Don't worry about her,' said Mike. 'Best for you to go and get some rest, don't you think?'

CHAPTER SEVENTEEN

Wind chimes reverberated through the house as Jeff strode through polish fumes to the front door. Mavis had been dusting for the best part of the day, in between preparing exorbitant amounts of finger food. If Jeff wasn't mistaken, she was doing anything to avoid sustained conversation. Neither of them had raised the subject of their son. Jeff glanced at his watch. The second semi-final was less than an hour away, as well as England's passport to the final. It had to be Joan and Martin.

'*Monsieur Eckersley*?' The man spluttered his name as if choking on a bone in an otherwise pleasant meal. Perched on his head, a baseball cap announced him as an All Star. A Converse All Star, whatever that meant.

Jeff nodded as he looked past the white-starred logo to a white van that had its engine running on the driveway.

'Him that I want,' said the man in a thick French accent. He turned and ran away.

Converse in name and in nature, thought Jeff, before watching him waddle back some seconds later. He swivelled the box hoisted on his shoulder and placed it on the ground with a thud.

'Delivery,' he announced, wiping his brow.

'At eight o'clock at night?' asked Jeff, but the man was already jogging back to his van.

'Delivery?'

Jeff jumped. He bent to pick up the box, not before Mavis had placed an espadrilled foot on the obtrusive item. Her toenails glistened light pink.

'A delivery of what?'

'Just some things I need. Nice nail polish, love.'

Jeff tugged at the box. It remained glued to the floor.

'You couldn't pick it up at the depot?'

Mavis's eyes bore into Jeff as he continued to examine the toenails on a foot that showed no signs of moving. He ventured a quick glance upwards. Mavis pushed her glasses up her nose.

'What depot?' asked Jeff, confused.

'The one in Toulouse. You were there the other day.'

'That depot.' Stalling for time, Jeff noticed movement out of the corner of his eye.

He turned to see Rémy coming down the drive. In the distance, Joan slowed her pace to waylay Martin. Joan's dislike of Rémy was becoming increasingly evident, that much was sure. Since discovering Mavis worked in the stockroom, Jeff harboured other worries. Had he inadvertently pointed the wasted injections enquiry in Mavis's direction by suggesting checking the security cameras? Whatever might have happened, it was surely an accident.

'Maybe that's where you were on Wednesday too?' said Mavis.

'Wednesday?'

'Mavis. Jeff.' Rémy approached them, armed with his usual pack of beers.

Mavis moved her foot with surprising rapidity and readjusted her hair.

'Come in.' Jeff scooped up the delivery box with a smile. To think he had been worrying all day about Rémy turning up tonight.

'Sausage roll?' Martin pushed a plate of beige pastry goods in Jeff's direction as he resumed his position on the sofa.

It had been a tense first half. England had ramped up their game after a goal by Damsgaard, only for the Danes to score an own goal. The tension of the match was one thing. If Jeff was rooted to his favourite armchair, it was because Mavis was chatting with Rémy right in front of the buffet table. He both feared and didn't want to know what they might be saying to each other.

'No pork pies?' asked Jeff. They were his favourite. Always had been. Mavis was definitely mad at him.

'Brexit,' replied Martin.

'Didn't Roy bring any over on his last run.'

Martin surveyed the room. 'Between you and me, he did, but I daren't buy any.'

Taking a sizeable bite of the warm sausage roll, Jeff frowned.

'I fancied a Melton Mowbray myself, but I'm in it up to my neck with Joan.'

Jeff raised an eyebrow in the form of a question, unsure of what that question was but feeling Martin uncharacteristically inclined to share.

'Been quoting EU meat regulations in her sleep for days. Lost her fucking shit with Roy when we bumped into him. Would have thought she'd single-handedly foiled Pablo Escobar.'

Pastry disintegrated in Jeff's mouth. His jaw became motionless. In seven years of knowing Martin, he had never once witnessed him criticise Joan. Nor heard him say 'fucking shit' despite many a disappointing football match. Martin took a slug of beer and fell into the sofa's protective cushioning. Jeff recognised a man who, when push came to shove, didn't really want to talk after all. He brought his attention instead to the buffet table. There was Mavis, still standing with Rémy.

All those questions about the depot, where had they come from? Even limiting herself to perfunctory conversation, Mavis was more accusatory than usual since that morning. Maybe Mystic Peg had been pulling those cards. And there he was, unable to remember what he had said a week ago. Or was it the upset of the previous evening? Mavis probably blamed him for David storming out and Jeff, if honest, did fear a repeat outburst. No amount of soap and water had been able to lift the green stain on the dining room wall. He had resorted to a lick of paint in the end. They hadn't spoken about it. They never did, did they? She'd seen the photo he had pulled out of the drawer. He knew she had.

Several times that day, Jeff had picked up the phone to call his son, losing the courage before pressing the green button. He'd been harsher than intended. He would find a way to say sorry. From what David had said before leaving, he still had something to tell them. As if losing his job wasn't enough of a surprise. Mavis had continued her knitting. Frenetic clacking of needles whilst waiting on the oven timer that afternoon. Jeff couldn't see it. Had there been a baby on the way, their headstrong son would surely have tried to hang onto his salary, whether he liked the job or not. The low dining room light caught Mavis's eyes as she threw her head back in laughter. The unmistakable high pitch of the Bee Gees floated into the living room, reminding Jeff of Mavis's everlasting smile. That smile he had first seen all those years ago in the cinema and the smile she so rarely shared with him anymore.

Martin tugged on Jeff's arm. 'They're back on the pitch.'

Jeff turned to the television. 'So they are.'

'You were miles away.'

Jeff nodded. Rémy and Mavis came through the double doors from the dining room together. Jeff turned up the volume on the television, cutting the Bee Gees short in their remonstrations. He knew he couldn't avoid talking forever. If he was going to do it, they had to be alone.

At fourteen minutes of extra time, the decisive penalty was scored that would ultimately take England to the final. Somewhere into the tense second fifteen minutes of obligatory extra time that followed, all hell broke loose around the subject of quiche Lorraine.

Didier sprang from a dining chair that had made its way into the living room. 'Peggy!'

Despite surprisingly good English, the final syllable pierced through the air, drowning out swathes of football commentary. Jeff had already inched up the volume but was now distracted. He studied Didier more closely. He had arrived at half-time with Peg, the doorbell's deafening wind chimes interrupting Jeff's sprint to the toilet. As he had ushered them into the house, stale cigarette smoke and pungent passive aggression from his blue number ten shirt had consumed Jeff. Bloody Platini strolling in, insisting he knew Rémy from somewhere. Just so the French could stick together on England's night.

Didier looked up at Peg. 'It's just—'

'There's nothing wrong with Mave's quiche,' Peg insisted. Having moved to a standing position, she towered over him.

'Leave it Peg, love,' Mavis shouted across the room, looking to Jeff for support.

Jeff had been trying to ignore the debate swelling to his and Martin's right. He cast an eye at an observant Rémy to the other side of the fray. He wasn't the only one trying not to intervene.

'I am only saying that there is no tomato in a quiche Lorraine.' Dismayed jazz hands hung from Didier's arms.

'There's whatever you bloody like!' Peg spat out the words like unwanted pips. 'That's the beauty of a quiche. You chuck in whatever's left in the fridge.'

Jeff doubted such a slapdash attitude to baking would go down well in a country whose cuisine had been decorated by UNESCO. He also wondered on Peg's insistence given her dietary preferences. He reached once more for the remote control to turn up the volume. Mavis snatched it out of his hands. The double doors that joined the living room to the dining room creaked open. In the doorway stood Joan, making Jeff realise her hitherto absence.

'I think you'll find I made those quiches, Didier. If you have something to say, say it to me.'

'Bloody hell. Here we go,' muttered Martin.

Joan looked emotionlessly down at Didier.

'Peggy simply asked me what I thought of the quiche—'

'At which point you smile and say it's delicious. Not bloody rocket science,' finished Peg.

'I was simply offering advice. All I am saying is I am not sure that the tomato, how do you say, imposes itself in the quiche.'

'And how does a tomato impose itself then, Didier?' Joan's voice resonated as if conducting a school assembly.

A smirk caressed Jeff's lips as Martin emitted a snort. Jeff returned his attention to the television screen. They both knew, and Martin more than most, it would be ill-advised to catch the headmistress's gaze. More importantly, they were now well into the second fifteen minutes of extra time. England only had to defend their way into the final.

'That's just it, Joan. The tomato does not. I mean, it should not, *quoi*! It does not belong here.'

From the corner of his eye, Jeff saw Joan inch closer to Didier. The boys on the pitch were holding firm. Jeff offered Martin a look of hopeful relief, it morphing into an eyeroll as Didier continued his analysis. Favouring expressions such as 'unfortunate wet texture' and 'would benefit from a little salt', Jeff wondered how Didier's brain had become so entirely disconnected from his mouth.

'Do you know who my mother was?' asked Joan.

'*Pardon*?'

'My mother headed up the Surrey W.I. for years, Didier. Donkey's years. Her shortcrust was the pride of Guildford. Neither man nor beast ever ventured to call her bottom soggy, or anything else for that matter.'

Silence descended on the room. Partly, as Didier found himself blindly navigating a wealth of English cultural references. Mostly, as Mavis had accidentally pressed the mute button on the remote control. Jeff glanced at his wife, her eyes imploring him to act. He ventured a hesitant look towards Joan, all the while keeping one eye on the game. Only one minute to go. With the double doors open and the commentary cut, the Bee Gees sang to an empty dining room. They were lost in a lonely part of town, and so it seemed was Didier.

'Joan, love,' said Jeff.

Joan glared back at him as she brought a finger to her lips. Would she be asking them to sit with their hands on their heads soon? The terrifying silence that graced the room was nevertheless impressive. 'You can't tell me the English can't cook something they invented, Didier.'

'The English invented the quiche Lorraine?' The arms that had retreated to Didier's sides flew back into the air.

Jeff and Martin edged closer to the silent television. The clock counted down the last seconds. The final was in reach.

'Didier, the French may think they have first dibs on all things food related, but do you really think they were the only people to mess around with eggs and pastry?'

Joan was in a three formation, flanked by Rémy and Peg. The Bee Gees screeched on the tragedy of the situation. The Gibb brothers were half-right. Didier, for his part, may have had people beside him, but he was definitely going nowhere.

'Peggy?'

'You're on your own, Didier. Not gonna lie to you. No one can digest your baguettes, but we wouldn't dream of telling you. Not polite like, is it?'

The clock stopped. Everyone flooded from the benches onto the pitch in a tidal wave of joy. Jeff stood, pulling Martin to his feet.

'It's all over,' said Martin.

'And it is now!' Jeff slapped his friend on the back.

'Too bloody right it is!' Peg cast a disdainful look at Didier.

Joan and Peg left the room, Mavis following on their heels. When Jeff and Martin stopped jumping up and down, a smirking Rémy and an outraged Didier faced them.

'Well, you English know how to make a party,' said Didier.

'But look on the bright side. Football is very nearly home.' Rémy smiled.

'*Et merci, toi. Fraternité? Mon cul!*' Didier glared at Rémy. 'I know where I've seen you before.'

Rémy shrugged.

'In Toulouse.' Didier pointed at Jeff. 'With that one. Whatever his wife doesn't know he's up to, you're involved in it too.'

Didier strode out of the living room with as much authority as his short legs would permit. Jeff caught Rémy's eye. He had known he couldn't avoid it all evening. More tests, Dr Watkins-Villeneuve had said that afternoon. There could be options. Jeff had fled the hospital, Rémy shouting after him. As Jeff now stared at Rémy, he remembered what the Frenchman had said about real freedom being won by disregarding that which lies beyond our control. A new silence consumed the room. It was one for which even the Bee Gees would have had trouble finding the words. Dr Watkins-Villeneuve had not only found, but elongated them, placing all the emphasis on the last syllable. Possible tu-*mour.*

CHAPTER EIGHTEEN

Mavis looked out of the passenger window as the car meandered out of Toulouse. Two hundred more doses administered that morning. Rémy said they had a couple more weeks to go but that initial results showed an increase in happiness levels in eighty percent of patients. Imagine that! Finding a way to make people never feel sad again. Mavis couldn't help but feel proud to be part of something that could make such a difference, especially in young people's lives. Look at their David! So het up with work. A baby, that would refocus his attention. That had to be his news. Surely he'd be back in touch once the dust had settled. Kicking off her sandals, Mavis admired her pink toenails.

'How was Joan this morning?' asked Jeff, in between whistling.

Mavis examined her husband with mounting curiosity. He never asked after Joan.

'I suppose she's still out of sorts?' Jeff insisted.

Mavis shook her head. One of Jeff's hands was on the steering wheel, the other drumming his thigh. He focused on his hand position whenever driving. The time fluctuated between ten to two and quarter to three, but the clock always had two hands. Jeff stopped at a set of traffic lights.

'So?' Jeff turned to Mavis. 'Joan?'

'What about Joan?'

'Is she okay after last night?'

Less than twenty-four hours had passed and neither of them had mentioned Quichegate, both having sloped off to their separate bedrooms. Peg had driven Mavis to the centre that morning.

'She wasn't there today.'

Neither Joan nor Martin had been at the hall. It was most unlike Joan to cancel last minute, despite Peg's nodding claims it all made sense because of a dream she'd had. A dream about monkeys. Sometimes Mavis decided it easier not to pursue conversation. She gazed at the changing traffic light. Once Didier had left the previous evening, they had found themselves alone in the kitchen — her, Joan and Peg.

'I've spent so much of my life giving lessons to others, maybe it is time for one of my own.' Joan had said, eyeballing Mavis.

Mavis had reassured her that quiche was a dish born out of necessity and whim. Joan had returned a sad smile, announcing what Mavis interpreted to be a truce. Never once returning to the subject of the security cameras, lingering doubts Joan may have harboured around Rémy seemed, all of sudden, far behind them.

'Dreadful state of affairs though?' said Jeff, bringing Mavis's attention back to the car.

Relieved at Joan's sudden change in attitude, Mavis was less clear when it came to her husband's uncharacteristic insistence on talking. One of his hands now drooped from his leg like a thirsty plant. Jeff and Martin had both been subdued after the game. Strange to think a heated debate around pastry could take the shine off the night England gained their place in the World Cup final. Or was it the European Cup? Mavis couldn't quite remember.

'All that business. Poor Peggy.' Jeff shook his head.

'Peg?'

'Didier the Baker. It's not right, is it?'

'What's not right?'

'Criticising Joan's baking. I imagine he's out?' Jeff's parched hand came back to life to imitate the slitting of his throat. 'So, is he?'

'Is he what?' Mavis stared at Jeff with mounting bewilderment.

'Toast.'

'Who?'

'Didier the bloomin' baker.'

'I'm not—'

'Good riddance, I say. Peg can do much better.'

Mavis's slow nod was greeted by a toothy smile. Jeff laughed and mumbled, 'A baker ending up as toast!' as he pressed a button on the dashboard.

'You've always said—'

An American rapper cut Mavis off, bursting out of the speaker to her right. Lose yourself in the music, he shouted. Lose yourself in the moment. Mavis wasn't sure she wanted to. What the hell was going on? Her eyes bore into the radio. Jeff never played music in the car.

Jeff stared, just like her, when the music cut and a number flashed up on the dashboard screen. Mavis recognised the country code. It was a UK number. She read the last four digits. Twenty-eight, twenty-eight. Their David.

Jeff searched in her eyes.

'Answer it,' she said.

Jeff nodded and pulled into a nearby lay-by. He tapped the green icon on the screen.

'Dad?'

The love that flowed spontaneously from Mavis's heart collided with the fear that had crystallised in her head over the past two days.

'David. Is that you, Son? I'm here with your mum.'

Mavis prodded at Jeff's arm, flapping her other hand in international sign language that invited him to lower his voice.

'You in the car? I can call back.'

'In a lay-by. We can talk.'

'You always shout when you're on Bluetooth.' David let out a small laugh.

Mavis released the breath she had been holding inside. David had laughed. A gentle laugh, not an angry laugh.

'Maybe I do, Son. I get a lot of things wrong.'

The same relief seemed to wash over Jeff. He joined David with a laugh of his own. A peaceful silence descended on the car.

'I—'

'It's fine, Dad.'

'I need to—'

'I didn't call for that.'

The silence returned.

Jeff stared at the screen as if trying to read his son. His right leg bounced. Mavis scrutinised the screen too. Maybe David was still angry with them after all. Her anger during dinner had been both out of character and inexcusable. Should she interject and say sorry? Jeff had already been cut off at the pass. Heat rose to her cheeks, the air conditioning having cut when Jeff turned off the engine.

'You said Mum's there too?'

Mavis caught Jeff's regard. A nod encouraged her to find some words. 'David, love.'

As she spoke to the screen, her gaze lifted to notice the black and white markings of a magpie. The plump bird pecked at the ground some metres ahead in the desolate lay-by. Its long fan tail flicked up and down. One for sorrow.

'Listen, I came the other night to tell you something. Something important.'

This was it. Mavis watched Jeff, waiting for him to answer.

'You still there?'

'Go on, love,' said Mavis.

'It's me and Jess.'

Mavis held her breath. Quite literally, as she brought two hands up to her chest and pressed hard. Two tails now bobbed up and down, the birds' black heads rummaging in the dust. Two for joy! It *was* the baby. Mavis reached for the button to lower the window. Electric, they were also deactivated.

'I'm not sure you're going to like this.'

Something wasn't right. Mavis widened her focus from the pair of magpies. Three for a girl, four for a boy. Come on. There had to be more around here somewhere.

'Me and Jess, we . . .'

Mavis stared at the dashboard screen, sweat accumulating in the small of her back.

'Just spit it out, Son!' said Jeff.

Mavis glared at Jeff and poked his right leg. Bouncing violently, it shook the whole car.

'We're getting divorced.'

'What about the baby?' shouted Mavis.

She could feel Jeff staring at her. He shook his head but said nothing.

'Baby?' asked David.

'I've knitted a matinée jacket.' Mavis's eyes bore into the screen until the numbers blurred into one.

'A what?'

'And booties.'

'Mum, I—'

'Divorced? You can't get divorced. Not with a baby.'

'But we're not having a baby, Mum.'

'It's that other woman?' shouted Mavis.

Jeff jumped in his seat.

'Woman?'

'From accounts. The one you're always having lunch with.'

Maybe lunching at will had never worked for any generation, young or old. Mavis turned to Jeff. His head shook more violently than before as he mouthed the word 'stop'.

'Dad? You still there? Is Mum okay?'

Okay? She was absolutely fine. It was David that wasn't. Divorced? What was he saying? You didn't just get divorced.

'Yes, Son.' Jeff raised his palm to Mavis, before bringing his hand to stroke his chin.

He seemed wearier than usual. Tired, and yet somehow more at peace with himself than Mavis had seen in a long time.

'I know you won't understand—'

'Did you see the football, Son?'

Mavis jabbed Jeff in the leg again. A leg that had stopped bouncing but chose to ignore her.

'Dad, I am trying to— '

'Life's a bit like football, you see. A competition. All

those rules and objectives we place on ourselves. In pursuing the final score, we forget to enjoy the match. We're so busy thinking of what we must be, we forget who we are.'

Mavis succeeded in attracting Jeff's attention.

'Forget who we are?' asked the dashboard screen but Mavis was caught in Jeff's piercing stare.

'You know what happens when you forget who you are?'

'Are you sure you and Mum—'

'Those around you forget who they are too. It's not fair on anyone really, is it? If you think this is right for you, then you're doing the right thing, Son.'

Mesmerised, Mavis stared at Jeff, her heart beating that little bit faster as her husband winked back at her.

Mavis edged towards Jeff's bedroom door. Dr Bourdon had explained at length that snoring is most likely to occur when the flow of air is obstructed by the relaxing of the throat muscles. She listened. Was Jeff already asleep?

The conversation in the car had performed somersaults in Mavis's head all afternoon while watching Jeff work the vegetable patch. So acrobatic was her mind, she had even cooked salmon for tea, thinking it a Friday. Examining Jeff like a microscope specimen, she had waited for him to enquire why there was no Thursday hotpot. The question never came. On the contrary, he had complimented her mushy peas. Erratic thoughts had then pursued her into the evening. Trying to follow a television programme about trout fishing, she had continued to scrutinise Jeff in his favourite armchair. Unable to broker a truce between the questions that bickered with each other, her head had started to ache. Jeff had finally retired to bed early, them both dodging those elephants once more. There were so many now, it was surprising she could see the television, let alone follow the intricacies of a fish's life.

Unable to rest until she resolved what on earth had got into Jeff, Mavis pressed her ear on the cold wood. What did he mean he had forgotten who he was? And that she had too? And why that wink? If it wasn't for never setting foot near the centre, anyone would think Jeff had been on those happiness injections. She held her breath and listened. What Dr Bourdon had been unable to say in layman's terms, Mavis had learnt from experience. The louder the snoring, the deeper the sleep. When it came down to it, resolving one thing would elucidate the rest: what the hell had Jeff been up to lately? She listened a little longer. Just to be sure. It was now or never. The door trembled with the rise and fall of Jeff's breath. He was definitely away with the fairies. Mavis pulled the key from her dressing gown pocket and made her way to the garage.

The strip light flickered and clicked twice before illuminating the room. Looking behind her, Mavis regretted her haste at leaving the door open. She returned to gently close it as halogen humming filled the garage. *You forget who you are. And those around you forget who they are too.* There had been no accusation in his voice, more understanding. Pausing for a moment, Mavis let her hand appreciate the refreshing chill of the metal door handle. Her mind came back to Rémy, as it tended to of late. Jeff was starting to sound like him, now she thought about it. Her eyes scaled the uninviting breeze block walls. Everything was incredibly tidy. Of course it was. She never came in here. This was Jeff's kingdom. Floor-to-ceiling metal shelving caught her eye. It supported numerous plastic boxes, all with lids of different colours and indicative, if Mavis knew Jeff, of an intricate coding system. So, where would he put it?

'Those little grey cells, Mavis,' she said out loud, remembering the Agatha Christie books of her youth and feigning a Belgian accent by stretching out the 'i' and the 's'.

Rémy reappeared in her thoughts. Maybe Joan had spoken to Jeff? Shared her suspicions before the truce had kicked in? Could he know about her spending time with Rémy? Mavis's eyes danced from box to box, from red to green to blue lids. What if Joan had found footage of Mavis's fall into Rémy's arms and shared it? But why would Jeff be so understanding? It didn't add up, nor did his casual acceptance of David's news. Since when was it fine and dandy to walk out on a marriage?

Semi-hidden behind a couple of bikes, something caught Mavis's eye on one of the bottom shelves. The corner of a box poked out from under an old sheet. Bearing no dust, it had all the appearance of having been recently placed there. Mavis displaced the bikes as quietly as she could. The floor cold and dusty, she brought the stool Jeff used to reach the higher shelves to the centre of the garage and dragged the cardboard box next to it. Hoisting her nightie, she sat down, grateful for the breeze that rushed up her legs. Was it the same box? A notched beak and wings shaped into arrows formed the logo she had first seen peeking out from beneath her sandal on the night of the football.

'Peregrine Deliveries,' she read out loud. This was definitely it. The box Jeff had been so desperate to hide from her. Didier's outburst may have distracted her, but only momentarily.

Straightening her back, Mavis took a deep breath and paused. It wasn't only curiosity eating her. Shame gnawed a similar-sized hole. She wasn't in the habit of doubting her husband, nor sneaking around, but he'd been acting so strangely of late. Disappearing to the other side of Toulouse, talking of depots in which he had clearly never set foot and all those excuses to not help out at the clinical trials. But then hadn't she been acting out of character too? She didn't ordinarily dine with other men. What had become of her? It had all started for David with the odd lunch special and look at him now. She was sure that Sam woman was involved in his divorce.

Mavis inhaled deeply. Straightening the folds in her nightie and letting the flimsy cotton cover her knees, her mind came back to Jeff. Remembering it was his behaviour and not hers that had brought her to the garage, she tugged on the box flaps that nestled under each other. It was more than curiosity and shame, wasn't it? It was also fear. Fear of what she might find, but it was time to face the music. She inhaled once more before pushing away the packing chips to see something immediately recognisable. An industrial-sized bag of Yorkshire Tea teabags. Hundreds of them.

'Where everything's done proper?' An ironic laugh chased the familiar strapline out of her throat.

Jeff was fond of stockpiling but why hide teabags? Maybe it was a decoy? The answers had to be elsewhere. Mavis delved deeper into what was becoming an unusual lucky dip. On hitting something hard, she pulled out not one, but two books, puffs of yellow polystyrene showering the floor.

'*Europe by Land and Sea: Travelling for the Aerophobic*,' she read out loud.

Then she caught sight of the second title and froze.

'*Dating after Sixty*?' Mavis addressed the empty garage for an explanation.

Endless possibilities swarmed her mind. Whatever she might have expected to find, it was certainly not what she had found. Leopards never change their spots, do they?

'The worst is so often true,' she said, once again attempting a Belgian accent and unwittingly gifting Hercule Poirot with Miss Marple's pessimism.

She arranged everything as she had found it. It all made sense now. Jeff was leaving her.

CHAPTER NINETEEN

Napoleon and Shirley eyeballed Mike as he stroked his chair's velvet armrests. His thoughts returned, as they had done several times, to his meeting with Cynthia. Bursts of phrases, Mae West's sunshine hair and that smile when he had mentioned Cynthia's TEDx Talks. Since when did the Organisation monetise its services, injecting people with goodness knows what, and qualify people's access to happiness according to age? *They refused to take the injections and they're too old to do anything with now. Leave those pensioners to it.* Those two lines lingered longer than the rest, Cynthia having spat them with such venom. He'd been waiting for her to juxtapose the two, tell him *Felixir* injections would avoid difficult choices when it came to prioritising. She hadn't verbalised it as such but the future was shaping itself into a two-tier system, with those refusing injections not qualifying for help.

Gab's absence from the office for the past five days had gifted Mike with extra thinking time. Project Toulouse wouldn't have been cloaked in such secrecy if it weren't for Gab trying to keep it under Cynthia's radar. But Cynthia had admitted she knew all about Billy Whizz dropping the file at their office. *We send agents out to anyone and everyone now, do we? On the wish of a cleaner who was passing through.* She had to be behind Project Toulouse too. But why? It was a run-of-the-mill file and she obviously didn't care whether Mavis or Jeff took the injections or not. She'd written them off before Rémy had even got to Toulouse due to their age. So why create a whole secret file, only to pull Rémy back early? Something else had to be going on. Could the answers lie with those same pensioners?

Mike rubbed his face and reached for the manila file on his desk. Bringing Rémy back wasn't the only thing Cynthia had told him to do, was it? She wanted him to let Gab know he was no longer needed. She wouldn't wait forever. He opened the file and stared at the reams of blue printouts divided into five clear plastic subfolders. Wedges of paper comprising lifetimes of events. Events that had shaped those people.

'Joan Bolt (née Baker),' read Mike out loud as he opened the first subfolder that came to hand. 'Born in 1948 in London. Daughter of Clarence Baker, advocate for better workers' representation and prominent Conservative MP. Upset backbenchers in 1946 by supporting Labour's move to repeal the Trade Union Act. Made famous with his slogan, *And nobody wants that!* Mother, Fannie Baker (née Fosse). Lifetime ban from Guildford Women's Institute at the age of thirty-four for winning cake competition through duplicitous means.'

Mike laughed as he turned the page. Fannie had tried to fool everyone by ordering her cake from a village half an hour away. The baker, as mischance would have it, was the judge's second cousin. Mike moved through the following sheets, his smile fading. An ectopic pregnancy at the age of twenty had been Joan's only chance at motherhood. Problems weren't detected until late on. An emergency operation had ended in a total hysterectomy, resulting in premature menopause. Not being able to have children had pushed her into teaching.

He stared into the park. Joan's life, like any other, had its share of trauma. Sadness that she had overcome and channelled into a positive path, shaping many young lives. A strong woman, and yet she had sacrificed things that would have made her happy along the way, her parents having moulded her into who they thought she should be. Organising the papers into a tidy pile, Mike put them back into their subfolder and moved onto the next.

'Martin Bolt. Born 1946 in Hertfordshire. Father, Thomas Clayton. American soldier. Returned to his family in Indiana after the war. Never knew of his son. Mother, Mabel Bolt, died suddenly in 1955. Rare and undetected reaction to medication. Death declared due to natural causes. Orphaned, raised by his aunt in Devon.'

Subsequent pages recounted a childhood of frequent hunger, Aunt Annie often refusing to feed Martin out of spite. A successful and quiet career as a forensic pathologist had ensued. No clues there as to the link between Project Toulouse and Cynthia's plans, not from what Mike could see. He moved onto the third folder, noticing this one weightier than the others.

'Peggy Davies. Conceived on a milk float in Llansamlet. Born 1949. Never knew her father, Alfonso Petulengro, a Romani traveller. Mother, Gwen Davies, medium.'

The Gwen Davies? Mike's face burst into a smile. Everyone knew Swansea Gwen. How had he not made the link? Peggy would also have the gift then. Mike double-checked the paperwork and nodded. Stronger than her mother's, as it happened. How had he missed that? Maybe Gab had read the file in more detail than him.

Mike returned to his reading. 'Broke a boy's nose for calling her a dirty gypsy. Thrown out of school. Left Wales.'

Mike scanned the next sheets. Having left home, the people and places comprising Peggy's life were numerous. Swept on a journey through Wigan, the Isle of Man, Bombay (before it became Mumbai) and Bangkok, Mike came to linger on several months spent on a boat in Yugoslavia. 1962 and a communal living experiment, Peggy had signed up with the love of her life, a certain Leaf (né Richard) Wilkins. It was on that same boat, moored off the island of Hvar, that Leaf had confided he was having a baby with her best friend. Mike looked thoughtfully into the air. It was probably what you called Croatia now.

None the wiser, Mike stretched his legs and yawned to refresh himself. When it came to Peggy Davies, there was a lot left to read but instinct told him the answers lay elsewhere. Gathering the blue papers on his lap back into their subfolder, Mike moved to the last two plastic folders in the file. He'd already read them several times and found nothing, but the yellow printout delivered to Rémy in haste had nothing to do with Joan, Martin or Peggy.

'Mavis and Jeffery Eckersley. Let's have another look here then.' He pulled out two wedges of blue paper and started to rifle through them.

'Mavis Eckersley (née Boyle). Born 1955. Daughter of Reverend Morris Boyle and his wife Mary Boyle (née Quinn). Only child. Born in Manchester. Met Jeffery Eckersley aged nineteen. Married. Two children, David and Matthew.'

Mike flipped to papers from the other subfolder. 'Jeffery Eckersley. Born 1953. Also in Manchester. Son of William and Ruby Eckersley. Mother left with depression when Jeff was eleven. Threw herself in the Ship Canal. Never found. Father sank into depression. Married aged twenty-one.'

Skimming through more papers told of times once Mavis and Jeff were married. 'June 1983 . . .'

Mike let the blue papers fall to his lap. So many moments, for all of them. Snatches of time, that had become life-changing events. Incidents that, as was often the way, had come to define them. Maybe the answers weren't here at all? These lives were no different to the billions of other lives they had on file at the Archives Office. *Leave those pensioners to it.* Cynthia's words echoed through the office, paining his ears. He hadn't got any closer to joining all the dots, but one thing had become even clearer. The truth lay in opposition to Cynthia's heartless dismissal. These files had been left for far too long. Why did people think life became easier with age? Certainly not for a generation that had been taught to bottle it all up.

Mike gazed out of the window, past Steve and his team still milling around, to the Records Office. His attention floated to the entrance to the grounds. Woven into the wrought iron gates, two ravens eyed each other knowingly under the curving reminder, *IMPOSSIBLE FOR A DEED TO BE UNDONE.* Impossible, of course, but those archives housed the universal truth that escapes so many. Child's play some might say, and for many, life is one long game of Buckaroo with them the mule. A water bottle, cowboy hat, lantern, some rope, a shovel, even a stick of dynamite; load yourself up with as many items as possible. All those life events, carry them with you, ruing and regretting the past and making sure you don't buck. How can the path ahead be simple when carrying so much weight? That's what people don't understand. Life isn't about trying to change what happens. It's about choosing what to carry with you, weighing you down, day in, day out. And yet, in today's race to the top, it is aspirational to take on more stress and worry, load that mule as much as possible. Promoted as 'resilience' and the essence of a productive workforce by people like Dr Cynthia Wolf, an expert in the very opposite. The audit didn't make sense, nor the recent changes at the Organisation. None of it. And that was before the absolute nonsense of fabricating an injection to make people happier.

Mike dropped the file on his desk. He let out a long groan, imploring Napoleon and Shirley for answers. He had gone to that meeting sure in the knowledge he would outwit Cynthia. How foolish of him. She hadn't been the slightest bit fazed. The opposite. She had seemed almost pleased with him for having worked her out. The beauty spot above her right eye had performed a celebratory jig on him mentioning her TEDx Talk. The same joy had illuminated her face on quoting Epictetus.

'*Men are disturbed not by things, but by the view which they take of them*. Tell me, how does that fit into our Power Poppy, Napoleon?' Mike addressed the cactus in front of him.

Cynthia, with her army of Johns, now there was a woman who was no Napoleon. The Frenchman had favoured annihilation as a military strategy; Cynthia one of pure exhaustion. She played an interesting game though. With her final card, she had come back to the oldest trick in the military handbook: divide and conquer. So, she wanted Mike to tell Gab he wasn't needed, did she? Mike's gaze fell on the empty orange chair opposite him. The dent in the cushioned headrest stared back. His stomach sank. He hadn't worked out Cynthia but she had misjudged him too. It *would* be kinder to liberate Gab from all this but did she really think he would throw his oldest friend and colleague under the bus? Mike knew she was playing with his sentiments. He wasn't stupid. He also knew a workplace that happily pushes one person into oncoming traffic rarely limits itself to one road accident. How he wished he had been at that meeting with Cynthia and the Johns, and the management meetings before that. Mike was convinced these changes had been mooted long before he had become aware of them. There was Gab not trusting him. Why hadn't he come forward sooner, Cynthia had asked. How? Thanks to a memo he had never even seen? Mike threw his feet onto the desk, sending thousands of dust particles into the air to taunt him.

'Billy bloody Whizz!' Mike shouted at the paper mountain now ruling an entire corner of the office, the wastepaper basket long since hidden. Their problems had all started with him.

Mike sank his fingers into the armrests, pushing at the wood under the mousse. His nails hurt as they dug deeper. He reached for Gab's Rubik's cube to fiddle with that instead. He wasn't ready to give up and concede. And he wasn't going to sacrifice Gab. He needed to move fast. Gab had already been out of the office for a few days. Mike knew he was working on borrowed time. If the situation at hand wasn't what he was used to, he had to approach it another way. What had Cynthia said about needing a cool mind at the Agency?

'The beauty is in the ever-changing colour combinations,' Mike said to himself, as he twisted the cube in different directions.

Keeping an eye on true north.

Our vision is sometimes challenged.

Men are disturbed not by things, but by the view which they take of them.

'Of course!' Mike threw the Rubik's cube on the desk.

He knew exactly where to find the answers. As he sprang from his seat, another piece of paper, yellow this time, fluttered from the Project Toulouse file to the floor. It was the information that had caused so much consternation some weeks back and was now the least of their problems. It was the printout that said Jeffery Eckersley would die the coming twenty-sixth of September.

CHAPTER TWENTY

'You've been acting strange.' Martin handed Jeff another beer. 'What was Didier on about the other night?'

It was ten o'clock in the evening but heat hung in the July air, as did Martin's expectation. They hadn't seen each other since the last match and were now stood impatiently outside the *Café de la Mairie* in Saint-Julien. The town was halfway between the villages in which the two friends resided, offered a wealth of amenities without having to go to Toulouse and, most importantly, an outdoor screen for the final of the Euros.

'Strange?' Jeff feigned incredulity as his eyes bounced around a crowd of blue number tens, hoping they wouldn't land on Didier. Jeff had some explaining to do. The evening had been cut short after Quichegate, as Mavis had coined it, but Jeff knew he couldn't avoid Martin's questions forever. Thankfully, Martin was a man of fewer words than Jeff. It had taken a full ninety minutes of play, two sets of extra time and several beers for him to even venture the subject. The penalties would start soon.

'Nothing you want to talk to me about?' Martin clinked his glass against Jeff's.

Jeff shook his head, doubting anything ever really got past Martin, not with the career he had. Talking of which, for him to be so insistent, maybe Jeff was looking worse than he thought. Jeff had invited Rémy tonight for additional deflection, what with him being up to speed with everything, even the latest news. Rémy was nowhere to be seen.

'They're coming back.' Jeff pointed to the screen as blue and white figures entered the pitch ready for the penalty shootout. England had maintained a 1-1 score right through extra time.

'Joan showed you, didn't she?' said Martin.

'Showed me?' Jeff stalled for time as the screen filled with more players. So, *that* was what Martin wanted to talk about. Of course.

'The security footage from the stockroom.'

What Joan had shown him had been a bit of a shock, but what was done, was done. The security footage was the least of his worries. 'Look, the Italians are up first,' said Jeff.

A silence fell on the crowd as all eyes turned to the pitch. A blue-shirted number nine fired the ball towards the goal. Straight into the deflective hands of the English goalkeeper. Martin and Jeff let out a cheer.

'I know you know,' said Martin.

Jeff shrugged, silently urging Harry Maguire to quickly take his spot for the next penalty. The footage was unexpected but had confirmed doubts Jeff had been entertaining for a while. The real question was what Joan wanted to do with it.

England scored again. They cheered.

'God, this is it!' Jeff grabbed Martin's arm, a wave of beer rolling out of his glass.

In that single moment, everything else faded into non-existence. Recent decisions, deliberation on how to announce the news to Mavis and whatever secrets a stock-room was ready to share, it all disappeared. The heavy evening air became weightless. Jeff stood alone facing the screen, cherishing the last flickering light of a long-burning dream. To see England once again hold a cup up high.

Italy scored. England missed. Even-stevens.

Martin and Jeff exchanged nervous glances.

Another goal to Italy. Another miss for England.

A football match can turn on a dime.

Then Italy missed.

Maybe it could turn again.

Then England missed.

It was all over.

Jeff's stomach dropped. He had only asked for one thing. One small thing. 'I don't believe it,' he said, as both men were consumed by the collective sadness that had no doubt descended upon the English wherever they were in the world.

'Not the result we'd hoped for. But then things don't always work out the way we expect.' Martin put his arm on Jeff's shoulder.

'How very true,' said a familiar voice, dropping, as was its way, the aitch.

Jeff and Martin turned to see Rémy. Clothed in a Hawaiian shirt covered in slices of pizza, he carried three beers.

'That's great you told Martin,' Rémy said.

'Told me what?'

Jeff froze. He found himself back in room 612 the previous day. A towering stone viaduct stared back.

'Not far from here,' Dr Watkins-Villeneuve had qualified, her red-framed glasses glancing at the same poster. 'People find it more soothing than bare wall.'

With every word delivered after that, Jeff had felt himself plunge into the rocky abyss below the Roman feat of engineering.

Confusion traced lines over Martin's forehead. Jeff shook his head at Rémy, who smiled back and gave an encouraging nod.

'Come on, Jeff. We're friends,' said Martin.

Jeff searched his repertoire of limited vocabulary. 'I've not been well.'

Martin started to nod. 'That's why you haven't been helping out with the drug trials?'

'I got my MRI result yesterday.'

Italian joy erupted like Mount Etna from the screen as a bubble encased the three men.

'There's nothing more we can do now,' Dr Watkins-Villeneuve had said, reaching for Jeff's arm.

Jeff grabbed one of the beers in Rémy's hand. Having searched for a more poetic form of words, he reverted to the simple, harsh two-word reality. The news he had been waiting to confirm before announcing it to Mavis. And tonight, he would tell her too.

'I'm dying.'

CHAPTER TWENTY-ONE

'We already know,' said Peg.

From the candlelit huddle, Mavis lifted her head to see the three men stumble into the dining room. Jeff wobbled. He'd been drinking again.

'You do?' Jeff's eyes darted between her, Peg and the tarot cards sprawled across the blue and yellow tablecloth.

'Football's not coming home. Gone to bloody Rome, in'it.' Peg's laughter bounced off the dining room walls.

Mavis and Peg had heard the result on the news, it no doubt the reason behind Jeff being half-cut.

'Where's Joan?' asked Martin.

'Popped out to the garden.' Mavis watched Martin stride past her. 'You three are back late?' She pushed her glasses up her nose.

Jeff had been acting odd since the semi-final. She'd tried to play along, coming up with the phrase Quichegate for a bit of fun, thinking with his guard down he might spill the beans. Nothing. All that sneaking around over the past few weeks, his strange behaviour and those books. A travel guide for the aerophobic indeed. Faced with his absolute horror of flying, enough was enough for Jeff. He was leaving France, leaving her, leaving this. He would crawl if he had to. Mavis had just been mentioning her findings to Peg with Joan out of earshot. Well, she'd shared the strange choice of books and left Peg to infer the rest.

'Stayed on for a few beers, love,' said Jeff.

She watched him try to focus on the pictures on the table.

'Come on, Jeff. Let's give it a whirl?' Peg nodded at the tarot pack.

Mavis smiled as the curveball winded her husband. Nice one, Peg. This would get to the bottom of it. Jeff searched the room for moral support. Martin was already in the garden. Rémy pulled out one of the dining room chairs for Jeff to take a seat, before taking his own opposite Peg. Was Rémy encouraging the reading? Had he worked it out too? Could he know of Jeff's plans and not have told her?

'Right, Jeff. We gonna do this?' asked Peg, already shuffling the cards. The table rocked as Jeff's leg bounced. 'Anything you want to know?'

'Nothing at all,' replied Jeff.

'Just see what you pick up?' suggested Mavis. She arranged her glasses once more. Jeff offered a questioning frown. She chose to ignore it. As Mavis watched Jeff watch her, a welcome breeze drifted through the gap in the patio doors. Jeff closed his eyes. Trying to sober up, no doubt, before his secret came out. Peg would see it in the cards. She always did.

Having placed a row of three cards on the table, Peg started to turn them one by one. The first card revealed a man in a red robe speaking to a crowd with what looked like a monkey at his feet.

'The magician. Things aren't all they seem, are they, Jeff?'

Jeff's leg bounced double time. He offered Peg the same questioning frown. Peg also ignored it. He had nowhere to run. Peg turned the second card. Two people contemplated each other, both holding a chalice.

'The two of cups. Maybe not being honest about certain things . . . with certain people?'

'What things?' asked Mavis.

Peg turned the final card. Three shiny swords leapt out. Mavis gasped.

'Didn't we have this card for you too, Mave? Great sadness for . . .'

Everyone looked at Peg as she ground to a halt mid-sentence. For a second, Mavis harboured the genuine fear her friend may have had a stroke.

'You know a Gab?' Peg turned to Rémy.

Mavis heard her own sigh of relief. Jeff looked at her as his leg slowed down a gear. She frowned back at him. He wasn't getting off the hook that easily. Why had Peg changed tack?

Rémy shook his head.

'Or a Gabriel?' insisted Peg.

Rémy continued to shake his head.

'You work with him?'

Again, Rémy shook his head. The breeze filtered once more through the gap in the patio doors, this time accompanied by raised voices.

'He's burning out,' continued Peg. 'You need to do something.'

'I heard he's not his usual happy self but . . .' Rémy let his sentence trail off as he turned towards the patio doors.

Snippets of angry voices gained in volume. In the glow of fairy lights, Mavis made out the silhouettes of Joan and

Martin on the patio, the latter gesticulating in a way she had never seen before. They both started to make their way towards the house.

'Not his usual happy self?' asked Peg, the only person in no way distracted by the noise. Mavis tried to tune back in.

'Sorry?' said Rémy.

'How would you know that? You don't even know this Gabriel.'

Rémy repositioned himself in his seat, Peg's gaze never leaving him. Not until the patio doors slid wide open. In strode a fury-fuelled Martin, followed by Joan.

'Enough with all these lies.' Martin's voice echoed through the dining room.

Mavis saw Jeff shake his head at Martin. Did Joan and Martin know about Jeff leaving too? She really was the last to know.

'For the love of—'

'For fuck's sake, Joan. Tell them.'

Mavis had never heard Martin swear, not even when Roy had come back from one of his trips having left Martin's chocolate Hobnobs in Dover. Her eyes moved to Joan, whose dishevelled white hair now matched her ashen face. What was it Joan had to say?

'Martin. No one wants—'

'Bleedin' well tell them.'

'No one needs to know about that security footage.'

'Footage?' Mavis turned to Rémy.

'Joan doesn't want everyone to know. So, I'm going to tell you. Let you all know what an embarrassment I am to my dear wife.'

'You?' asked Mavis.

'It was me that wasted those injections.'

'Why would you do that?' asked Peg.

'I only wanted somewhere to store my chocolate eclair. It was a hot day. It was never a problem when I worked at the lab.' Martin's attention dropped to his feet.

Rémy's finger traced lines around the olives adorning the tablecloth.

'Not on purpose,' insisted Joan. 'Just doesn't bloody think. I mean, who needs to know about this other than us?'

'You might have used the fridges. Doesn't mean you left them doors open.' Peg's voice silenced everyone as it travelled across the room.

'Maybe not your accident,' said Jeff.

'Maybe not an accident at all, eh Rémy?' Peg tried to eyeball Rémy across the table.

Rémy remained entirely focused on his finger tracing. What was going on between the two of them? Mavis couldn't work it out. She watched Jeff observe the same comments ping-pong across the table, apparently as lost as her. Two spectators oblivious to the rules of the game.

'How can I continue to be president if everyone knows?' shouted Joan, bringing everyone's attention back to her. 'How dare you, Martin!'

'How dare I? I spend my life trying to keep you happy, Joan. We all do.'

Mavis and Jeff now joined Rémy's close inspection of the tablecloth. Absolutely no one wanted to be called into a marital spat that had been so long coming. Mavis stole a quick glance to see Joan go to speak and Martin raise his hand to silence her.

'I've had it, Joan. Up to here.' Martin brought his hand a few inches above his head. Measuring in at a good six foot three in socks, everyone understood he was well and truly done. 'Life's too short for your stupid little feuds. No one gives a shit.' He marched around the table, squeezed Jeff on the shoulder and left the room.

All eyes returned to Joan. Her gaze lingered on the empty doorway through which her husband had ducked to pass. Mavis scrambled to regroup her thoughts. The silence was broken by the longest of wails. Joan's bracelets scored the patio doors as she slumped to the floor.

'This is all I bloody need.' Jeff pushed himself out of his chair.

'Jeff!' Mavis glared at her husband to silence him as she and Peg stood to help Joan.

'For Christ's sake! Too much to ask, is it? A quiet moment in my own damn house.' Jeff left the room in Martin's wake.

CHAPTER TWENTY-TWO

Mike slowed his pace as he passed the crowd gathering under the shade of the large tree. A peal of bells resonated through the park before tolling. Seven times. The usual silence then tried to reign but was quickly peppered with the beeping of mails arriving on mobile phones. With an increased workload and further staff cuts, people had taken to multitasking meetings and correspondence. Crazy really. The first chapter of their training manual covered the incapacity of the human mind to focus on more than one thing at a time. Mike dropped his gaze in short prayer. The ceremony was about to start. Those bells were meant to be heard. Far and wide. It was another goodbye. Another agent being sent out on a mission. Few were those paying attention that day. That was all about to change. Of course, their work would continue as it always had. Happiness was not a limited, monetisable commodity. How foolish to think it had ever been in question. He couldn't stop. He had to find Gab.

He sped down the path, light bouncing off the translucent pavement. He felt in his pocket to make sure the paper was there. He had found it after not too much searching. It all made sense now. He just needed to show Gab. Then, together, they would speak to Cynthia. Mike didn't stop when he came to the river, but instead waved at H. That's what he called the old man who sat on the bank scribbling away. His white cat idled over to brush up against Mike's legs. Mike smiled, as he always did, at the feline's extra toes that resembled thumbs.

Where *was* Gab? Mike scanned the full length of the river. He could hear the waterfalls around the bend. Gab liked to watch trout, the glistening of their silver scales as they rose from the water most relaxing to him. Up near the waterfalls, the current was at its strongest and the fish aplenty. It was as good a guess as any as to where his colleague might be. Mike rushed on, reflecting as he often did on how trout, by swimming upstream and against the current, are often considered to possess that sought-after superpower of resilience. The thing is, they have to swim that way. It's the only way they can breathe. People are different. They could be carried by the current of life, but they refuse. Instead, they battle the natural flow, all the while gasping for air.

A familiar figure walked towards him.

'Gab!' Mike broke into a run as he pulled the piece of paper out of his pocket. 'I know what's going on.'

Gab smiled. He appeared the most serene Mike had seen him in some time.

'Look, it's the original memo. I found it in the bin. It was still there, what with Billy Whizz never coming back.'

'Here one day—'

'Gone the next. Yes, I know. Anyway, that's not what's important.' Mike unfolded the piece of paper. 'It was all a test, Gab.'

'A test?' Gab examined the crest-headed memo.

'It says here, *never before have we seen such levels of depression and anxiety as so many are pushed into fear and insecurity*. But can't you see? That is exactly what they have been doing to us.'

'Certainly bloody have.'

'No! Don't you get it? Look at these lines here: *we are called to ask if happiness should in fact be viewed as a limited commodity, reserved for some and not others.'* Mike glanced at Gab as he continued, *'The time has come think differently.'*

Gab nodded.

'It's not asking us to *believe* those things but was designed to immerse us in a conditioned experiment. Put us in the same scenarios as those we are trying to help. Help us to not become detached from the realities of what is happening out there,' continued Mike.

'Walk a mile in my shoes?' Gab laughed and slapped Mike on the back.

'That's the reason behind those clinical trials. Those injections are what would make happiness a commodity, reserved for some and not for others. It was presented as a solution to incense us.'

'Looks like you worked it all out.'

Mike's breathing quickened with excitement as he continued to explain his findings. 'They were never questioning our mission, rather asking us to consider how we keep people focused on true north. Look at this, Gab.' Mike pointed to the crest at the top of the memo.

'You told me he was the smart one.'

Mike jumped. He met with a beauty spot jigging above a right eyebrow and a set of perfectly straight, white teeth, as Cynthia came to stand next to Gab. What on earth was she doing here?

'So, you spotted it then?' Cynthia took the memo out

of Mike's hand with a proud smile. 'Clever to change the Latin translation on the crest from *As above, so below* to—'

'*As below, so above*, I know,' said Mike. He frowned as Cynthia continued her explanations, his eyes bouncing between her and Gab.

'It's never been done before, an organisation-wide experiment like this. West Taylor Fisher isn't a consultancy firm. It's an acting agency.' Cynthia tapped on the memo in his hand. 'But desperate times called for desperate measures.'

Mike thought back to Cynthia's office and the poster on the wall. 'West as in Mae West?'

Cynthia nodded. 'Set up by some of the best. I hope you can forgive me, Mike?'

Mike felt his shoulders loosen. He hadn't got her completely wrong after all. 'So, you *are* an expert in flow states,' Mike mumbled as he turned his entire attention to Gab. There was only one reason they would be stood together as bold as brass. 'I don't believe this, Gab. You *were* in on it all along?'

CHAPTER TWENTY-THREE

Snoring rippled through the house, Joan set for one hundred years of slumber. Unlike Jeff's usual jackhammer, her efforts were comparable in volume and annoyance to a food blender. Not one of the expensive German ones, more the cheaper end of that same market. The ones they announce on offer in Lidl on Wednesdays. Sleeping Beauty had consumed her body weight in Bombay Sapphire once Martin had left, making the trip to Mavis's sofa the previous evening nothing if not a struggle.

Mavis cupped her mug of tea and examined the allotment, her enjoyment of the strong brew tempered by exasperation at the number of ratatouille jars Jeff's abundant bounty would necessitate. Her crossword book lay in front of her, unopened. She glanced to the sideboard, her muscles tensing at the memory of curry throwing. Jeff had reached his limits and was leaving. Maybe she had too. The ugly clock stared back at her, its ticking thankfully ceased and hands immobile. Equally frozen in time, the photos surrounding the clock were anything but silent. Laughter burst out of the two scruffy-haired boys with their cheeky smiles. They had all been happy once. That happiness had been taken away from them. Mavis's thoughts came back to her husband. Sleeping Beauty hadn't heard Jeff leave earlier that morning. Mavis had. The creaking of the bedroom door, the house shuddering as the front door slammed, the car engine coming to life. In many ways she'd been glad to not face him. Not immediately, in any case. Her recent questions begged answers, but, when push came to shove, the reality scared her. Was Jeff ever planning on bloody telling her? Her gaze lingered a moment longer on the smallest of the two boys, Matthew. The old photo taunted her, reminded her of what she had lost. And why it was her fault. Maybe it would be the same with Jeff. He would disappear from one day to the next, and no one would ever talk about that either.

Mavis's phone pinged, pulling her back to there and then. Snoring continued to undulate through the house, the steady blending now occasionally interrupted by bursts of pulsing. Mavis snatched at her phone, not wanting to wake Joan. She flipped it open, consulted the new message and let out a gasp. She scrolled to 'P' in her contacts.

'No need to help out with the trials today,' said Mavis as soon as Peg answered.

'Morning, Mave.'

'Rémy texted. No need for any of us to go. He won't be there.'

'Mave, I think we maybe need to—'

'You were right, Peg. Things aren't all they seem.'

Mavis pictured the second book buried in the polystyrene unlucky dip. The one that had hurt her most, *Dating after Sixty*. Maybe they weren't happy. The one thing she hadn't seen coming was Jeff leaving her for someone else. Not at their age. Alone to fend for herself? The truth was, Mavis didn't believe she could. She'd never had to.

'Listen—'

'You said he was lying. It was in the cards.'

'I said he wasn't being entirely honest.'

'Jeff's leaving. Having an affair, or at least trying to.'

Laughter burst out of the phone. 'Jeff?'

'Only wolves and penguins, you said.'

'I'm not sure I said your Jeff—'

'I've started thinking differently since spending time with Rémy. When I am with him, I find something I thought I had lost.'

Silence graced the line. Mavis pulled the phone away from her ear, thinking the connection might have been cut.

'And he gives you it back?' asked Peg.

'It all started when he came.'

'Happiness doesn't come from outside, Mave. It comes from within. That's what people don't get. You make your own.'

'You said me falling over wasn't an accident. Maybe it is all planned. Rémy is here because Jeff is leaving.'

Peg let out another short laugh.

'I don't see why you find this funny, Peg. You of all people—'

'I'm just not sure Rémy is actually who he says he is.'

The mantel clock stared at Mavis, its hands stuck at two and ten.

'Whatever he is, he's invited me over to his houseboat.'

It was quiet down by the canal. Gravel crunched underfoot as with every step Mavis asked herself the same two questions. Why was she going to Rémy's houseboat? And what was she going to do about Jeff? Not seeing him that morning had put potential discussion on hold but she couldn't avoid it forever. Or maybe it was simply too late? Something dug into the ball of her foot. Mavis winced. A stone must have made its way into her sandal. She paused, thought about stopping. As quickly, she resumed walking, imagining Jeff's wispy hair a full three strides in front of her. Maybe she hadn't been that honest with him lately either but never would she have thought him capable of leaving her. You didn't do that, did you?

One of the seven sacraments, marriage is a lifelong partnership. She could hear her father's voice echoing around the church. He would be turning in his grave. Look at David, though. All the youngsters did it now, separate. She had called him back. Apologised, and kept a neutral silence in response to him announcing he was starting a bakery. Baking bread! Sourdough, to be precise. Modern bread was no longer bread, he said. All refined grains and sugar.

Mavis stopped to lean on a tree, the tiny stone having made itself impossible to ignore. Bark pinched her hand. She shook her foot. In any case, all the evidence was there when it came to Jeff, even if Peg was now backtracking. So, why was Jeff stalling on telling her? If it hadn't been for her own investigations, she would be none the wiser. Mavis jerked her foot harder, also wanting to oust her mixed feelings. Like balls of wool, tangled emotions had become tricky to unravel, all hiding their true colours. The stone dislodged itself. She placed her foot back on the ground. A sharp pain travelled up her leg. 'Aaah!' The stone had firmly wedged itself into her heel. How dare Jeff go behind her back like that!

Mavis hobbled to a nearby bench. As she bent to remove her sandal, sunlight skimmed the canal. Rolling free, the intruding stone disappeared into the gravel path and she let the calm waters transfix her. She reclined, stretching her limbs to warm them and returning to the other question on her mind. Or rather, the other person. Peg was right about Rémy not being all he seemed. Just a flirt Mavis had first thought. Then she had got to know him. He had looked inside her, understood her, and something about the last few weeks had changed her. Life had taken on different colours. She wanted to be happy. She could live in the present, she realised now, without forgetting her Matthew. Without having to go back to that sad place. Why *had* Rémy invited her today? In an instant, she was back in his strong arms. Her face nestled in his wiry chest hair, Saint Christopher clung to her chin. Mavis straightened the pleats of her skirt several times and stood to continue her journey. Before changing her mind.

A black hull came into view. Its anchor claws reached out as if to abduct her. Mavis stopped, silence replacing the crunching of gravel. It was only her and the crustacean. In the stillness came ripples of nausea. Then, crushing waves of fear. Maybe this wasn't a good idea after all, even though it was nothing more than coffee and a chat. That was how David had ended up getting divorced, one coffee too many. He hadn't said as much, but he'd stopped mentioning that woman. That was sign enough. On the other hand, Jeff was leaving anyway, wasn't he? Wasn't it fear of uncertainty that had always held her back?

Mavis inched towards the boat.

'Carpe Diem!' shouted the crustacean.

Wasn't that what Dame Judi Dench had tattooed on some part of her? Not her bottom. That was that pop star from Newcastle. Somewhere else. It didn't mean seize the day though, did it? More pluck the day. Never pluck a fruit before it has ripened. Was it even for the plucking? Pluck, pluck, pluck. Look what happened to Eve with that bloody apple . . .

'Enough!' muttered Mavis.

She took a deep breath and encouraged herself towards the walkway. An earthy smell played with her nostrils as she wobbled her way onboard, opened the door and descended the first few steps into the living area.

Laughter and a sickly smoke greeted her.

Mavis stopped in her tracks. 'Jeffery?'

CHAPTER TWENTY-FOUR

'Go White Lightning! Go White Lightening!' sang Jeff as he watched Mavis enter the cabin. 'Even I don't snore like that.'

Arms danced in front of him. Jeff realised they were his own. What were they doing there? He let them fall. A wave of exhaustion washing over him, he slouched into the sofa. A red tip glowed on Rémy's deep inhale. Smoke trailed around the cigarette like late evening mist enveloping a beacon out at sea. The smell of diesel played with Jeff. Time to set sail. All aboard! He remembered Mavis, abandoned on the jetty. He looked back to the stairs.

'You want to talk about Joan?' Mavis stared at him.

Jeff admired his wife. Statuesque. Beautiful. Maybe a little annoyed. He did want to talk about Joan, didn't he? Why was that? He couldn't quite remember. Rummaging the corners of his mind led to wailing. How could he forget? Hours of it before Joan had fallen asleep. He frowned. Why would Mavis be so angry? It wasn't him that had snored all night. He needed to lighten the tension.

'You heard the noise on that woman? Bet Dr Bourdon would have a field day with her!' Jeff snorted.

'I left her on the sofa . . .' Mavis's voice trailed off as, inhaling deeply, her eyes traced a path around the cabin.

Jeff felt himself about to set sail again.

Mavis's head twisted and locked him in its sights. An osprey's yellow gaze eying its prey. 'Bloody hell, Jeff. Are you smoking that wacky baccy?'

'Wacky baccy?' Rémy smacked Jeff on the arm.

'Not sure they call it that nowadays, love.' Jeff attempted to sit up, his laughter now choking him.

'You seem to know a lot about it all of a sudden.'

'Ganja!' shouted Rémy, the elongation of the final vowel making Jeff laugh harder.

Jeff sank further into the sofa. As his amusement abated, the likely reason behind Mavis's annoyance made a slow reappearance. He had left the house whilst she was sleeping that morning, not telling her where he was going. Rémy had texted him, suggesting he had something to take the edge off. Drugs were no long-term fix, he had insisted, but he had a little something that might help Jeff find his words. Time was, after all, running out. It wasn't that Jeff didn't want to tell Mavis what was going on. He had simply been waiting to know what exactly he was telling her. Make it as easy as possible for her. Once his worst fears had been confirmed, the minimal words he possessed had made a frightened dash for it. Not least on seeing Joan take up residence in the living room. Jeff inhaled on the joint Rémy passed back to him. He thought about offering it to Mavis, only then noticing her face had fallen into a frown. The room span. Jeff closed his eyes, letting the waves lick the boat. They'd be in Ireland soon enough. The salt pinched at his skin. He let himself float.

Part of him had known all along. An indescribable

feeling that the test results wouldn't be good. A sentiment he had wanted to label as his usual pessimism, but that felt distinctly different. That was why he had started his preparations: the allotment, the deliveries, the plans. Then he had bumped into Rémy outside the hospital, quite by chance, before that consultation. Rémy had seemed to know too. Now, all Jeff needed to do was speak to Mavis. But she was here, wasn't she? Jeff opened his eyes to search for her. There she was, perched on the stairs. Not an osprey, but his little bird. She was frightened. Like that magpie from the garden. Endings and rebirth. He needed to hold her, like the magpie. Jeff beckoned for Mavis to come and join him, his dead hand falling on the sofa. Medicinal, Rémy had said. There was nothing wrong with medicinal usage, not in cases like this. It was good, whatever it was. Maybe the afterlife felt like this?

'You believe in heaven, don't you, love? Your dad would have given you that.' Jeff flung out an arm to point at a picture on the wall of a man in a red robe. A monkey at his feet, the man held a wand up to the sky.

'Heaven?' Mavis descended the final stair and came into the cabin.

Jeff had never really believed. But when you're on the verge of leaving somewhere, it's funny how the question keeps popping up as to where you're going next. He and Rémy had been talking about it. They'd talked about a lot of things during his hospital visits. 'A place we go,' he resumed.

Mavis continued to stare speechlessly at the wall. Did she recognise the picture like Jeff had? It was one of Peg's tarot cards. She had pulled it last night for him.

'What is that picture?' asked Mavis.

'The magician,' said Jeff.

'Where the spiritual meets the physical. Universal

energy contained in the individual.' Rémy's hands traced lines from the ceiling to the floor.

'Heaven and Earth?' Mavis finished her question with another frown.

'As above, so below.' Jeff's gaze lingered on the magician's wand that Rémy had explained connected two worlds.

'As below, so above,' completed Rémy.

Jeff lifted his arm to high five Rémy. His eyes stretched open as the clapping sent an echo around the cabin. This was good stuff, but maybe too strong. It didn't sound that plausible on hearing himself say it out loud.

'Are you saying what happens down here could also happen up there?' asked Mavis. 'I hope not.' She sat on the edge of the sofa.

Every force had its equal and opposite, didn't it? But why would anyone want to bring Earth up to Heaven. Mavis was right. Absolute nonsense. Jeff had heard these drugs could do funny things, people throwing themselves off all kinds of places. It wasn't a long drop into the canal. He had always been a strong swimmer. They had had to swim a hundred metres with all their clothes on to join the Sea Scouts. Maybe he could swim to heaven? Jeff turned to Rémy, slouched on the sofa with his eyes closed. He'd have to ask him later. Jeff tried to focus on Mavis. He had to tell her what he had to say.

'What the bloody hell is going on, Jeff?'

Damn it. Not only had he worried her, she was edging back into annoyance. He'd played this all wrong. Her gaze dropped to his shirt. It was the one Rémy had been wearing the last time they were all here. Lots of tiny planets floating in a dark blue sky. Rémy had given it to him and Jeff, like Rémy, had chosen to fasten only half its buttons. He had to admit, never one for any kind of fashion statement, he was looking good.

'Sexy, isn't it?' Jeff slapped Rémy on the tummy by means of a thank you. His head lolling, Jeff turned to Mavis. '*The Sky at Night*. Always hated that bloody show.'

'You used to love watching it with your dad.'

'Just wanted him to love me.'

The line seeped out of Jeff like a slow puncture. Once released he could almost see it whizz around the room, like one of those fireworks they used to make at the factory where his dad had been foreman all those years ago. Why had he said that?

Mavis reached out to touch his arm. Too far away, her hand fell on the velvet upholstery. 'It was hard for him when your mum died, love.'

Tears welled. Come closer, he wanted to shout. He needed to feel her touch. Jeff's throat tried to constrict. The tsunami inside pushed to break free.

'She never died, Mavis. She upped and left one summer. We never knew where she went.' Jeff turned to the red-robed magician on the wall. 'That summer we went to Ireland with Scout camp. I didn't understand it properly until your dad made you marry me. You were trapped too because David was on the way.' The magician's unflinching stare bore into Jeff. 'I was never enough for her to stay. And I'm not good enough for you either. You should have bloody well left me years ago.'

CHAPTER TWENTY-FIVE

Every muscle in her body contracted, fixing Mavis to the spot. On the verge of leaving her and Jeff had the gall to say they had been forced to marry each other. It was her that should have left him, was it? That would have made life easier for him, wouldn't it? Had he ever loved her? Even now, he couldn't come out with it and tell her he was leaving. Talking nonsense instead about his mother. Upped and left? Ovarian cancer, that's what she'd had. That's what Jeff had always told her. Speaking ill of the dead like that. That was the thing with these drugs. Got you saying and thinking all sorts. Or so she'd heard. And since when did Jeff not like *The Sky at Night*! Or have any inclination to discuss heaven? One foot out of the door and he thought it would be funny to wind her up?

She couldn't look at him. Her hands cramped. Her knuckles whitened as she gripped her legs. Those questions she had been happy to avoid earlier that morning had been joined by more. Together, they made a merry dance in her head. All these weeks of sneaking around to find Jeff here? Arm in arm with Rémy like they were best friends. She dug her nails into her thighs and studied her feet. Her toenails glistened back, mocking her. Why on earth had Rémy invited her here to see this? She had been such a fool to think he found her attractive. He'd been Jeff's accomplice all along. Distracting her attention so Jeff could get on with leaving her. Should have bloody well left him, should she? All well and good saying that now.

Mavis lifted her head, ready to give Jeff a piece of her mind. For the first time in fifty years of marriage, she saw him cry.

CHAPTER TWENTY-SIX

Tears burned Jeff's cheeks. Mavis looked up, her eyes finding his. She seemed more lost than ever. He wanted to reach out and tell her it would all be fine, but it wouldn't, would it? And he hadn't even told her why. Instead, he had blurted out his secret shame, leaving her wonder why the hell he had never told her before. Why would you tell the woman you love that you are unlovable? That one day your own mother woke deciding she didn't want you. Sat hidden on the stairs, he'd heard his father's drunken ramblings, claiming it had all changed the day Jeff had arrived. Jeff closed his eyes. His mind oozed out of his ears, expanding to fill the room. Medicinal, Rémy had said, and Jeff had let himself be persuaded. What did he have to lose? Rémy had been right in one sense. In that moment Jeff felt nothing. All twinges of recent weeks had gone. But releasing pain had freed space for angst. All he had ever wanted to do was to protect Mavis, but he couldn't.

It was just like back then.

That blustery June day, the lights had flickered in the

poorly heated lecture hall and the windows had rattled ominously. Jeff's throat had grown sore at having to speak over the noise. He had never believed in natural foreshadowing. He had, however, every faith in the mathematical models Didsbury John was working on for numerical weather prediction. Michael Fish, the weatherman, had chirpily dissuaded any overreaction to the anticyclone moving over Scotland, but John had declared this would be the worst storm of their lifetime. Four years later, the great storm of 1987 would ultimately take that title, but Manchester was indeed about to see hailstones the size of golf balls. Jeff's first thought had been to call home to let Mavis know but they'd had a row over breakfast, and slow traffic had already made him twenty minutes late.

Jeff addressed the room of young faces, elaborating on extending the sequence of digits in pi. Digressing, as he often did, he spoke of Turing and his later work that linked the patternless, irrational number to a myriad of patterns in nature, not least zebra stripes. Talking of the great man, he hoped future generations more tolerant than their predecessors, but also found it reassuring to know there was order everywhere. Even in places you thought there could never be, like in pi. Then Jeff saw Maggie, the department secretary, peering in through the window. She beckoned him, making the shape of a phone with her hand and bringing it to her ear.

The mini cab drove as quickly as it could, the driver pushing Jeff a cigarette and offering to turn down the radio once he learnt the destination.

'Leave it on,' Jeff insisted, wanting the distraction.

The high pitch of Michael Jackson reminded him of David teaching Matthew to moonwalk in the living room. Pleasant thoughts that inexplicably troubled him that day. He tried to evacuate the worst of his fears in the trails of smoke he puffed into the car. They regrouped to choke him. Exiting the cab, he ran the last hundred metres as rush-hour traffic backed up before Manchester Royal Infirmary.

'I need to see a doctor.' He addressed the young woman behind the desk. She peered at him, with limited patience, from under a white paper cap. 'I'm sorry, it's my wife. An accident, they said.'

'Mr Eckersley?' She cast a look towards her colleague.

'Come with me, would you?' said the second nurse, her dark blue dress pinched in at the waist by a swathe of elastic. She reached out to him.

'What's wrong?' Jeff's raised voice caused heads to turn.

Her fingers dug into his arm.

His feet rooted him to the ground.

'Mr Eckersley—'

'Where's my wife? I want to see my wife.'

'She's still in surgery, Mr Eckersley.'

The hand tugged at Jeff, reminding him there was a certain inevitability to events. It encouraged him to be led, forcing him into the realisation that he was in no position to resist, shout down or ignore. There had been a car accident and Mavis was injured. He already knew that much from the call. Now, he had to let the doctors do their work. Trust they could save her.

'The doctor will be with you soon,' said the nurse, guiding him into a windowless, white room and placing a hand on his shoulder before leaving.

The wind howled outside. Jeff played with the change in his pocket. As he paced the room, he guessed the coins on size, before pulling them all out to siphon off the half-pennies and put them in his other pocket. The boys liked to buy sweets with them. A row of four green chairs, attached one to the other, helped Jeff focus on the after. Not the now. When all this would be over and him, Mavis, David and Matthew as they always were. The four of them. A family. Together like the chairs. Children needed their mothers. He chose to not sit. He paced some more. He waited, all the while wondering why they didn't decorate the walls. Pictures would be better than sinking into this white emptiness.

'Mr Eckersley?' The door swung open and a middle-aged man dressed in scrubs introduced himself as Dr Ram. He gestured towards the row of chairs, inviting Jeff to sit.

'Is Mavis okay?' Jeff remained standing, not wanting to sit on what had, in his mind's eye, become the Eckersleys. He dived into the deep brown eyes in front of him, searching for any kind of clue. Was the news good or bad?

'Your wife has a broken pelvis, Mr Eckersley and has suffered severe internal bleeding,' Jeff heard himself gasp. Reaching for the seats behind him, he fell into the unwelcoming plastic. Into the chair on the far left he had imagined to be him. 'But we have stabilised her. You'll be able to see her soon.'

Jeff rubbed his face. On dropping his hands, he noticed Dr Ram still looking at him, his middle-aged spread now occupying the chair to the far right.

'It's about your son, Mr Eckersley.'

'My son, what do you mean?' Jeff shook his head, checked his watch. David and Matthew. 'Gosh. It is late.' A cold sweat consumed him. He motioned to stand. 'I have to pick them up.'

Dr Ram reached out to touch Jeff's forearm. 'I'm sorry, Mr Eckersley. We tried everything.'

'What?'

'Your son Matthew was in the back of the car.'

CHAPTER TWENTY-SEVEN

Snoring rose from Rémy but Jeff seemed to be coming around. He mumbled about having to be strong for her, like his own father hadn't been able to be for him. Then he'd said his name, 'Matthew.' And 'I'm sorry. I'm so, so sorry.'

Mavis stared at the magician on the wall.

'Mummy, can we be quick so I can get back for art?' She heard Matthew's small voice. He tapped her on the shoulder.

Tick, tick, tick, the indicator drummed as she waited to turn at the junction. To her right, several bins lay overturned on the pavement. The trees that lined the street bent in contorted submission to the howling wind.

'We'll see. It's the only appointment the dentist had left. And you want to sort out that toothache, don't you?' She turned to Matthew in the back seat. 'Let's put that song on you like. Pass me your cassette.'

'I don't think we should go today,' he said, though his hand reached through the gap in the front seats to pass her Michael Jackson's *Thriller*. 'It's too windy.'

'Too windy?' Mavis laughed as she turned to ruffle his hair, before squeaking open the plastic box and pushing its contents into the cassette player.

It was 'Billie Jean', his favourite. It was on side one. A click echoed around the car as the cassette slotted into place, reminding her of her seatbelt. *Clunk click every trip*. They'd had the announcements for a while now. It had been made law that January and she kept forgetting. She pressed rewind. As the whirring started, she reached for her seatbelt. A car beeped behind her, making her jump. Offering an apologetic wave, she pushed quickly into first gear and turned the corner.

'Where's Michael, Mummy?' Matthew was standing in the gap between the two front seats.

'Sit down, love. He's rewinding.'

Mavis changed from first to second. A car glued itself to her bumper. Click. The cassette finished rewinding. She waved to the car behind, asking it to slow down. She passed into third gear. *Clunk click every trip*. She still hadn't put her seatbelt on.

'Watch me moonwalk now, Mummy.'

'Matthew, I've asked you to sit down. Just listen for now.'

Mavis tried to catch her son's attention with her arm as she noticed the car behind her get closer in the rear-view mirror. A Ford Escort. She pressed the play button on the cassette player. Silence, broken only by the beeping behind her. She looked at the rectangular flap, then back to the rear-view mirror. What the bloody hell did he want now? Michael Jackson burst out of the speakers. Mavis jumped. Recovering, she turned a second corner onto Foxglove Lane.

'It's too loud, Mummy.'

She felt for the volume dial, eyeballing the man now

gesticulating wildly in her rear-view mirror. What was his problem?

She looked ahead.

A centuries-old trunk lay fallen across the road.

Mavis tried to swerve, caught the indicator stick with her sleeve. There was nowhere to swerve to. They careened forward, straight into the trunk, the bonnet crumpling like an accordion. In her peripheral vision Mavis saw her little boy. Propelled out of the front of the car. Felled like the tree.

She felt Jeff watching her. She was in Rémy's boat, that's right. Mavis pulled away from the magician, Jeff's eyes locking with hers. There were the tears. Those tears she had wanted to see thirty-eight years ago when Jeff had said those five words forever etched on her memory. *He didn't make it, love*. It wasn't that Jeff hadn't held her hand as she started to cry. He'd offered words of consolation as the doctor had filled the silence in his own way. *Winds, the speeds of which we haven't seen in the UK for over twenty years. How can you predict such a thing? Accidents happen. I'm so very sorry. Rest, Mrs Eckersley. You need to rest.* She had closed her eyes. In the darkness, the smell of rain-drenched tarmac had clung to her nostrils, a hole had started to form in her heart and all she could hear was the deafening sound of the indicator.

Tick, tick, tick.

Jeff never shed a tear that day, or any day after that. He blamed her, just as she blamed herself. And now here they were, Jeff stoned and on the verge of leaving her. Was this how he was going to tell her it was over?

CHAPTER TWENTY-EIGHT

'The last few weeks have been horrendous, watching you pretend to slide into depression. How could you do this to me?' Mike shouted at Gab, his hands dropping defeatedly to his sides.

Gab put his arm around Mike's shoulder, pulling him so close that his curls tickled Mike's chin. 'I wasn't pretending, Mike.' His voice was a whisper. 'I thought this was all for real. That our great Organisation had lost sight of the essential. I took that memo and everything else on face value. I suppose I lost my shit. Ye knaa what ah mean leik!'

'This really isn't the time for your Geordie.' Mike tried to pull away, Gab holding him in place.

'Seriously, Mike. Maybe I could see everything was wrong but I haven't been able to demonstrate a cool head like you, not by a long shot. I got to a dark place.'

Until then, Cynthia had been a quiet observer. She moved back into view as they opened the circle to include her. 'We secretly slipped instructions on the drugs trials into the Toulouse Club for English Pensioners file without Gab knowing. He wasn't lying to you there.'

'And there was me changing the name to Project Toulouse to keep it quiet!' Gab laughed.

'You and Gab were meant to find out at the same time, just as you did. But once we saw the effect the trials, coupled with everything else, had on Gab, we had to intervene.' Cynthia placed a hand on Gab's arm. 'It wasn't meant to go that far. We would never endanger anyone's mental health for the sake of an experiment. Thanks to Rémy—'

'Rémy?' asked Mike.

'He's the one who raised the red flag.' Cynthia smiled at Gab. 'Would you believe, he came to see me after something Swansea Gwen's daughter told him.'

'Cynthia was about to call off the entire experiment, but I asked her to continue. Leave you the chance to work it out. I knew you would.'

'And you did.' Cynthia laughed. 'Once Gab was up-to-speed with everything, it even provided us the opportunity to see how far you would go.'

'But you stood firm, Mike,' said Gab. 'I want to thank you for never giving up on me. So many would have in your position, just to keep hold of what's theirs.'

'And the workplace can really be that bad?'

'Worse than you think, Mike. People have become a commodity. The more profit companies make, the greedier they get. Always wanting more for less.'

Mike rubbed his face. Gab was okay but it was all such a lot to take in. 'And *Felixir* fits in too, right?'

'People may have become a commodity but, by exerting more and more pressure on them, so has happiness. And you know what the definition of a commodity is. Something that can be bought—'

'Or sold,' finished Mike. 'So, we won't be resorting to injections?'

Cynthia shook her head.

A test after all that, but a test based on reality. This was what they were up against now? Life was difficult enough without making it harder. They would certainly have to rethink their approach to cases.

'But you kept your eye on what matters the whole time, Mike.' Gab patted him on the back.

'It's true.' Cynthia clapped her hands together. 'Everyone's really impressed. Can you imagine how hard it is for people to do that in the same situation? Impossible to keep focused on what is truly important when you are being put under more and more pressure, all the time your self-esteem eroded by those who pay you salary.'

'To the point where you think you aren't good enough to work anywhere else,' finished Gab, a knowing look in his eye. He put his arm around Mike again. 'Without you, we would never have got to the bottom of all this. That's why you're taking over as Director.'

'Director?'

'Of the Agency.'

'You've proved to us you are exactly the person for the job. Top management all agree you should lead on strategy going forward,' said Cynthia.

'But where are you going?' Mike asked Gab.

'Nowhere. Just got other things I want to pursue alongside work.'

'What other things?'

'Playing the trumpet. Maybe baking some bread.'

'Like Daft Punk?'

'It was actually Groove Armada I was thinking of.'

The two men paused for a second to catch each other's attention. Gab laughed and reached out to high five. 'Who's at hand?'

'The WHO is at hand!'

'And *those pensioners*?' said Mike. 'You still haven't told me how Project Toulouse fits into this? It must somehow.'

Cynthia laughed. 'Buying into the idea you are too old for happiness is one thing, but the older generation also has a role to play in what is being allowed to happen in the workplace nowadays.'

Mike frowned at Cynthia. How could they influence something they weren't even part of? He went to ask the question but was cut off by Gab.

'We need you to work with Rémy.'

'Rémy?'

They had to be joking, didn't they? Rémy may have raised the flag about Gab, but he'd been his usual unpredictable self in Toulouse.

'He'll be back soon. Start thinking on the strategy moving forward and you'll see how this all fits together once he's back. There have also been some excellent results from the *Felixir* trials.'

'Hang on a minute, I thought we all agree there is no happiness drug? That *Felixir* was just part of the experiment?'

'Part of the experiment, yes, but we can't ignore the results,' replied Cynthia.

'The results?'

'Ten thousand people across twenty-five different European countries and—'

'It wasn't just Toulouse?'

'Oh no, we've had agents right across Europe. Rémy has been coordinating it all for me.'

'Has he now?' Mike knew Rémy had been hiding something else that time he went to visit him in Toulouse. 'So, this *Felixir* works then? How come? What's in it?'

'Everything you'd expect, I'm afraid.' Cynthia winked at Mike. 'When Billy came to me, I sent him straight to

Gab. It gave us the age profile we needed and happened to be in one of the cities we were targeting.'

'Everything . . . Hang on a minute, what did you say? Billy Whizz came to you? So, he isn't one of your actors?' Mike wondered if he wasn't more confused than ever.

'No, he said he was the cleaner. Called that because—'

'Of how quickly he whizzes through the place.' Gab frowned at Mike.

'Anyway, what with Mavis and Jeff's son's story, we couldn't have planned it better if we tried.'

'Matthew?' asked Mike, remembering the accident.

'No, the other one,' said Cynthia.

CHAPTER TWENTY-NINE

The more Jeff thought about it, it was odd for her to turn up on the boat like that. And she hadn't uttered a single word since him breaking down in tears.

'Why *are* you here, Mavis?'

Mavis's caressing of the sofa turned into frenetic skirt straightening. Jeff glanced at Rémy, whose chest rose and fell in a light slumber. Snippets of that morning's conversation came back to him. Talk of how things were better out than in. Maybe the truth about his mother leaving was more of a curveball than anticipated. Whatever was in that funny cigarette, it had the effect of a highly potent truth serum. He had always felt insecure, from the first moment he had seen Mavis. Wondered if he was good enough for her.

'So, this is where you've been sneaking around the past few weeks?' asked Mavis.

'Sneaking around?' Jeff laughed.

'All this!' Mavis threw a hand in the air, only for it to land with a dull thud on the sofa.

'But what is this?' Jeff attempted the same swinging

motion. He watched Mavis try to follow his arm's stunted path. 'Life, Mavis. What does it all mean?'

The little bird he had seen all those years ago in the cinema sat in front of him. No longer happily chattering but frozen in fear, as if she was now the one head-to-head with a keen-eyed osprey.

'I'm not sure that stuff is good for you, Jeff.' Mavis nodded towards the ashtray.

'Are you happy, Mavis?'

'You're fed up, aren't you? That's what this is about.'

'I feel happier than I have in a long time.'

Jeff examined his wife, the irony of his comment not lost on him in light of his recent crying. She was still tetchy. On the attack. Why *was* she here? It must have been Rémy who had invited her. Of course it was. He'd been badgering Jeff for days to tell her.

'I've been a big scaredy cat, haven't I?' Jeff found himself imitating a feline before dropping the hands that had transformed into paws back into his lap.

'It's not funny, Jeff!'

He was losing her. He needed to focus. What did he want to say? 'In my life, I've been trying to stop bad things happening by not doing anything at all.'

Mavis's eyes narrowed. 'And now it's time to do those things?'

'If it's not too late.' Jeff reached out to her.

'And when exactly were you planning on telling me all this?' Mavis stood and started to pace.

Jeff followed her sandals as they squeaked around the cabin's wooden floor. He knew the conversation wouldn't be easy but this was way more difficult than he'd imagined. Rémy had said honesty was the way forward. Not only telling Mavis about the scan results, but about everything he had been too scared to share. There was little time left, but there was some. Her lips shimmered. That shade of pink she favoured more recently. Jeff's attention dropped to the red blouse she had also taken to wearing of late. Her hair was pinned back from her face to reveal pearl droplet earrings. And Jeff uncovered for himself the truth Mavis was determined to hide. Rémy must have been spending time with Mavis too.

'You didn't come here to see me,' said Jeff. 'You had no idea I was here. You came to see Rémy.'

CHAPTER THIRTY

Mavis's breathing stopped, as did her pacing. Her legs refused to work. She remembered the driftwood in Peg's kitchen. *What we think, we become*. She *had* come here to see Rémy. Some fanciful notion that it wasn't too late to have some fun. What with Jeff leaving anyway, she might as well make the most of it. That it wasn't fair for him to leave her on her own. What had she thought would happen? Her eyes bore into her sandals. That she would trip into Rémy's arms again? Her father wouldn't only be turning in his grave. He was probably clawing his way out as they spoke.

'Came to talk about the trials.' Mavis turned away.

'You came all the way here on your own?'

Mavis's gaze rested on the row of high windows and the decking outside. 'Caught a train, then a taxi.'

'A proper taxi? Anyone can claim they're a taxi nowadays. Not that Uber thing David uses?'

'For goodness sake, Jeff!' Mavis's hands flew into the air as she swung back around. 'Suffocating. That's what David called you and he's right.' Deep inside, a familiar and yet altogether new voice encouraged her to continue. 'You haven't trusted me since the accident. I know you think it was all my fault. That I ruined everything.' The words that had haunted her day and night made a dash for freedom. 'That I killed Matthew!'

'Killed Matthew?'

'But sometimes things just happen, Jeff. Things you can't control.' Her father's stern face hovered behind the latticed wood. The creaking step of the confessional pushed back at her knees. 'I've believed for all these years it was some punishment for us falling pregnant when we weren't even married.' Jeff went to speak. Mavis raised her hand. 'But it's not my fault. I need to let it go.'

Mavis felt lighter. Things did sometimes happen. Things you couldn't control. Events not linked in any way to whatever your parents had told you were past mistakes. Sinful errors for which only God could forgive you. And maybe she had been driving but how could she have known about that tree? No one could have known what would happen that day.

'I knew what would happen that day,' said Jeff.

Mavis stared at her husband. What *was* that stuff he'd been smoking? Could he read her thoughts now too? A shaft of light caught a silver medallion hanging from her husband's neck.

'Didsbury John told me,' whispered Jeff.

'Didsbury John told you what would happen, did he? Didsbury John barely knew what day of the bloody week it was, head always in a computer. Now you're telling me he could predict the future. You spend half your time taking the mickey out of Peg!'

Anger burned in Mavis. After so many years, was this all he had to say? Jeff hadn't wanted to listen when it had happened, and he still didn't. Didsbury Bloody John!

'It was my fault, Mavis, not yours.'

'What are you talking about, Jeff?' Anger faded into concern at what seemed like delirium taking hold of her husband. Mavis glanced around the room. He hadn't been taking anything else, had he? They say it's a slippery slope, once you start.

'John predicted the worst storm to hit the British Isles in forty years.' Jeff's voice disappeared into another whisper.

Regaining her seat on the sofa, Mavis leant in as if trying to find the words Jeff had lost in the silence. Dropped, perhaps, down the side of the cushions. 'You're not making any sense, Jeff.'

'I should have called you. John said to stay indoors. He'd modelled it all. I should have known. The man was a genius. But we'd had that fight. I was still annoyed.'

Mavis nodded slowly. They *had* fought that morning, before Jeff had gone to work. David had fallen in the garden, cut open his hand and come to Jeff crying. Jeff had called him mardy, told him boys shouldn't cry, making David cry even more. 'Start crying now and you'll be crying forever,' he had said.

Mavis had called Jeff thoughtless, not fit to be a father. He had slammed the front door behind him.

Mavis shook her head. A fresh batch of tears gathered on Jeff's lower lids before spilling out to stain his sunken cheeks. This time Mavis didn't turn away. She reached out to hold her husband's face because she recognised that cloying, penetrating damp. It was pain. A lifetime of pain. Those blue eyes that had first twinkled at her in the picture house locked with hers. Sticky water gathered in the gaps between her fingers as the light caught what she now recognised as Rémy's Saint Christopher necklace around Jeff's neck. Knee-deep in water, a man carried a child. *Saint Christopher Protect Us*.

'Are you serious, Jeff? You think our whole lives hinged on one phone call you didn't make?'

Jeff tried to talk but seemed unable.

'Other people went out that day too. The difference between us and them wasn't a phone call. They simply didn't drive down that street at that time.'

'But I didn't do my job, Mavis. I let you both down.'

CHAPTER THIRTY-ONE

The cabin sank into silence. Still holding his face in her hands, Mavis stared at him. Jeff searched for the words he had spent a sleepless night preparing.

'I don't want to stop you anymore, Jeff.'

'Stop me?' Jeff felt his back straighten.

'I could have been a better wife. Allowed myself . . . us to be happier.'

'You've been—'

'No, let me finish. I know you're leaving me.' Mavis's hands dropped from his face.

'You do?' Jeff's body stiffened once more. He held onto the breath he hadn't managed to exhale. She knew he was dying? Her calm acceptance of the news had Jeff in a neck lock. They had drifted but he hadn't realised to what extent.

With a loud thud Rémy fell off the sofa. Jeff looked to the floor to see the ashtray had fallen with him.

Rémy coughed from a cloud of grey ashes as he massaged his head. '*Putain!* Just tell her, Jeff.'

'But she knows.' Jeff looked back at Mavis.

'*Mais non!* She found the books in the garage. She knows about your meetings in Toulouse.'

'You told her?'

'How would you know about the box?' Mavis turned her attention to Rémy.

'Shrewsbury was a difficult mission, but you two!'

'Shrewsbury?' Mavis frowned at Jeff.

'It's near Birmingham, love.'

'I know where it is, Jeff. What's it got to do with you?'

'Well, nothing. At least I don't think so.' Jeff turned back to Rémy as Mavis took his hand.

'*Rien, absolument rien* to do with Shrewsbury. Nothing. *Nada*. This is about you two telling each other what's going on. I've never had such a difficult case.' Rémy rubbed his face.

Case? What did he mean by case?

'You mean these clinical trials?' asked Jeff. Mavis clasped his hand tighter. She shrugged and nodded at Jeff to continue. 'The World Health Organisation sent you, right? Are you not keeping up with targets?'

Rémy's eyes scaled upwards. 'Look, I'm not meant to tell you this, but I'm running out of ideas. I come from the other one.'

'The other what?' asked Jeff.

'The other WHO! The World Happiness Organisation.'

Laughter burst out of Jeff. 'The World Happiness Organisation, is that a thing?'

A smile tickled Mavis's lips.

'I was sent down here to help you and your friends. And now I need to get back. My boss is in burnout. Everything's a bit up in the air. I mean it's all a bit of a mess if I'm honest with you.'

'The boss of the World Happiness Organisation is feeling unhappy?' Jeff pouted his lips and titled his head.

Wide-eyed, Rémy shook his head.

Looking to the fallen ashtray, Jeff wondered how long the effects of Rémy's 'medicine' may last.

'I don't understand what this has to do with Jeff?' asked Mavis, frowning.

'Please tell her, Jeff.'

This was it. He had to tell her. Jeff searched for something in the cabin on which he could focus. There were no ticks. No tocks. Just silence. He took a deep breath, cupped Mavis's face in his hands, as she had his. 'I am leaving, love, but not how you think.'

'Not by land or sea? I saw the book.'

Jeff guided her eyes heavenwards with his. He tried to conduct the words fighting in his mind towards the gentlest of replies. A poetic symphony that would make his news more delicate on the ear. Maybe even make her smile because Mavis's smile was the most beautiful thing he had ever known. In the confusion, the simple two-word truth decided it had been silenced for too long and trumpeted out of him.

'I'm dying.'

CHAPTER THIRTY-TWO

Jeff's words landed with a thud just above Mavis's navel.

'No, I don't think so, Jeff.' His hands dropped to her shoulders to pull her to him. She tensed her back. 'There's nothing wrong with you.'

A groan rose from Rémy, still on the floor.

Dying? Mavis ran her hands down the pleats in her skirt. She scratched her thighs with her nails. Could she feel that? This wasn't real. It couldn't be.

'It's cancer, Mavis. It has spread.'

'But you're never ill.'

Mavis let her head fall onto Jeff's shoulder. He smelt differently to usual. Did death have a smell? Was it lingering, waiting to take her husband away? She nestled further into his neck and inhaled. Not different, unfamiliar. It had been so long since she had been this close. She tried to breathe more of him. Staccato breaths attacked her throat. A damp Hawaiian shirt clung to her cheek. The door banged shut as Rémy disappeared up on deck, his footsteps thundering above them. Jeff was dying.

'Why didn't you tell me before?'

'They've been doing lots of tests. I wanted to know what exactly I was telling you, love.' His fingers traced a delicate path through her hair. 'And I wanted to make sure everything would be okay for you when I'm gone.'

'How much—'

'Who can say? Well, actually Rémy can. September the twenty-sixth.'

'What?' Mavis pulled her head up from Jeff's shoulder.

Her husband's eyes creased into a smile. 'Rémy says that's when I'm off.'

Mavis's mouth fell into a gaping hole.

Jeff laughed. A rumble at first, it spluttered out of him like a motorbike kickstarting, before building into a growling roar.

She nodded at the ashtray. 'You don't believe that stuff about a happiness organisation, do you?'

'God, no. He's as mad as a badger, love.' Jeff's laughter subsided as a serious air brushed over him. 'But he's also the wisest person I've ever met. We've wasted too much time ruing over the past, don't you think?'

Mavis nodded. She stroked Jeff's tired face.

'I thought happiness was about avoiding anything bad happening to you. But maybe life's big events are unavoidable?' said Jeff. Mavis followed his gaze over to the red-robed magician whose eyes had never left them. 'What we think of as the filler in life, those moments in between the big events, that's where our real opportunity for happiness lies. That's the bit we control because we decide how we want to play it.'

Mavis nodded, realising Rémy had been having the same conversations with Jeff as with her. 'We still have some time.'

'We do.'

The white lie she had told earlier about why she had

come to Rémy's boat gnawed at her. An itch she needed to scratch. Wasn't that what they had always done? Hidden the truth from each other. She turned to Jeff. 'Maybe I did see something in Rémy these past few weeks I thought I could no longer find in you.'

'And something we could no longer see in ourselves?'

Mavis let Jeff pull her to him once more. Kicking off her sandals she edged further onto the sofa to lay her head on her husband's torso. Riding the rise and fall of his breath, she inhaled him again. Wiry hair tickled her nose. Rugged, male chest hair. A cold, well-worn Saint Christopher kissed her chin. The punch she had felt in her stomach dissipated into a steady fluttering that she remembered from that first meeting at the picture house. Nothing to do with hunger, indigestion or caffeine, she recognised it for what it was as the whole cabin started to sway.

'Is that diesel I can smell?' said Jeff.

Out of the row of sunshine-filled windows, Mavis watched a Hawaiian-clothed Action Man steer the boat away from the canal path.

CHAPTER THIRTY-THREE

An eager crowd smiled at Mike in the packed hemicycle, from the midst of which Gab combined a wave and a thumbs up. Mike adjusted his headset, pulled the microphone to his mouth and admired his white trainers. They glowed an almost ethereal white. A spotlight shone on the freestanding letters W, H and O to the back of the stage. Where the bloody hell was Rémy?

'Welcome.' Mike's arms prickled as his voice quietened the hall.

He clicked on the remote control to start his presentation. Gab grimaced at the introductory slide entitled: *The World Happiness Organisation: Our Vision*. Mike smiled. The blue background wouldn't help but Cynthia had explained no colour was more calming or consensual. Except maybe yellow, but that didn't show up as well on screen. Before continuing, he cast a glance to the side of the stage. Rémy had promised they would coordinate before the presentation. Nothing. Only to then announce, via Gab, he'd been waylaid as Jeff's funeral had been pushed to Sunday. Typical Rémy. He probably wasn't going to show at all.

'Let's start with a question.' Mike extended his arm to the crowded room. That's how all good presentations worked. He'd done his research. You had to get the audience involved. 'Why is our caseload so high? What do you think is making people unhappy today?'

'Fear of missing out,' shouted a voice from the back. 'People thinking about everything they haven't yet done.'

'FOMO used to kick in at about forty, didn't it? But it's starting earlier,' agreed a second voice.

Heads nodded across the hemicycle.

'Is there really more uncertainty than ever before?' asked someone else. 'Or is it just twenty-four-hour rolling news making people think that.'

Mike nodded. 'You're right. And the marketing industry is pushing people into grasping at happiness whilst they can. Life is one big sushi bar. If you don't snatch what you want as it sails by on the conveyer belt, it may not come around again.'

'Or someone else might grab it!' shouted Gab.

Laughter rippled through the room.

'Exactly.' Mike felt the tension in his body start to leak out of his feet. 'But that's not the whole story. Some workplaces have become more toxic than we realised. And that's tapping into this need for instant gratification and fear of missing out. Let's run the footage.'

Pointer in hand, Cynthia nodded. As the lights dimmed, Mike cast a final glance towards the side of the stage. Understanding that Rémy had been on a wider mission, Mike had initially reprimanded himself for not having trusted him in Toulouse. He had wanted to collaborate but, faced with silence, those same doubts had quickly pushed their way back up like weeds. Mike had since spent hours in the Archive Section of the Records Office, collating and cross-referencing snippets from offices around the world. To be honest, working solo suited him. One thing he had learnt over the past few weeks, however, was to never assume you know everything.

The compilation footage started to the backdrop of 'Happy' by Pharrell Williams and Mike turned to the screen. The first shot of a sparse, dimly lit office broke into a montage of brightly painted, open-plan floors where employees perched on round balls that were good for their posture or simply stood at high desks that facilitated no seating whatsoever. The footage continued. With impressive agility, a tanned CEO in San Jose demonstrated the slide connecting floors in his online marketing emporium. His pastier counterpart at their European HQ in Dublin scaled a fireman's pole in record time. In Prague, coders played pool, whilst AI engineers in London favoured darts. Whether the offices were in Barcelona, Brussels or Budapest, employees could be seen racing cars on video screens, playing pinball or scratching their heads to compile the ultimate fantasy football team.

The audience exchanged confused glances. Perfect.

The footage stopped. The music too. A cityscape from what could have been any world capital appeared on screen. The camera zoomed in slowly. Like a thief, it entered one of the skyscrapers via a floor-to-ceiling window on one of the higher floors. An expanse of wooden parquet and a full wall interpretation of the Tree of Life filled the screen.

'Come and balance your chakras between twelve thirty and one o'clock on Tuesdays,' whispered a long-haired man to an empty room. Sat in the lotus position, he beamed at the screen. 'It's on the company. Remember it's important to ensure work-life balance.'

The man closed his eyes. The camera left the room as it had arrived. From the silence emerged the melancholic strings and percussion of REM's 'Everybody Hurts'. Air left the hemicycle on a collective inhale. Exactly the impact Mike had intended. Smiling at Cynthia, he glanced in passing at the side of the stage. Still no one.

The camera scaled up to the roof of the same building to zoom in on a conversation between two women. Behind them, red neon letters spelt the word WAFFLE, the effs styled into a hashtag. Further proof, if any needed, that food is an endless source of inspiration when it comes to company names, not least for this social media platform. As the colleagues drank oat lattes, hair whipped their faces.

One woman put her arm around the other as she started to cry. 'What do you mean they aren't giving you a pay rise?'

'They said there's a freeze.'

'But you had a promotion. And the board managed to pay themselves big, fat bonuses.'

'Can't say much though, can I? Simon reminded me I'm *always* leaving early to pick up the kids and we haven't met our quarterly targets yet.'

'But you put in at least 45 hours a week. You think you're screwed. I'm never leaving this place. I've just signed a twenty-five-year variable rate mortgage, haven't I.'

'You get that mail from HR?'

'Free yoga? Like we've got time to even fart.'

The two women started laughing, as one wiped away her tears. The camera zoomed out of the conversation to crawl its way down the building. A spider searching its next fly. Mike watched a mesmerised audience as it inched into another office. Elbows welded to the desk and head in hands, a woman yawned. The name plate beside her read *Chief Human Resources Officer.*

'Mental health,' she said to a colleague, as she ran her hands through her cropped hair and rolled her eyes. 'Here we go. The CEO says we need to be talking about it more. Let's link it into our core value of resilience and put a few breathing exercises on the Intranet.' The man opposite noted every word she said on a pad. 'And there's what's-his-name upstairs. We're still offering yoga, aren't we? That's something we can put in the Annual Report.'

The spider was on the move again. The camera entered the toilets on one of the lower floors. A man in a suit licked his finger, picked up the last traces of white powder on the shelf under the mirror and rubbed it into his gums.

'What the fuck is going on?' asked the man beside him. 'Why did you storm out?'

'*A number of my peers doubted my capacity to lead.* That's what they told me.'

'But look at your results. You're smashing it.'

The man wiped his nose with the back of his hand. 'It was you, wasn't it?' He glared at him.

'For fuck's sake, Ian. Come on, you know what we have together. That stuff is making you paranoid.' The colleague tried to approach once more.

'It's this place making me paranoid,' said the man, planting a kiss on his cheek and leaving.

As the door creaked shut, left alone, the other man reached for his phone and tapped out a message. The camera homed in on twelve angry words, spat out in capitals: FUCK. IAN KNOWS. BUT WITH THESE CUTS, IT WAS ME OR HIM.

The camera panned up to a starry sky.

'This is what we are up against,' said Mike, as the footage came to an end and the auditorium lights came up. 'Over the last few weeks, we have only had a taste of how it can be glossed over.'

'A nice taste at *Bjorn and Bread*!' shouted someone.

'It explains why our caseload is so high,' added another, more seriously.

'Hang on a minute. This is all footage of workspaces. Are you saying we should only focus on the working population from now on?' asked Gab.

Mike's jaw tensed. Was that what he was saying? He hadn't thought to resume it that way. Why was Gab frowning?

'No, not at all,' said Cynthia to Mike's left.

Not at all? Cynthia's stare bore into him. That day down by the river, she had said the older generation had their part to play, hadn't she? Mike had never got to the bottom of it. He'd reread the Project Toulouse file but, with no help from Rémy, had become quickly absorbed in workplace footage and forgotten. Of course, they wouldn't favour the young. They had never favoured some over others. Happiness was a finite resource available to everyone, not a select few. That was what the whole audit had been about. Mike's head started to spin. He had led everyone to a false conclusion. The lights burned his hair. He couldn't see into the auditorium anymore. What had he missed? He dragged his gaze around the stage, trying to find words, his toes cramping as they scrunched together in his trainers.

'How about the intergenerational aspect? Didn't you tell me we had to consider that too?' The voice from the back of the room stumbled on the aitch. A figure walked down the flight of stairs that cut through the middle of the seating and led to the stage. 'Sorry I'm late. Terrible traffic.'

Laughter erupted across the auditorium as heads craned.

Rémy? About bloody time.

'Shall I pick up from here?' Rémy stepped onto the stage and slapped a hand on Mike's shoulder.

Mike stared at Rémy's shirt and frowned. He had come to understand the Frenchman conveyed subliminal messaging in his tailoring but found himself confused by what appeared to be mini quiches.

Rémy followed Mike's gaze. 'Often many versions of a story, don't you find? And invariably the truth a combination of them all.'

Mike laughed nervously. Cynthia nodded and smiled. What did he have to lose? Better late than never, he supposed.

'Happiness is an immutable concept, life isn't.' Rémy addressed the audience. 'There are even many versions of the same life depending on who is looking at it. I want to introduce you to a young man who used to be an important part of one of those toxic workplaces. Do you know what kept him there for so long before breaking free?'

'The money?'

'The kudos?'

Rémy shook his head and nodded at the screen. 'I've lined up some more footage. Can we play it, please?'

A whisper of incomprehension danced around the room. The lights dimmed. Mike turned to see an interview on a breakfast news show.

'Good Morning. I'm Anna Mackay and on *Today!* this morning we are delighted to have David Eckersley with us,' announced a Scottish presenter, smiling at the camera.

Jeff and Mavis's son? Cynthia had said there was a link to David but Mike had never found it. He glanced over at Rémy who winked back at him.

'Firebrand at Forty, David, that's what *Forbes* called you. But since leaving your career in the pharma industry, you've been, how can I say, rather *vocal* about the failings of your ex-employer. Can you tell us more about that?'

'We need to speak out more. Challenge the system.' David ran a hand through his fringe and smiled. 'But we get trapped in it.'

'Trapped? You've had a very successful career haven't you, clinically trialling drugs. Maybe weren't known as the *easiest* boss yourself?' The presenter tilted her head and smiled.

'Sure, I bought into it once. Thought to get ahead, you had to blend in. Felt lucky to have a well-paid job, not in a position to complain. I was grateful for the studies my parents had paid for and reminded of the opportunities they never had. Then one day I realised I was living the life they wanted for me. Or at least I thought they did.' David threw his head back and smiled. 'And so I decided, fuck that!'

The presenter laughed nervously. 'So, what changed?'

'The company tried to make me buy into a set of values.'

'And you left because you didn't share them?'

'I got fired for divulging they were hiding the truth. For wanting to act for the greater good, rather than the pursuit of money.'

The presenter's eyes darted from camera to camera. 'It's been great to have you on the show, David, but I think we may need to move on to the weather.'

'The people will know,' said David. 'It's coming.'

'And here's Miriam with what looks like a cold front.'

The camera panned across the studio, before the footage stopped and the lights went up.

So, Project Toulouse did fit into all of this. The generational divide. It was as old as time. How on earth had Mike missed it? From one generation to another, we inadvertently keep ourselves, but also our children, trapped in unhappiness. But what did David mean? What was coming?

'And that is why we will continue to focus with as much dedication on each and every case, no matter what age,' said Rémy, nodding at Mike.

Rémy took a bow and made his exit as applause filled the room. Mike smiled out at the crowd. He had been foolish to judge Rémy. Maybe he did go about things differently but that's what allowed another perspective. Just like parents and their children attack life in different ways. Mike's eyes locked with Gab's and he understood what he had glimpsed over recent weeks, but not fully appreciated: the trepidation of saying no to what everyone else says is right for you. The recipe for happiness had not changed, its sole ingredient being true to yourself. The future strategy meant coming back to basics, with everyone, however old or young. Just like they had always done.

Mike ran across the park and slapped Rémy on the back. 'Why did you leave so quickly? I wanted to talk to you.'

'Look, I'm sorry I wasn't in touch before. It was really tough in Toulouse trying to get everything to align before coming back.'

'You did a great job though.'

Rémy snorted. 'So good you came to visit me?'

'I didn't know the full story, did I?'

'I was sworn to secrecy.'

'I suppose so, but even when it came to the bit I *did* know about, I had to wonder why you went straight in on the Four Noble Truths and Buddhist notions of craving and hankering with a Mancunian pensioner.'

'Sex is just part of nature, Mike. And I go along with nature.' Rémy winked.

'That a fifth noble truth for the French?' Mike laughed.

'Let me tell you, there was a lot of banging around on that boat every night. No idea what Jeff and Mavis were doing in the kitchen.' Rémy laughed, sucking Mike into a dizzying view of his tonsils.

Mike nevertheless noticed a hint of tension. He hadn't been able to fully trust Rémy, had he? His attention came back to Rémy's shirt. On closer inspection, it displayed a full range of finger food. Sausage rolls interspersed the quiches and, if Mike wasn't mistaken, the odd pork pie. Many versions of pastry, various shades of the same. Rémy was right. Truth is a complex thing.

'Well, you certainly proved there's no such thing as can't. That fall in the stockroom was all planned, right?'

'Of course,' Rémy paused in thought. 'But Swansea Gwen's girl is good. She realised I was behind Mavis's accident and leaving the fridge doors open. Leaving the blame with Martin seems to have helped his marriage but it's a shame to have fed into Peggy's doubts about her gift.'

Mike had been to see the Forecast Analysts. 'Don't worry about Peggy,' he said. 'It's all in hand.' His face cracked into a smile, it fading on thinking how close Gab had come to burning out. He pulled Rémy into a bear hug, the Frenchman disappearing into his armpit.

'Everyone loved your presentation.'

'Thanks.' Mike reached for his head, thinking he was still wearing his headset. It had been something to walk that stage.

'It was weird getting back in the field, you know,' said Rémy, pulling Mike out of his thoughts. 'What they had started to call work-life balance has been rebranded as work-life integration.'

'Sounds like Cynthia's flow state.'

'In an ideal world, yes. But not when external objectives and profit are still attached to it. Home working, hybrid working, working leave . . . it mixes everything into one cohesive existence of indistinguishable parts, making people feel grateful for sacrificing their private life to their employer.'

Mike frowned.

'Think about it, Mike. White light, what is it?'

'A combination of all colours?'

'Exactly, all those colours coexisting independently. See those guys over there,' Rémy looked towards the artists sat in their usual spots in front of the Treasury. 'What if they took their palettes and mixed all the colours, would they get white?'

The artists shrugged in time with Rémy, albeit too far away to follow the conservation. Maybe it was a Mediterranean tic that simply activated itself periodically, irrelevant of the subject matter.

'Probably more of a sludge?' replied Mike.

'Colours take on their true beauty when they are given room to breathe. Life's about to get very sludgy. Work-life integration will be the biggest marketing scam of a generation. Well, the second.'

Mike looked at Rémy. He still hadn't mentioned clinical trials but from what Cynthia had since shared, ninety-nine percent of participants had felt significantly happier. David had alluded to something coming out too, hadn't he?

'The first biggest scam will be *Felixir*?'

'Well, it worked, didn't it.'

'It did.'

'And people will be livid once they know what's in it.'

'But how will they know? Is there something you're not telling me?'

'*Moi*?' said Rémy, as Gab's heavy tread announced his arrival.

'Is that quiche Lorraine?' Gab studied Rémy's shirt. 'Nothing the English can't do with pastry is there? Come with me.' He winked. 'They're unveiling the new company motto.'

The three men interlocked arms and wandered towards a gathering crowd. Chatter and laughter had returned to the park. The German played his violin and beamed the broadest of smiles, no doubt believing people had congregated for him. He paused mid-music to let the starling, that was sat on the scroll, finish the refrain. A piercing noise reverberated around the park, the microphone on the impromptu wooden stage the culprit. Numerous people covered their ears as a bespectacled man in a black polo neck sent deafening bursts into the crowd on counting to three.

'*Verdammt noch mal!*' said the German, stamping his foot and causing the starling to jump a few inches before landing back on the scroll.

'There's Steve.' Gab pointed to the stage.

'Thank you all for coming.' Steve's amplified voice echoed around a silenced park. 'Unveilings are often showier moments than this, but with events over recent weeks, it's time to get back to the simple. Without further ado, guys, please.' Steve motioned behind him.

Several long ropes pulled at a billowing, red satin sheet. It fell like a handkerchief to reveal the organisation's new two-worded motto: THINK DIFFERENTLY.

'I've seen that somewhere before,' said Mike.

'He wanted it without the 'ly' but that wouldn't have made grammatical sense. I can't tell you the trouble they had. A right tug-of-war. These creative types!' said Gab, his voice now a whisper.

'Does sound familiar, doesn't it?' Rémy's face disintegrated into a frown.

'I think I like it,' said Mike. 'That's what we all need to be doing now. I'm going to pull together a charter for the citizens of the world.'

'Let's call it the Toulouse Agreement!' said Rémy.

'Like the Paris Agreement?' asked Gab.

Mike smiled. 'If we can have an agreement on climate change, surely we can do the same for mental health?'

'But no governments and corporations in charge?'

Mike shook his head. 'It's time for people to reclaim their power. Watch this space.'

CHAPTER THIRTY-FOUR

'Jeff did like to know what he was doing for the week.'

Ignoring Joan's take on Jeff being buried on a Sunday, Mavis admired the Bolt whiter-than-white hair now glinting a delicate salmon pink. The cold air inside Saint-Julien's cavernous church licked Mavis's arms. September sun threw coloured shards of light through the towering stained-glass windows. The sun that brought them here.

'Lovely service, Mavis.' Martin stretched an arm around his wife. The hand that skimmed Joan's bottom en route escaped neither woman. Joan fought to hold in a smile.

Mavis nodded. It had been a lovely service. All those hymns she had learnt by heart as a child and yet new to her today, every single one sang in French. Logical really, but she hadn't set foot in a French church before today. Or in any church since her father had rushed a set of vows in front of a select committee. She looked past her friends. What would she do without Jeff?

Mavis thought on the past eleven weeks. On leaving Toulouse, their route had run parallel to the motorway.

Once they had passed Castelnaudary and Carcassonne, they had entered deep tranquillity, peppered only with sleepy villages, stone locks and birdsong. In between welcoming the many mallards, swans and herons who visited the canal to cool off, Mavis had helped Jeff develop an Excel spreadsheet called *Bucket List* on Rémy's laptop, before sailing all the way south to the Etang de Thau where the flamingos nested. Mavis had called Peg to let her know the news and ask her to check on Joan, forgotten on the sofa. Speaking with her friend, Mavis had attributed Jeff's eleven-week prognosis to the doctors rather than Rémy. It was strange not to round up to three months, Peg had concluded, but still a good ten days more than Mickey Rourke and Kim Basinger had been gifted, so best to make hay while the sun shone.

A smile caressed Mavis's mouth as a ray of blue light caught her eye. She was pulled into a rocky sea and the trailing robes of Saint Christopher on one of the windows. There he was again. Thick blond hair hanging over his face, Christopher smiled at the boy on his shoulders. Jeff was with Matthew. And she would be fine too, wouldn't she? Mavis searched the church for David and found himself drooping in on himself on the pew opposite Jeff's coffin. On leaving Toulouse, despite a ticking clock, it had felt like an eternity stretched before them. After a week or so, the Excel spreadsheet had pulled them back to terra firma. Jeff had wanted to see his son.

'David?' Mavis stroked the fringe flopping over his eyes. Her other beautiful boy.

'I judged him for so much, Mum. That stupid argument over dinner. I didn't know he was ill. Vulnerable.' David let his head fall on her shoulder.

Vulnerable. God, how Mavis hated that word. It was used nowadays to describe anyone in poor health and everyone over sixty. One thing she had learnt over recent weeks was, whatever your age, life when lived to the full was synonymous with vulnerability. Your only other option was to shy away from the film. Hide behind your hands and miss what is meant to be your unique footage.

'Sometimes we keep things to ourselves to protect others, love. And you've had your own worries,' said Mavis.

'Dad told you everything?'

Mavis nodded. Jeff and David had spent a lot of time together before palliative care had taken Jeff permanently to bed. In the kitchen of all places, a room Jeff never visited as a rule. David had gone head-to-head with his bosses at the pharmaceutical company on wanting to release data into the public domain. Data he said would change lives, but company lawyers had intervened, accusing him of breaching non-disclosure agreements and threatening him with lawsuits. Lawsuits that would break him financially. Apparently you couldn't talk openly about what you did at work anymore.

'I had Stockholm syndrome for a long time when it came to that company. And then my conscience got the better of me. It was the best decision to leave, Mum, and I might have also found a way to ease my conscience too.' David laughed. 'Dad was good at bread, you know. It's all about precision, baking.'

Mavis nodded, unsure of what burnout had to do with Sweden. That's where Stockholm was, wasn't it? She'd read on the Internet that you couldn't get happier people than the Scandinavians. In any case, it was a relief to see her son opening up. David was a pure product of her and Jeff. Doing what others expected of him and bottling things up until they had nowhere to go but fester inside. He also had more time ahead of him. Time for a second chance. Mavis smiled at Sam, who reached over David to take her hand.

'Lovely service, Mavis. Your husband was a wonderful man.' Sam's eyes scaled the domed ceiling. 'Here's hoping there are some good matches on up there.'

Mavis squeezed Sam's long, slender fingers. What her mother would have called piano player's hands, they were out of sync with the rest of him. Sam from accounts, as it had turned out, was a six-foot-two-tall Adonis of a man from Nigeria and an even more avid football fan than Jeff. The four of them had spent a lot of time together over the past few weeks, often with visits back to old football matches as they snacked on experimental variants of sourdough.

'Dad liked you,' said David, squeezing Sam's other hand. 'I don't know why I thought he wouldn't accept you.'

Mavis smiled. How they had all underestimated Jeff. The two of them had watched *9½ Weeks* one night on the canal boat after Mavis had searched the Internet for the actors Peg had mentioned. Once Rémy was asleep up on deck, of course. That scene where the couple were attacked when mistaken for homosexuals had left Jeff quite upset about people's intolerance.

'Didsbury John was seeing some fella called Turing when he was younger, you know? Something to do with zebra stripes, your dad said. But you couldn't talk about it back then,' said Mavis.

'The guy who taught you and Dad Mah-jong?'

Mavis shook her head. 'You're thinking of Hong Kong John.'

'Didn't he crack the Enigma code?' Sam asked.

'Well, I'm not sure what he did before he left Hong Kong, love.' Mavis squeezed Sam's hand, noticing him exchange smiles with David.

Mavis felt herself smile too. She and Jeff had watched the rest of that film. Not all the antics were for them, but they'd had fun with a makeshift blindfold and some mint choc chip ice cream hidden at the back of Rémy's freezer.

'Well, let's hope your Jeff doesn't bump into Maradona up there. I think we can all agree that if God was to have a hand in anything, it wouldn't be a football match.'

'What was that?' Mavis swam in Sam's brown eyes.

'God wouldn't get involved in the result of a football match, would he? A match changes from one second to the next. That's why it's so exciting.'

Didn't he sound like Rémy? Mavis and Jeff had shared eleven joyous weeks, give or take a day, because Jeff had died, just as Rémy had said he would, on the twenty-sixth of September. Having both dismissed Rémy's ramblings as the talk of a stoned man, and Rémy never returning to it, she and Jeff had nevertheless kept the date in the back of their minds. It had rolled around like the smallest of stones, not in an irritating way but more as a constant reminder to seize the day. Because it turned out it was for the plucking.

'Have you seen Rémy?' asked Mavis.

'That guy who looks like my old Action Man?' David motioned behind him. 'He told me to tell you goodbye. Peg and I were talking to him outside.'

Mavis sat in Jeff's armchair after the wake. The house echoed with loneliness now everyone had gone. Why hadn't Rémy stayed until the end of the service? He'd called them one of his cases. If had decided it time to leave, their case must be closed. Was this it for her then?

Things were looking up for everyone else. Joan and

Martin had announced they were heading to the south coast for a few months. They'd always fancied naturism, Joan had said. She didn't seem to care that, on calling the World Health Organisation, she'd been told they'd never heard of *Felixir*, insisting they never undertook clinical trials of any kind. She was even ceding the T.C.E.P. presidency to Roy in her absence. Talking of whom, Peg and Roy had clicked. As it turned out, he had a bit of 'the gift' himself. Could see dead people, he said. Insisted Jeff was right next to Mavis. And to think all the time she'd known him, Mavis had simply thought Roy a bit boss-eyed. A tear trickled down her cheek. And then another, in a slow race to nowhere. Just like her, now Jeff was gone. Because he was gone, wasn't he? Whatever Roy said. She sank into the empty space surrounding her. This was it now.

Rule Britannia! flooded the house. Mavis jumped and brought her hand to her chest. Had the radio turned itself on? Her eyes darted around the room. Jesus Christ! She should have paid more attention to Roy. Her hand fell to her lap. A smile traced its own path. He'd only changed the tune on the doorbell, hadn't he? It *was* Jeff. In his own way. Fancy that! Mavis pushed herself out of the armchair to answer the door.

A vaguely familiar man stared back at her. On his head sat a white baseball cap. Around the black star curled the words CONVERSE ALL STAR, whatever that meant. His eyes flipped between Mavis and the brown envelope in his hand as he abandoned the struggle to pronounce her name.

'*Lettre*,' he said, pushing the envelope at her and pointing to a screen on a handheld gadget. '*Signature*.'

Mavis waited to be handed a signing implement, an uncomfortable silence descending on them both. A waggling finger indicating it unnecessary, Mavis traced a freehand scribble. The man nodded and ran to a white van Mavis now noticed parked at the top of the drive. A Converse All Star? Didn't seem fond of conversing of any kind. She shut the door and inspected the letter in her hands. Recorded delivery from the UK. What could that be?

Mavis passed through the living room to the dining room. There was more light there for reading. On her way, she noticed a handwritten address, admiring the cursive lettering that curled up on itself like a snake on the capital E of Eckersley. It couldn't be the tax people, could it? Death was an expensive business but David said he would manage all the paperwork. She was pretty sure HMRC didn't have time for fancy calligraphy. Settling into one of the dining chairs, she slid her finger into a tiny opening and dragged it along the length of the envelope. Several pieces of A4 paper fell out in one go, attached together by a bright purple paper clip. Mavis examined the logo at the top of the first sheet of A4. Three black blocks, each containing a chunky white letter. Why on earth would the BBC be writing to her? Mavis held her breath as she read.

Dear Mrs Eckersley,

We are delighted to announce that you and Ms Peggy Davies have been accepted as one of our teams in Season One of our new travelogue programme, The Only Way is by Land or by Sea.

This season we will be asking our teams to race each other from the northernmost to the southernmost point of Europe, using only land or sea transport and on a budget of £2000. Attached is a preparation pack giving you some more detail.

We were particularly interested in your profiles for many reasons and, of course, are always keen to represent a thoroughly diverse demographic in all our programmes. We can't wait to meet you both. Alison in our team will be in touch with you shortly to answer any questions you may have before we start filming next spring.

Yours sincerely,

Ruby Engel
Assistant Producer

Diverse demographic? David had explained that hiring women represented the pinnacle of what they now called 'diversity' in some companies. Older people were also considered good at budgeting, now Mavis thought about it. Her face broke into a grin. A travel show? Her and Peg? Mavis reread the letter. Not simply a travel show, but a competition. Like the *Bake Off*? Without the cakes, of course. What *would* they eat?

'*The Only Way is by Land or by Sea*,' Mavis read out loud.

So that's what Jeff had been up to. No planes, then? That would have suited him a treat. *By land or by sea.* Mavis shook her head. To think on Rémy's boat, Jeff had explained the book away as a delivery for Peg and Mavis hadn't asked any more questions. Peg had kept this quiet. She must have known for Jeff to have signed them up together.

Mavis let the papers drop to the table.

What we see as irrational in life are often events laid out in advance. That's what Rémy had explained, wasn't it? Deep inside we know what we have to learn and events are sent to take us there. Maybe Jeff dying was one of those events. Like Matthew leaving all those years ago.

Accompanying David and Matthew behind their sandcastles, Jeff smiled at her from the sideboard. With his thick, floppy fringe, he sat at his desk at Manchester University. Her eyes scaled the Great Pyramid of Giza towering next to him, a memento of their visit. It was a printout from the Internet, not a photo. Catching a plane would have been a bridge too far. But you didn't need to fly to Egypt anymore. Mavis had found virtual tours online. As they had navigated their way around the ancient tomb, Jeff had explained something called the golden ratio had been used to design it, maybe pi too. The irrational number wasn't a one off at all. It can be found everywhere, from animal markings to architectural wonders. All part of a bigger plan.

Mavis grasped the edge of the tablecloth to pad the tears that splattered the letter. She held the paper up to her face, needing to reconnect to Jeff. Fragments of the past rocked her insides, leaving her tears to dry into the same deserted loneliness. She understood some things but, after a lifetime together, life without Jeff felt like guiding a boat without a rudder. One question kept popping up too. If Rémy really was from a World Happiness Organisation, could it be managed from above? What if the bigger plan was actually God's plan all along? Mavis had fallen out with the big guy some years ago but Jeff had found his way back towards the end, in his own way.

'God has to exist,' he had declared, on passing from the pyramid's King's to Queen's chamber. 'Probably not an all-powerful, aging white man, that's just Western, patriarchal delusion. But there has to be a greater power at play, a force capable of hiding order in such apparent disorder. Think about it, only a genius could have invented pi.'

Maybe the question wasn't where Rémy came from or why. What mattered was what he had brought them. He had certainly taught her and Jeff a lot. Given them some last wonderful weeks together. And now she must go it alone, with those lessons tucked away in her pocket. That's just the way it was. That was why their case was closed and Rémy had left.

Tick tock, tick tock.

Jeff's mum's clock was repaired, back in its rightful place.

Tick tock, tick tock.

Placing the letter on the table, Mavis slowed her breathing to hear the ticks, but also the tocks. Those in-between beats where life doesn't lead you by the hand, but you decide where you want to lead it. That was the key to it all really, not just the World Happiness Organisation. Life and everything in it is whatever you want it to be. It is simply a question of how you decide to react. Mavis looked to the vegetable patch. Summer past, the bright reds and yellows had departed. Green shoots peeked out, suggesting a winter bounty. New beginnings, that's what Jeff was trying to give her with this competition. Conversations with Rémy filtered back to her. Those from when he had first arrived. All that stuff about craving, expecting things to be a certain way but riding the waves of whatever else is sent. Here she was, stood at the foot of one almighty wave. Even if it meant getting a bit wet in the process, was she going to hunker down and let it drench her or try and ride it? She picked the letter back up and pulled it towards her chest. Jeff was helping her move on, wasn't he? This was his parting gift to help Mavis attack those waves. Her own rudder.

CHAPTER THIRTY-FIVE

'What's this place called again?' asked Peg. Phone to her ear, she peered out at Mavis from a full-length, orange puffer jacket that gave her all the appearance of a sleeping bag on legs.

'North Cape, love.' Mavis rubbed her gloved hands together, as she looked over at Damien, *The Only Way is by Land or By Sea*'s Director, wondering when they might start filming.

His barrel-shaped torso, Mavis had decided, had more to do with constant nibbling on miniature forms of chocolate than winterwear that had more togs than Peg's. Wearing a canary yellow coat, Damien was, in many ways, a human representation of the midnight sun he was preparing to film, were it not for the permanent air of worry he concealed with difficulty behind a pair of black-rimmed glasses.

'Nordkapp,' Mavis belatedly offered the Norwegian name.

Having flown into Honningsvåg via Oslo the previous day, all participants had been asked to congregate around the tall metallic statue everyone called *The Globe*. The TV crew wanted to get shots of the nightless nights particular to that part of the world, as well as interview snippets with the contestants before the race started in two days' time.

Mavis smiled at Peg, whose thumbs up suggested she would soon finish her conversation. Peg and Roy had been dating since Jeff's funeral, much to the vocal discontent Didier shared with anyone in the village brave enough to buy a baguette. Hell hath no fury like a French baker scorned.

'Ten minutes everyone!' shouted Damien, milling amongst a throng of people, cameras, microphones and cables.

Mavis breathed in the chilly Arctic air. Wind whistled around the empty plateau as her attention floated on the wide-open sea. It had been several months without Jeff now. Thirty-four weeks that coming Sunday. Every day memories took her back to the past. Small things, like the half a spoon of sugar in her morning tea, crossword clues about football, the apron hanging in the kitchen that David had bought Jeff or the pair of blue-checked slippers stored neatly under the bed. And, of course, the bigger things like the seventy-four jars of ratatouille in the garage.

'Roy says hi.' Peg waddled over to Mavis. 'And your Jeff says not to forget your sunscreen.'

Mavis stared back. The chilly four degrees predicted by Peg's smartphone on leaving Toulouse airport seemed about right.

'Before you say it, he said it's less to do with the temperature and everything to do with UV levels.' Peg slapped Mavis on the arm, laughter bursting out of her.

Small memories of Jeff were indeed reinforced by Peg having a direct line to him. Mavis smiled at the oppressive sky. A blanket of cloud hovered overhead, spitting rain.

'Is he alright, Peg?' Mavis, searched for the right words. 'I mean, is he happy?'

'Like a pig in shit, love. Wants you to focus on this race. Says he's stargazing with a Billy?'

Mavis smiled.

'What?' asked Peg.

'That's Jeff's dad.' William Eckersley, but everyone called him Billy Whizz, what with him being foreman at the firework factory. Nice to think they had found complicity up there.

'Your Jeff's bloody chattier than I ever heard him alive. Takes them a while to settle in when they get up there but now he's on a roll.' Peg rolled her eyes. 'When's this thing starting anyway? Desperate for a piss.' Peg gave Mavis an excited poke.

'Doesn't matter, we know the start of our route anyway.'

They had decided that their best bet would be to hitch-hike south, then take the motorway straight to Oslo, or cut into Sweden. They couldn't decide exactly until they knew where their next checkpoint was. That was how it worked. Following a series of planned checkpoints, you only discovered the next destination on reaching the previous one. The finishing line was at Cape Trypiti on the Greek island of Gavdos.

Peg rubbed her hands up and down Mavis's arms as if heating someone else would allow her to feel warmer.

'Kendal Mint Cake?' Mavis rummaged in her pocket.

Peg's nose wrinkled at the white block that emerged. Another surprise from Jeff. On revisiting the garage, Mavis had found the box in the same place as last time, the polystyrene popcorn replaced by endless provisions. The two books and teabags had been joined by the Kendal Mint Cake, Imodium, an eye mask, a travel-size crossword book and one of those towels that isn't really a towel but does dry you, sort of. Mavis had brought pretty much everything with her, apart from the two flares. Roy had insisted they wouldn't be allowed to check them out of the country. He knew about that kind of thing.

'Thank Christ we weren't up here in March,' said Peg, dancing from foot to foot.

An early spring start to the race had slid into May. Peg had said it would. It was cold now. It would have been in the minuses in March. Damien had insisted that delaying was due to them being three camera operators and one sound technician down with the flu. Mavis had concluded that no one really did want to freeze their nuts off. Peg's words, not hers. It was great to get started. Mavis had been craving distraction. The *Felixir* clinical trials had continued until Rémy's departure, even though she had never returned to the centre, what with Jeff having limited time. The results had not yet been released, however, testing undertaken on thousands of people across Europe despite the World Health Organisation's persistent denial. Even so, that Wyn Jones on the news was already calling it 'a medical miracle', insisting that 'sadness was soon to be a thing of the past'.

'I've never heard such guff,' Peg had said, 'and from a Welshman at that!'

'Isn't no more sadness a good thing?' Mavis had asked.

'It's impossible, Mave. Think about it, you can't have happiness without sadness. Like you can't have love without hate. They only exist because they have their equal and opposite.'

'But you helped with those trials like me?'

'And I'm glad I did,' Peg had said with a wink. 'You'll see, Mave.'

Mavis wondered what else Peg knew. Fragments of

conversation from the night of Joan's breakdown had returned. It was as if Peg had always known there was more to Rémy, not that either woman had ventured the subject. Peg did, however, have both renewed faith in her abilities and caution in terms of what she shared.

'It doesn't always help people to know things ahead of time,' she had confided on the plane. 'If you know what is going to happen and use that information to change the course of events, how can you predict the event in the first place? It's all a bit chicken and egg.'

Rémy's insistence on happiness being controlled from within had started to make sense to Mavis, as did what Peg said about happiness and sadness having to coexist, in a way. So, how did you explain the results they had witnessed with their own eyes during the *Felixir* trials? People were definitely happier. Talking of Rémy, they'd had no news from him. Mavis had never mentioned his talk of a World Happiness Organisation but everyone had agreed, without concluding Rémy's exact origins, that he had diddly squat to do with pharmaceuticals. None of it really added up but it wasn't important. The discussion might come up again with Peg, as and when she was ready. Or maybe it never would. Another thing Mavis had learnt was to let things happen in their own good time.

'Listen up everyone!' Damien's voice reverberated across the windy plateau. 'Could you all stand up there near the globe and look out to sea? We're going to start filming some of the intro.' Two yellow arms wafted in the direction of the statue that sat on a swathe of concrete. 'Ideally we want to get the sun shining through the sphere, silhouetting you all.'

'Damien, love, have I got time for a quick wee?' Peg pointed at the grey bunker of a visitor centre in which they had drank coffee and watched a panoramic film.

A reluctant nod accompanied the appearance of a mini KitKat. 'The rest of you make your way up then.'

Mavis waved Peg off and wandered towards the globe, eyeing up the other contestants as she went. She smiled at Greg and Doug. In the hotel bar the previous evening, they had explained, in intricate detail, how they were both on sabbatical from what they called 'one of the Big Four'. Unsure what that meant, and with Peg's access to the Internet limited as she had forgotten to ask for data roaming, Mavis had politely enquired.

'A professional services consultancy,' Doug had said. 'The thing is—'

'Not everyone likes consultants,' Greg had continued, 'but sometimes you need someone from outside to come in with a fresh pair of eyes.'

Mavis had nodded, feeling better informed but none the wiser. Nice enough couple, albeit Greg had a tendency to finish everyone's sentences, not just his partner's.

Next to them was another couple from Hertfordshire. Somewhere near London, Peg had said. Mavis wasn't sure if they had introduced themselves by name. Slightly older, their two kids were at university and they were craving adventure. Mavis also recognised Jayne with a 'y', as she called herself, pulling the headphones out of her son's ears. A single mum, she was on the show to bond with Bryan, also with a 'y'. Peg said he had millions of followers on YouTube, whatever that entailed. Whatever it was, it wasn't enough for Jayne. After four Chardonnays, she had declared the show a last-ditch attempt at carving him any kind of future.

On arriving at the top of the short flight of concrete stairs, Mavis pulled out her travel crossword book from her pocket. One clue had eluded her on the bus there.

'Entrance, seven letters,' mumbled Mavis.

Maybe opening? Or Ingress. Or could it be arrival?

'Enchant?'

Mavis followed the voice to see a man walking up the steps to her right. He hadn't been in the bar the previous evening. She had, however, noticed him at the back of the bus.

'As in en*trance*?' He moved the emphasis to the last syllable. 'I do love a good crossword. Don't think we've met?' A gloved hand stretched out to take hers.

'Mavis.' Her hand slotted in his.

'Stanley.'

Thin with kind eyes, Stanley stood a good foot taller. Mavis thought there something of an older Benedict Cumberbatch about him, before deciding a deerstalker could make Ronald McDonald resemble Sherlock Holmes.

'From Wythenshawe,' he said.

'Urmston,' Mavis smiled, shaking her fellow Mancunian's hand.

'Fancy having more than one Northerner on the show. Now that is progress.'

'Quiet on set please,' shouted Damien. 'And action!'

Mavis and Stanley turned towards the show's presenter. He used to play Doctor Who from what Peg had said. Mavis had seen him more recently on that game show. That one with the wheel. Jeff never could stand him.

'Here we are at the most northerly point in Europe and at the very end of the European land mass.' With his back to them, the ex-Doctor Who explained to camera the premise of the show.

'Don't you think that looks a bit further north?' asked Stanley, pointing his iPhone compass in the direction of another stretch of headland.

Mavis shrugged as she followed his gaze. Earwigging on a discussion in the bus from the hotel, she had learnt of lingering uncertainty as to where Asia stopped and Europe started. In between crunching on two mini Lion bars, Damien had explained that, covered in ice and Russian soldiers, Franz Josef Land had never been under much consideration as a starting point. The team had also eliminated somewhere called Svalbard. The Norwegian archipelago's proximity to the North Pole made for difficult filming and practicality had usurped technicality to bring them to Nordkapp. Whatever piece of land Stanley had spotted, Mavis had the feeling it didn't offer the same filming opportunities as the midnight sun illuminating a man-made metal globe.

'Back!' said Peg to a prolonged 'Shhhh' from Damien. Rolling her eyes, she dropped her voice to a whisper. 'I got a postcard for Joan and Martin.'

Mavis scanned the picture of a troll superimposed on a cliff edge and nodded. Having since understood the lack of clothing entailed in naturism, she hoped it wouldn't encourage reciprocal communication.

'Who's your new friend?' asked Peg with a wry smile.

Mavis turned to see Stanley awaiting an introduction.

'This is Stanley. He's here with—'

'His wife?' Peg searched the congregated contestants.

Mavis felt sure Peg would have noticed him without spouse on the bus.

'Recently widowed, love. I'm here with my granddaughter, Jodie, but I wonder if she's not a bit taken with that YouTube lad.' Stanley nodded his head in the direction of Bryan with a 'y' who now shared one of his ear buds and his full attention with a long-haired brunette. Two highly drawn eyebrows announced a permanent state of surprise, in sharp contradiction to the boredom that traced the rest of Jodie's young face.

Mavis smiled as she sank into her scarf. The grey

blanket of cloud seemed to be lifting. As her gaze fanned out over the borderless ocean, all she could feel was infinite space.

'Right,' said Damien, addressing them from lower down on the concrete plateau, 'let's—'

'Get back to the hotel?' Greg turned to walk back to the bus.

'No!' A chocolate wrapper rustled in Damien's pocket. 'Get you to stand in teams a metre apart so we can film the opening credits.'

'A metre?' asked Stanley, turning to Mavis.

Throwing a glance heavenwards, Mavis let out a laugh. 'It's two to three strides, love.'

PRESS RELEASE

Miracle happiness drug nothing more than a placebo

Astonishing results for Felixir's mysterious European clinical trials: 99% of patients record feeling happier but injections contain only saline

A revolutionary drug to "actively eliminate sadness from everyday life", Felixir was tested on 10,000 patients across twenty-five different European countries last year. With the World Health Organisation still refuting the claims it is behind Felixir, the mystery thickens as data leaked today reveals a staggering 99% of patients documented feeling happier over the course of the trials. Even more surprisingly, the same data reveals all patients were given saline-based placebo injections.

"Secret testing was bad enough. Admitting a chemical compound was never developed and administering whatever you want to unwitting patients makes a further mockery of the pharmaceutical industry," said a spokesperson for the European Pharmaceutical Alliance, who accused the World Health Organisation (WHO) of negligence last year for "seeking medical pathways without the involvement of the pharmaceutical community".

Despite several pharmaceutical giants voicing their outrage over social media, as shares witnessed a steep drop on the European exchanges, participants are unanimously positive in their feedback.

"It's crazy to think, we went through all that for nothing," says Gunter, 45, a participant from Stuttgart, Germany. "But I did feel happier after the eight weeks. I also made some great friends. We still meet up and have even started a cycling group."

"I'd be angry about it if I didn't feel so much happier," adds Paula, 54, a participant at the trials in Florence, Italy. "Something about answering those questions every week made me focus on the good things, rather than the bad. I still ask myself every evening, What was the one thing that made me happiest today?"

"This is a breakthrough, and one the pharmaceutical industry will want to silence at all costs, as Felixir demonstrates on a massive scale what's called the placebo effect," explains David Eckersley, former VP Clinical Trials at Ganz Pharmaceuticals, revealing that he was fired from his job last year for threatening to expose similar data findings. "Placebos are used in all drug testing and consistently achieve interesting results. The mind is a powerful thing. In this case, people were told they could feel happier and they believed it. It's that simple."

"It's interesting to see Felixir was never labelled an anti-depressant, but a drug to eradicate sadness. Sadness is not a disease and cannot be eradicated," adds the European Centre for Mindfulness. "Pain is certain but suffering optional. We are delighted to see a study that underlines the control an individual can take over their own happiness."

As the debate rages, everyone remains puzzled by the data being leaked, rather than published. Moreover, it was not released online but by a round-robin memo to Europe's leading media establishments, datasets printed and delivered in manila files to their doors.

A spokesperson for the WHO contacted WPW in response to today's news, sharing the following statement:

"These trials do raise a broader question. Placebo drugs aren't a cure-all and we are not dismissing the role of pharmaceuticals in healthcare provision. The time has come, however, to think differently and seriously explore all pathways to better mental health."

- ENDS -

GET A FREE HAPPINESS CALENDAR!

If you enjoyed this story and want to keep in touch, I'd love you to join my mailing list.

Just sign up at lougibbons.com and receive a free HAPPINESS CALENDAR as a welcome gift!

You'll also be the first to know about new releases and special offers, as well as receiving the occasional newsletter.

ENJOY THIS BOOK?

There are a lot of books out there. I write what I enjoy, focus on topics I consider important and spend time creating characters based on no one in particular but who we all recognise from somewhere!

You can't please all of the people all of the time but if this book struck a chord with you, how about leaving a review?

Gaining visibility in a crowded market is hard, good reviews make it easier. If you have five minutes to spare, please drop a few kind words online, on whatever platform you prefer to use.

Many thanks!

ACKNOWLEDGMENTS

This book wouldn't have been possible without a number of incredible people.

Firstly, thanks to family and friends who believed in me when I said I wanted to write novels and continue to encourage me every step of the way. I won't list you by name; you know who you are and you're all fabulous.

Secondly, a big thank you to Natasha Bell. Your insightful mentoring definitely put the 'ultimate' in *Jericho Writers' Ultimate Novel Writing Course* and helped me turn the beginnings of an idea into 75,000 words. I also give you full credit (but no commission!) for the final title.

Equally important in bringing the World Happiness Organisation to life was the support and contribution of my course mates: Ann, Bec, Dan, Derek, Dervla, Nia, Yvette, and, not forgetting, Wendy, who is sadly no longer with us. I wish you all the writing success you deserve.

A special shout-out to the team behind making this book look glorious enough for its debut and giving me the means to promote it. To Vicki Heath Silk for the creativity and vision behind its fantastic cover, to Rachel Eley for her sharp eye and attention to detail, and to my old friend, Pierre Cabrol, for everything web-related and only ever being a quarter of an hour away.

My gratitude extends to my advance readers and street team. I'm the slowest beta reader ever so, believe me when I say, your time and involvement mean so very much. And a special thought for Becky boo, thanks to whom my favourite time of the day will forever be quarter past three.

On a final note, if you are reading this, you've more than likely just finished what is my first novel. My heartfelt thanks go also to you. What is a book without readers?

SOME QUESTIONS

Which characters or situations did you find relatable? How did the book make you reflect on your own life or the lives of those around you?

What do the interactions between Mavis and Jeff reveal about long-term relationships and how they can change over time?

The book suggests that happiness comes from within rather than from external sources. Do you agree with this perspective? How does the story illustrate this idea?

The story emphasises the power of the mind in determining happiness. Do you think this is a realistic portrayal of human psychology? How does this idea resonate with your own experiences?

The novel calls into question modern ways of working, suggesting people have become a commodity. To what extent do you believe this to be true?

Did the idea of intergenerational conflict, created by parents (consciously or unconsciously) seeking to impart their own experience or desires on their children, strike a chord with you? And can it ever really be avoided?

What key lessons or messages did you take away from the book? How might you apply them to your own life or mindset?

What is the World Happiness Organisation?

ABOUT THE AUTHOR

Born in Manchester, Lou grew up in Wales and now lives in the south of France with her favourite people and cat.

For a large part of the week, she writes for multinationals on subjects ranging from medical devices to supply chain management. It's fun, but a couple of years ago, a question started to niggle her: what would it be like to write about some of the other - let's say more quirky - stuff in her head. After a year-long novel writing course, the World Happiness Organisation was born and she hasn't looked back!

When she's not writing, Lou loves nothing more than cycling, doing up old houses and - when the opportunity presents itself - hiking up smouldering Icelandic volcanoes.

lougibbons.com